Gentleman Junkie

BOOKS BY HARLAN ELLISON

NOVELS

The Sound of a Scythe [1960]
Web of the City [1958]
Spider Kiss [1961]

SHORT NOVELS

Doomsman [1967]
Run for the Stars [1991]
All the Lies That Are My Life [1980]
Mefisto in Onyx [1993]

GRAPHIC NOVELS

Demon with a Glass Hand
   (adaptation with Marshall Rogers) [1986]
Night and the Enemy
   (adaptation with Ken Steacy) [1987]
Vic and Blood:
The Chronicles of a Boy and His Dog
   (adaptation with Richard Corben) [1989]
Harlan Ellison's Dream Corridor [1996]
Vic and Blood: The Continuing
Adventures of a Boy and His Dog
   (adaptation with Richard Corben) [2003]
Harlan Ellison's Dream
Corridor Volume Two [2007]

SHORT STORY COLLECTIONS

The Deadly Streets [1958]
Sex Gang (as Paul Merchant) [1959]
A Touch of Infinity [1960]
Children of the Streets [1961]
Gentleman Junkie and Other Stories
of the Hung-Up Generation [1961]
Ellison Wonderland [1962]
Paingod and Other Delusions [1965]
I Have No Mouth & I
Must Scream [1967]
From the Land of Fear [1967]
Love Ain't Nothing But
Sex Misspelled [1968]
The Beast That Shouted Love at
the Heart of the World [1969]
Over the Edge [1970]
De Helden Van De Highway
   (Dutch publication only) [1973]
All the Sounds of Fear
   (British publication only) [1973]
The Time of the Eye
   (British publication only) [1974]
Approaching Oblivion [1974]
Deathbird Stories [1975]
No Doors, No Windows [1975]
Hoe Kan Ik Schreeuwen
Zonder Mond
   (Dutch publication only) [1977]
Strange Wine [1978]
Shatterday [1980]
Stalking the Nightmare [1982]
Angry Candy [1988]
Ensamvärk
   (Swedish publication only) [1992]
Jokes Without Punchlines [1995]
Bce 3bykn Ctpaxa (All
Fearful Sounds)
   (unauthorized Russian publication only) [1997]
The Worlds of Harlan Ellison
   (authorized Russian publication only) [1997]
Slippage [1997]
Koletis, Kes Kuulutas
Armastust Maalima Siidames
   (Estonian publication only) [1999]
La Machine aux Yeux Bleus
   (French publication only) [2001]
Troublemakers [2001]
Ptak Smierci (The Best
of Harlan Ellison)
   (Polish publication only) [2003]

OMNIBUS VOLUMES

The Fantasies of Harlan Ellison [1979]
Dreams with Sharp Teeth [1991]

COLLABORATIONS

**Partners in Wonder: Collaborations
with 14 Other Wild Talents** [1971]
The Starlost: Phoenix Without Ashes
(with Edward Bryant) [1975]
**Mind Fields: 33 Stories inspired
by the art of Jacek Yerka** [1994]
**I Have No Mouth, and
I Must Scream:
The Interactive CD-ROM**
(co-designed with David Mullich
and David Sears) [1995]
2000ˣ
(host and creative consultant of National
Public Radio episodic series) [2000-2001]

NON-FICTION & ESSAYS

Memos from Purgatory [1961]
**The Glass Teat: Essays of
Opinion on Television** [1970]
**The Other Glass Teat: Further Essays
of Opinion on Television** [1975]
The Book of Ellison
(edited by Andrew Porter) [1978]
**Sleepless Nights in the
Procrustean Bed Essays**
(edited by Marty Clark) [1984]
An Edge in My Voice [1985]
Harlan Ellison's Watching [1989]
The Harlan Ellison Hornbook [1990]

SCREENPLAYS, ETC

The Illustrated Harlan Ellison
(edited by Byron Preiss) [1978]
Harlan Ellison's Movie [1990]
I, Robot: The Illustrated Screenplay
(based on Isaac Asimov's story-
cycle) [1994, 2004]
The City on the Edge of Forever [1996]
**"Repent, Harlequin!" Said
the Ticktockman**
(rendered with paintings by Rick Berry) [1996]

RETROSPECTIVES

**Alone Again Tomorrow:
A 10-year Survey** [1971]
**The Essential Ellison:
A 35-year Retrospective** [1987]
(edited by Terry Dowling with
Richard Delap and Gil Lamont)
**The Essential Ellison:
A 50-year Retrospective** [2001]
(edited by Terry Dowling)

AS EDITOR

Dangerous Visions [1967]
**Dangerous Visions:
35th Anniversary Edition** [2002]
**Nightshade & Damnations:
The Finest Stories of
Gerald Kersh** [1968]
Again, Dangerous Visions [1975]
Medea: Harlan's World [1985]
**Jacques Futrelle's "The Thinking
Machine" Stories** [2003]

THE HARLAN ELLISON
DISCOVERY SERIES

Stormtrack by James Sutherland [1975]
Autumn Angels by Arthur Byron Cover [1975]
**The Light at the End of the
Universe** by Terry Carr [1976]
Islands by Marta Randall [1976]
Involution Ocean by Bruce Sterling [1978]

THE WHITE WOLF SERIES

Edgeworks.1 [1996]
Edgeworks.2 [1996]
Edgeworks.3 [1997]
Edgeworks.4 [1997]

Gentleman Junkie

by Harlan Ellison®

EDGEWORKS
an A B B E Y offering
in association with
E-Reads®

GENTLEMAN JUNKIE
AND OTHER STORIES OF THE HUNG-UP GENERATION
is an Edgeworks Abbey® Offering in association with EReads.
Published by arrangement with the Author
and The Kilimanjaro Corporation.

First EReads publication: 2009
EReads website: www.ereads.com

Harlan Ellison website: www.harlanellison.com

Aside from naming a child after someone, dedicating a book is the purest way of saying thank you and you've been important in my life. I never do it lightly. The first edition of this book was dedicated:

> For FRANK M. ROBINSON, who
> has helped, rescued, and even cried
> sad, dark tears; in friendship.

But years pass, and while the debt a dedication pays does not diminish in value, time separates friends; and the time machine that is a book permits the correction of oversights and omissions. So this new edition refurbishes the thank you to Frank and adds:

> For RACHEL, with love.

"There is no use writing anything that has been written before unless you can beat it. What a writer in our time has to do is write what hasn't been written before or beat dead men at what they have done."

ERNEST HEMINGWAY, 1936

"Society and man are mutually dependent enemies and the writer's job [is] to go on forever defining and defending the paradox — lest, God forbid, it be resolved."

ARTHUR MILLER, 1974

"The purpose of fiction is the creation of a small furry object that will break your heart."

DONALD BARTHELME

Contents

Foreword

by Frank M. Robinson

Harlan Ellison is a talent. He could, if he desired, be a fairly hilarious stand-up comedian, a more-than-decent balladeer, a respectable jazz musician, or what-have-you.

He makes his living at none of these.

He's a Writer.

This is an easy thing to say, and a very difficult thing to be. You have to have a certain talent to begin with, and then you have to develop it.

You develop it by first giving up your regular job because, as you quickly find out, serious writing is a full-time proposition and steady employment saps your strength and enthusiasm — so you take part-time jobs in bookstores, libraries, and beaneries, and you write in the early morning hours when the rest of the city is sound asleep (few people in the rest of the city have talents they want to develop).

You develop your talent by living on crackers and beans, by washing your own clothes and stringing them up on a wire in the john, by wearing the same shirt for a week and sleeping on your pants to give them a crease, and by living in a roach-ridden third-floor walk-up where there's only one water tap and the water's the same temperature come summer or winter — cold.

You develop that talent by writing like mad every free moment you have; by stealing away a few of those moments to read what's been written by other people; by submitting material to every magazine you know of, even if they only pay in packets of birdseed, and by being thrown bodily out of publishers' offices as well as agents'.

A lot of writers go through exactly this.

Ellison did.

A few writers have the guts and stamina to claw their way up from the bottom and finally Make It.

Ellison did.

All writers worth their salt (and despite what they go through) develop an empathy and a compassion for people and realize what so few outsiders do: that the characters you read about in fiction are not much different from the people you meet in Real Life, the acquaintances you make and the friends you love. It's not so much the material you work with, it's the view you take.

Ellison realizes this.

Read the following stories and you'll know what I mean. Harlan Ellison writes about the golden people, the tarnished people — Spoof and Marty Field and Tiger and Frenchie and Irish and the kids who hang out in the college sandwich shop — the little people with big problems who are no different from the people you know if only you could see the forest for the trees.

To take issue with an old saying, the rewards of virtue are a good deal more than virtue itself — of all the things in this world that do pay off, hard work heads the list. Exactly where the Big Time begins is hard to say — where does Wealth start and Poverty end, the interminable chain of scrounged meals and tiny, stuffy rooms get replaced by a decent diet and a Room with a View? In one sense, the Big Time for Ellison is only a page away. "Daniel White for the Greater Good" has been sold to the movies (what sort of job they'll do, I don't know, but if they're half as honest as the author, it will make Hollywood's pap look like . . . pap), a number — literally, plural — of novels are scheduled for early publication, and others have been inked on contract. Hard work pays. So does Talent.

And so does Truth. Ellison does not hide the fact that the hurtful youth and background of Marty Field in "Final Shtick" are his own, that Ivor Balmi of "Lady Bug, Lady Bug," is another dimly-realized facet of his own personality. In fact, like with any good author, most of his characters are partial reincarnations of himself. Literature is not found like raisins in the bland oatmeal of the Middle Classes. Authors with something to say are not Typical American Boys who have been raised in the soft and tender wombs of Suburbia. More often than not they've been kicked in the groin by life, and the scar tissue will always show.

So now the party's over and it's time to meet all those people behind the masks.

Frank M. Robinson, coauthor,
The Glass Inferno

Introduction

The Children of Nights

"Race of Abel, drink and be sleeping:
God shall smile on thee from the sky.

"Race of Cain, in thy filth be creeping
Where no seeds of the serpent die.

* * *

"Race of Abel, fear not pollution!
God begets the children of nights.

"Race of Cain, in thy heart's solution
Extinguish thy cruel appetites."

from *Cain and Abel;*
Baudelaire: FLOWERS OF EVIL

Writers with their books are like fickle daddies with their children. There are always favorites and less-than-favorites and even (though daddies would *never* cop to it) ones they hate. They love this one because it sums up the totality of their worldview, and that one because it has the best stretch of sustained good writing, and that one over there under the cabbage leaf because nobody else loves it . . . the runt of the litter.

I love this book shamelessly because it was the book that

was most pivotal in changing my life. Not once, god bless it, but three times. And having it back in print again after it's been out of print for a while fills me with such good feelings, I'd like to let them bubble over, to share them with you.

The first time this book turned me around, it wasn't even a book; it was merely a random group of stories, uncollected, published here and there in a variety of magazines that ranged from the then-prestigious *Alfred Hitchcock's Mystery Magazine* to the sexually cornball men's magazines of the fifties, magazines like *Knave* and *Caper*. You see, I started writing for a living in 1955 when I got booted out of college for diverse reasons and went to New York. At that time, I wrote a lot, and I didn't always write very well. Learning one's craft, in any occupations save writing and doctoring, permits a margin of error. If you're a plumber and you fuck up, the worst that can happen is that a pipe will break and you'll flood someone's bathroom. But writing and doctoring leave the evidence behind. And a bad story is liable to become as stinking a corpse as a surgeon's slip of the knife. Both come back to haunt you years later. (At least doctors get to bury their mistakes.)

So among the hundreds — quite literally hundreds — of stories I wrote to keep my hand in the game — detective yarns, science fiction, fantasies, westerns, true confessions, straight action-adventure stories — there are only a handful that I can bear to face today. Every once in a while I'd write a piece that meant something more to me than 10,000 words @ 1¢ a word=that month's rent and groceries. (Yes, Gentle Reader, there was a time in this land, not so far dimmed by memory, during which a normal unmarried human being could live quite adequately on $100 a month.)

Of those random stories that still stand up well, I have included four in this book: "No Fourth Commandment," which was later freely (*very* freely) adapted as a *Route 66* segment and, while I can't legally prove it, seemed to form the basis for a very fine but sadly overlooked Robert Mitchum motion picture; "The Silence of Infidelity," which I wrote while married to my first wife, Charlotte . . . and while it never actually happened to me, I can see it was a kind of wish fulfillment at the time; "Free with This

Box!" which *did* happen to me, and fictionalizes the first time I was ever inside a jail . . . a story that probably sums up the core of my bad feelings about cops even to this day, though I have more substantive reasons for my negativity in that area; and "RFD #2," a collaboration I wrote with the talented, marvelous Henry Slesar. Henry, incidentally, will be better known to readers as the man who created and wrote the enormously successful daytime television drama *The Edge of Night*.

There are others, of course. One cannot write three hundred stories in three years and not come golden at least a few times. But up till 1957, I was strictly a money writer who had not yet reached the pinnacle of egomania your humble author now dwells upon; a place that would have permitted me to think that what I was doing to stay alive was anything nobler or more fit for posterity than mere storytelling.

But I was drafted into the army in 1957, and time for writing was at a premium. So I wrote only stories that I *wanted* to write, not ones I *had* to write to support myself or a wife or a home. And from 1957 through 1959 I wrote "No Game for Children," "Daniel White for the Greater Good," "Lady Bug, Lady Bug" and eight others in this book, most of which I sold to *Rogue Magazine*, then based in Evanston, Illinois, a suburb of Chicago.

Writing those stories was the first time this book altered my life, even before they were formally a book. They brought me an awareness of how concerned I was about social problems, the condition of life for different minorities in this country, the depth of injustice that could exist in a supposedly free society, the torment many different kinds of people suffer as a daily condition of life. It was to form the basis of my involvement with the civil rights movement and antiwar protests of the sixties, my commitment to feminism.

Those stories showed me that if I had any kind of a talent greater than that of a commercial hack, I had damned well better get my ass in gear and start demonstrating it. So, when I was discharged from the army, and went to Evanston to become an editor for *Rogue*, I concentrated on writing the sort of stories best typified by "Final Shtick" in this book.

Things didn't go well for me in Evanston. The man I worked

for at *Rogue* was the sort of man who kills souls without even realizing the purely evil nature of what he's doing. My marriage had long since become a shattered delusion and after the divorce I proceeded to flush myself down a toilet. That was when Frank Robinson rescued me the first time.

Since Frank did the Foreword for the original edition of this book, and since it is reprinted in this edition, I'll digress for a moment to tell that story, as a demonstration to those of you who may not understand the real meaning of the word, what constitutes genuine friendship, the single most important rare-earth commodity in life.

Having been married to Charlotte for four years of hell as sustained as the whine of a generator, I was in rotten shape. I didn't drink or do dope, but I started trying to wreck myself in as many other ways as I could find. Endless parties, unfulfilling sexual liaisons with as many women as I could physically handle every day, dumb friendships with leaners and moochers and phonies and emotional vampires, middle-class materialism that manifested itself in buying sprees that clogged my Dempster Street apartment with more accoutrements and sculpture and housewares than the goddam Furniture Mart could hold.

And I wasn't writing.

One night, I threw another of my monster parties . . . almost a hundred people . . . most of whom I had never met till they waltzed in the door. A lot of beer, a lot of music, a lot of foxy coeds from Northwestern, lights, laughter, and myself wandering around trying to find something without a name or description in the flashy rubble of another pointless night.

Frank showed up. He was the only one who had thought to bring a contribution to the bash. A bottle of wine. We walked into the kitchen, to put it in the pantry, to be drunk lots later by whatever few human beings survived the animal rituals in the other rooms. We walked into the pantry and stood there talking about nothing in particular, just rapping beside the shelves groaning under the weight of Rosenthal china, service for a thousand.

At that moment, I heard a crash from the living room, and left Frank in midsentence. I dashed in, and some drunken pithecanthropoid I'd met at a snack shop called The Hut was standing silently and slope-browedly midst the ruins of a five-hundred-dollar piece of sculpture. He'd boogied into its pedestal and knocked it into a million amber pieces. Not a sound could be heard in the room. Everyone waited to see if I'd commit mayhem in response to this barbarian assault on my property rights.

"Chee," he mumbled, "I'm sorry. I dint see it, I'll pay ya for it."

The lunacy of the remark from an impecunious college student scrounging off his parents just to keep him out of the army and in a school he didn't like, was infuriating. I flipped, as expected. "You asshole!" I yowled. "Pay me for it? If you could pay for it — and you'll never be able to save that much money even if you get your pinhead out into the workpool — where the hell do you suppose you'd find another one, schmuck? They don't sell that statue in Woolworth's, for chrissakes! Some artist labored a year to cut it out of stone, you brain-damaged clown!"

And then I turned around and stomped back to the kitchen and Frank in the pantry, still waiting to finish his sentence. I was burning. Frank took one look at me and started talking. Softly.

"Look at you," he said. "Just take a look at what you're turning into. You're killing yourself. You're all hung up on owning things, crying over a broken statue, screaming at people you don't even know. You're going to die if you don't pack all this in, start writing a new book, and get the hell out of Chicago!"

He talked for a long time. And I suppose it was time to listen. After a while, I flashed on the simple truth that you can change your life, if you make a sudden, violent commitment without stopping to rationalize why you shouldn't. And I reached past Frank, and took down a stack of Rosenthal plates, perhaps twenty of them, one hundred dollars each, these days. And I stepped out of the pantry and stood in the kitchen doorway facing into the dining room, looking through into the living room, and without thinking about it I let out one of the most lovely, full-throated, 180-decibel primal shrieks ever heard on this planet . . .

And began skimming those lovely, expensive plates at the walls. The first one hit with a crash that brought the whole party to a standstill. Everybody turned to stare at the nut. I kept flinging plates. Into the dining room, into the living room, into the crowd, through the front windows with a smash and shattering joy that could be heard all through the neighborhood. And when I ran out of plates I went and got more. People were dodging the china, ducking and trying to decide whether they should bolt from the house or try and restrain me. Frank was behind me as someone moved on me, and I heard him yell, "Leave him alone!" They backed off, warily.

Each piece of crockery I kamikaze'd was like a link of a chain breaking. And when I'd had my fill of throwing plates and anything else in that pantry that I could pull loose, I rampaged among the partygoers, screaming wordless and senseless imprecations, ordering them out of the house. Now! Get out! Get your fucking deadbeat asses out of here! Split! And Frank stood in the kitchen doorway, smiling.

I didn't go to bed that night.

I began my first novel in years, SPIDER KISS. I wrote damn near five thousand words that night.

Next day I started selling my furniture.

That week I tendered my notice at Rogue, sold off everything I couldn't carry in a U-Haul trailer attached to the back of my Austin-Healey, packed up my manuscripts and my clothes, kissed all the girls goodbye, hugged Frank and showed him the letter from Knox Burger at Fawcett Gold Medal paperbacks saying he wanted a look at the novel, and motored out of Chicago for New York and a return to saying yes to life.

Well, that was the beginning of an uphill climb; a climb that took two years and had some backsliding but finally took me out of the toilet; a climb that produced SPIDER KISS and MEMOS FROM PURGATORY and, happily, GENTLEMAN JUNKIE.

Which brings me to the circumstances that produced the second time this book altered my life. And the second time dear Frank Robinson saved my soul. I wrote about it in brief in the introduction to another collection of my stories, but sequentially that segment comes right here in the story, so I'll just quote the part that fills the gap. Just remember these items: after being in New York for eight months, I remarried and was offered another job by the same creep I'd worked for in Evanston; this time editing a line of paperbacks. I took the job, though I loathed the man, because I had a wife and her son from a previous marriage and I *thought* I was whole and rational (but wasn't), and a steady job seemed the thing to go for. Friends, that is never a good reason! Take it from me . . . I've *been* in that nasty box.

Anyhow, here's what happened:

It was September, 1961.

It was one of the worst times in my life. The one time I'd ever felt the need to go to a psychiatrist, that time in Chicago. I had remarried in haste after the four-year anguish of Charlotte and the army and the hand-to-mouth days in Greenwich Village; now I was living to repent in agonizing leisure.

I had been crazed for two years and hadn't realized it. Now I was responsible for one of the nicest women in the world, and her son, a winner by *any* standards, and I found I had messed their lives by entwining them with mine. There was need for me to run, but I could not. Nice Jewish boys from Ohio don't cut and abandon. So I began doing berserk things. I committed personal acts of a demeaning and reprehensible nature, involved myself in liaisons that were doomed and purposeless, went steadily more insane as the days wound tighter than a mainspring.

Part of it was money. Not really, but I thought it was the major part of the solution to the situation. And I'd banked on selling GENTLEMAN JUNKIE to the very man for whom I was working. He took considerable pleasure in waiting till we were at a business lunch, with several other people, to announce he was not buying the book. (The depth of his sadism is obvious when one learns he subsequently *did* buy and publish the book.)

But at that moment, it was as though someone had split the earth under me and left me hanging by the ragged edge, by my fingertips. I went back to the tiny, empty office he had set up in a downtown Evanston office building, and I sat at my desk staring at the wall. There was a clock on the wall in front of me. When I sat down after that terrible lunch, it was 1:00 . . .

When I looked at the clock a moment later, it was 3:15 . . .

The next time I looked, a moment later, it was 4:45 . . .

Then 5:45 . . .

Then 6:15 . . .

7:00 . . . 8:30 . . .

Somehow, I don't know how, even today, I laid my head on the desk, and when I opened my eyes again I had taken the phone off the hook. It was lying beside my mouth. A long time later, and again I don't remember doing it, I dialed Frank Robinson.

I heard Frank's voice saying, "Hello . . . hello . . . is someone there . . . ?"

"Frank . . . help me . . . "

And when my head was lifted off the desk, it was an hour later, the phone was whistling with a disconnect tone, and Frank had made it all the way across from Chicago to Evanston to find me. He held me like a child, and I cried.

That was the second time for this book. It was the sorry little helpless weapon the human monster used to send me right to the edge. But the book was published, to very little fanfare. Oh, notables like Steve Allen and Charles Beaumont and Leslie Charteris praised the hell out of it, but those were in prepublication comments that were used on the splash page of the book itself. There were virtually no reviews.

Frank's comment in the Foreword that this was the verge of the Big Time seemed a hollow bit of reassurance from a friend. Nothing much happened with the paperback. It sold well, but made no stir among the *literati*. And my hopes sank that I'd ever be anything more than that commercial hack who'd starved in New York in 1955. You can go on ego and self-hype only so long. Then you need something concrete.

Which brings me to the *third* time this book changed my life. In a way so blindingly clear and important that it has colored everything since.

I left Evanston and Chicago and the human monster, and with my wife and her son began the long trek to the West Coast. We had agreed to divorce, but she had said to me, with a very special wisdom that I never perceived till much later, when I was whole again, "As long as you're going to leave me, at least take me to where it's warm."

But we had no money. So we had to go to Los Angeles by way of New York from Chicago. If I could sell a book, I would have the means to go West, young man, go West. (And that was the core of the problem, not money: I was a *young* man. I was twenty-eight, but I had never become an adult.)

In a broken-down 1957 Ford we limped across to New York during the worst snowstorm in thirty years.

Nineteen hundred and sixty-one was the year the bottom fell out of a lot of lives, mine among them. And when I walked into the New York editorial offices of Gold Medal Books, the paperback outfit to which I'd sold SPIDER KISS, the outfit I was going to try flummoxing into buying a book I hadn't written yet, just so I could stay alive and try to salvage my sanity, it was with the sure sense of being only moments away from the unincorporated limits of Tap City. I'd been writing short stories and stuff for maybe a half-dozen years, and a writer — no matter how pouter-pigeon-puffed his ego — can go only so long on self-esteem. He has to have someone with clout say, "Boy, you got a talent." No one had said it to me, though editors had given me money and published what I'd written.

When I walked into those offices, suddenly all the doors to the cubicles where galley slaves pored over galley proofs slammed open, and I was surrounded by people slapping me on the back and shouting things like, "Well done," and "You lucky SOB," and finally Knox Burger, the senior editor, ploughed through and demanded to know, in his crusty but loveable manner, "How much did you pay her to write that?"

Write what, I asked, looking more pixilated than usual. The Parker review, of course, he responded. *What* Parker review? The one in the January *Esquire*, you lox, he said. A snake uncoiled in my stomach. Ohmigod, I thought, Dorothy Parker has said something terrible about me in her book review column. It was as close as I have ever come to fainting.

I dashed back into the corridor, and unable to wait for the elevator, took the stairs three at a time, down the fourteen floors to the lobby, where I caromed off two patrons leaving the newsstand, and dragged a copy of *Esquire* from the stack.

There, on page 133, the great (and I do not use the adjective lightly) Dorothy Parker, the literary colossus whose works were already legend, whose most pointed mˆots had long since become aphorisms to be collected by Auden and Kronenberger, whose style and taste had helped make the *New Yorker* and the Algonquin Round Table focal points for the literarily aware, there, on page 133, Dorothy Parker had taken 86 lines to devastate Fannie Hurst's "God Must Be Sad" and 25 lines to praise an obscure little book of short stories by a twenty-six-year-old paperback writer.

"Mr. Ellison (she wrote) is a good, honest, clean writer, putting down what he has seen and known, and no sensationalism about it.

"In the collection is a story called 'Daniel White for the Greater Good.' It is without exception the best presentation I have ever seen of present racial conditions in the South and of those who try to alleviate them. I cannot recommend it too vehemently . . . Incidentally, the other stories in Mr. Ellison's book are not so dusty, either."

That, from the author of "Arrangement in Black and White," one of the earliest and, even today, one of the most perceptive fictional studies of racial prejudice.

Sometime later I came unfrozen, unstuck, and almost unglued. Can you understand what that kind of praise does for a writer who (like Willy Loman) has till then been out there on only a smile and a shoeshine? Ray Bradbury can tell you; he got *his* from Christopher Isherwood, and it *made* his reputation. It's like the first time a girl says yes. It's like the first time a female realizes she doesn't have to be some guy's kitchen slave to lead a fully-realized existence. It's like Moses getting the tablets.

This book, through the medium of Dorothy Parker, a writer whose credentials were so unassailable, not even the ugliest academic cynic could contest them, had altered my life. I was no longer all alone in my opinion of my worth. I was no longer a writer ambivalently torn between the reality of being a commercial hack and the secret hope that he was something greater, something that might produce work to be read after the writer had been put down the hole. GENTLEMAN JUNKIE, for the third time, had worked a kind of magic on my existence.

But there was more.

James Goldstone, a Hollywood director, read "Daniel White for the Greater Good" and took an option on it for a film. The money helped get us out of New York, and start toward the West Coast.

Several months after the review appeared — and to this day I have no idea how that ineptly-distributed paperback from a minor Chicago house, the only paperback she ever reviewed, came into her hands — I came to H*O*L*L*Y*W*O*O*D to live, if one can call Olympian poverty living. And several months after that I met a chap who said he knew Charles MacArthur, who knew Alan Campbell, who was married to Dorothy Parker, and I fell to my knees begging for an introduction. So the jungle telegraph sent out the pitiful plea, and in short order the word came back that Mrs. Campbell would be delighted to have me call at her residence on such-and-such a Sunday afternoon.

Was there ever a supplicant who trembled more in expectation of burning bushes or *mene mene tekels* scrawled on a wall? Literally festooned with rustic bumpkinism (bumpkishness? bumpkoid? oh dear, how he does go on!) I took along my copy of the Modern Library edition of her collected short stories. In a probably vain attempt to save myself from the *total* appearance of a brain damage case bumbling down the road of Life, I hasten to add that not even when I was in the presence of John Steinbeck or Jacqueline Susann did I ever contemplate asking for an autograph.

But this *was*, after all, Dorothy *Parker*, for God's sake!

I was received in the little house on Norma Place, just off Doheny, where Dorothy Parker and Alan Campbell were entering (what no one had any way of knowing was) their last years together, with a warmth and affection seldom found even in acquaintances of long standing.

Miss Parker was small and lovely and a trifle wan-looking. She engaged me in conversation that lasted well into the evening. (She was also quick to point out that Norma Place had been named after Norma Talmadge, and though it doesn't bear much relevance to anything in this introduction, she seemed to want me to know it, and I feel compelled to pass it on to you.)

I was certain her invitation and her friendliness were the sort of grand gestures offered by the great to the nongreat and that she had surely forgotten what it was I'd written that had first set me onto her, but in the course of discussion she remarked on my paperback at considerable length, quoting entire paragraphs that had stuck with her. I was tangle-tongued and drunk with awe. She really *had* liked the book. In a burst of exploding *chutzpah* that (as Miss Parker would have put it) belonged on display in the Smithsonian, I asked her if she would autograph her book. She smiled softly and said of course. And she did. And it was not till I was all the way home later that night that I opened the flyleaf of the book and read: "To Harlan Ellison — with admiration, envy, and heartfelt wishes that I could be as good a writer as he is — "

Dorothy Parker died a year later. I'm not sure. I think it was only a year; maybe it was a little more.

I can only remember that day on Norma Place, with the shadows deepening — for the day and for that little woman — and think of how she took a moment out of her life to validate mine. Dorothy Parker and this collection of stories. They have put their mark on me. We pass through numberless moments of life, all but a few of them mere time-marking: and occasionally something happens, or something is said, or a face turns toward you, and everything is different. The world is a strange and gorgeous realm you've never seen before. This book has done that for me three times.

I owe this book a great deal. It came from me, it comes back *into* me, it is my fiber and my courage and the stamp of approval that carries me through bad reviews and shitty times and all the anguishes to which we are heir.

And now it is back in print. I have removed the introduction I wrote to the first edition, because it simply doesn't hold any more. This introduction is the one that fits this dear little book now. (And I've removed one story from the original, "The Time of the Eye," because it's available in another collection and I don't want you to feel fleeced in even the smallest particular. But I've substituted "Turnpike," which is a nice little yarn, and you can't find it anywhere else, so you don't even lose the wordage.)

Like my other books — but especially with this one that means so much to me — I offer these thoughts and dreams for your pleasure. These stories are my children of the nights. The nights all alone at the typewriter.

HARLAN ELLISON
Los Angeles

Final Shtick

SHTICK: n.; deriv. Yiddish; a "piece," a "bit," a rehearsed anecdote; as in a comedian's routine or act.

I'm a funny man, he thought, squashing the cigarette stub into the moon-face of the egg. *I'm a goddam riot.* He pushed the flight-tray away.

See the funny man! His face magically struck an attitude as the stewardess removed the tray. It was expected — he was, after all, a funny man. *Don't see me, sweetie, see a laugh.* He turned with a shrug of self-disgust to the port. His face stared back at him; the nose was classically Greek in profile. He sneered at it.

Right over the wing; he could barely make out the Ohio patchwork-quilt far below, grey and gun-metal blue through the morning haze. *Now I fly,* he mused. *Now I fly. When I left it was in a fruit truck. But now I'm Marty Field, king of the sick comics, and I fly. Fun-ee!*

He lit another, spastically, angrily.

Return to Lainesville. Home. Return for the dedication. That's you they're honoring, Marty Field, just you, only you. Aside from General Laine, who founded the town, there's never been anybody worth honoring who's come from Lainesville. So return. Thirteen years later. Thirteen years before the mast, buddy-boy. Return, Marty Field, and see all those wondrous, memorable faces from your oh-so-happy past. Go, Marty baby. Return!

He slapped at the button overhead, summoning the stewardess. His face again altered: an image of chuckles for replacement. "How about a couple of cubes of sugar, sweetheart?" he asked as she leaned over him, expectantly. *Yeah, doll, I see 'em. Thirty-two C? Yes, indeed, they're loverly; now get my sugar, howzabout?*

When she dropped them into his hand he gave her a brief, calculated-to-the-kilowatt grin. He unwrapped one and chewed on it, staring moodily out the port.

Think about it, Marty Field. Think about how it was, before you were Marty Field. Thirteen years before, when it was Morrie Feldman, and you were something like a kid. Think about it, and think what those faces from the past recall. How do *they* remember it? You know damned well how they remember it, and you know what they're saying now, on the day you're returning to Lainesville to be lauded and applauded. What is Mrs. Shanks, who lived next door, remembering about those days? And what is Jack Wheeldon, the childhood classmate, thinking? And Peggy Mantle? What about Leon Potter — you used to run with him — what concoction of half-remembered images and projections has he contrived? You know people, Marty Field. You've had to learn about them; that's why your comedy strikes so well . . . because you know the way people think, and their foibles. So think about it, baby. As your plane nears Cleveland, and you prepare to meet the committee that will take you to Lainesville, dwell on it. Create their thoughts for them, Marty boy.

MRS. SHANKS: Why, certainly I remember Marty. He was always over at my house. Why, I believe he lived as much on my front porch as he did at home. Nice boy. I can remember that little thin face of his (he was always such a frail child, you know), always smiling, though. Used to love my Christmas cookies. Used to make me bake 'em for him all year 'round. And the imagination that child had . . . why, he'd go into the empty lot behind our houses and make a fort, dig it right out of the ground, and play in there all day with his toy guns. He was something, even then. Knew he'd make it some day . . . he was just that sort. Came from a good family, and that sort of thing always shows.

EVAN DENNIS: Marty always had that spark. It was something you couldn't name. A drive, a wanting, a something that wouldn't let him quit. I remember I used to talk with his father — you remember Lew, the jeweler, don't you — and we'd discuss the boy. His father and I were very close. For a while there, Lew was pretty worried about the boy; a bit rambunctious. But I always said, "Lew, no need to worry about Morrie (that was his name; he changed his name, y'know; I was very close with the family). He'll make it, that boy. Good stuff in him." Yeah, I remember the whole family very well. We were very close, y'know.

JACK WHEELDON: Hell, I knew him *before*. A lot of the other kids were always picking on him. He was kinda small, and like that, but I took him under my wing. I was sort of a close buddy. Hell, we used to ride our bikes real late at night, out in the middle of Mentor Avenue, going 'round and 'round in circles under the street light, because we just liked to do it. We got to be pretty tight. Hell, maybe I was his best friend. Always dragged him along when we were getting up a baseball game. He wasn't too good, being so small and like that, but, hell, he needed to get included, so I made the other guys let him play. Always picked him for my side too. Yeah. I guess I knew him better than anybody when he was a kid.

PEGGY MANTLE: I've got to admit it. I loved him. He wasn't the toughest kid in school, or the best-looking, but even then, even when he was young, he was so — so, I don't know what you'd call, *dynamic* . . . Well, I just loved him, that's all. He was great. Just great. I loved him, that's all.

LEON POTTER: Marty? The times we had, nobody could match. We were real crazy. Used to take bath towels and crayon CCC in a triangle on them, and tie them around our necks, and play Crime Cracker Cids. Kids, that should have been, but we were just fooling around. You know, we'd make up these crimes and solve them. Like we'd take milk bottles out of the wooden boxes everybody had at their side door, and then pretend there was a milk bottle thief around, and solve the case. We had good times. I liked him lots. It'll be good seeing him again. Wonder if he remembers me — oh, yeah, he'll remember *me*.

There they go, the vagrants, swirled away as the warning plaque lights up with its FASTEN SEAT BELTS and NO SMOKING. There they go, back to the soft-edged world where they belong;

somewhere inside your head, Marty Field. They're gone, and you're here, and the plane is coming in over Cleveland. So now think carefully . . . answer carefully . . . *do* you remember?

As the plane taxis up to Cleveland Municipal Airport, do you remember Leon? Do you remember Peggy, whose father owned the Mantle apple orchards? Do you remember Evan Dennis who tried to raise a beard and looked like a poor man's Christ or a poorer man's Van Gogh? Do they come back unfogged, Marty Field, who was Morrie Feldman of 89 Harmon Drive, Lainesville, Ohio? Are they there, all real and the way they really were?

Or do the years muddy the thinking? Are they softer in their images, around the edges. Can you think about them the way they're thinking about you? Come on, don't hedge your bets, Marty Field. You're a big man now; you did thirteen weeks at the Copa, you play the Chez Paree and the Palace. You get good bait from Sullivan and Sinatra when they want you on their shows, and Pontiac's got a special lined up for you in the fall, so you don't have to lie to anyone. Not to their memories, not to yourself, not even to the Fates. Tell the truth, Marty, and see how it sounds.

Don't be afraid. Only cowards are afraid, Marty, and you're not conditioned to be a coward, are you? Left home at seventeen, out on a fruit truck, riding in the cab right behind the NO HITCHHIKERS sticker on the windshield. You've been around, Marty Field, and you know what the score is, so tell the truth. Level with yourself. You're going back to see them after thirteen years and you've got to know.

I'm cashing in on the big rock 'n' roll craze, slanting songs at the teenagers. The way I figure it, they've exhausted the teen market, and they're going to have to start on the preteens, so I'm going to beat the trend. I've just recorded my first record, it's called "Nine Years Old and So Much in Love." It's backed with "Ten Years Old and Already Disillusioned."

Okay, Marty, forget the sick shticks. That's what got you your fame, that's why they're honoring you today in Lainesville. But that's dodging the issue. That's turning tail and running, Marty. Forget the routines, just answer the questions. Do you remember them? The truth now.

You're about as funny as a guided tour through Dachau.

Another bit, Marty? Another funny from your long and weirdie repertoire? Or is that routine closer to the truth? Is it a subconscious gag, Marty, babe? Does it set you thinking about Evan Dennis and Jack Wheeldon and all the rest from the sleepy, rustic town of Lainesville, just thirty-one miles from Cleveland in the so-called liberal heart of the great American Midwest?

Is it the truth, as you descend the aluminum staircase of the great flying machine, Marty Field?

Does it start the old mental ball game, that remark about Dachau, where they threw Jews into furnaces? Does it do something to your nice pseudo-Gentile gut? That gut that has been with you since Morrie Feldman days . . . that heaved on you when you had the nose job done to give you such a fine Gentile snout . . . that didn't complain when the name was changed legally. Does it bother that gut now, and give you the hollow, early-morning-chilly feeling of having stayed up all night on No-Doz and hot, black coffee? Does it bug you, Marty?

. . . . ve haff an interesting phenomena in Chermany today . . . you'll haff to excuse the paint under my fingernails; I've been busy all night, writing "goyim go home" on the doors of cathedrals . . .

Oooh, that was a zinger, wasn't it, Marty. It was a nice switch on the synagogue-swastika-painting bits the papers have been carrying. Or is it just that, Marty? Say, how the hell did you ever become a sick comic, anyhow? Was it a way of making a buck, or are you a little sick yourself? Maybe a little angry?

At what, goddam you, get outta here and let me alone!

Why, at your past, Marty, babe. Your swingin' past in good old we're-honoring-Marty-Field Lainesville.

Is that the axe, sweetie? Is that why you keep swingin'?

Shut up. Let me alone. It's a gig, that's all, just another gig. It's a booking. I'm in. I'm out. I take their lousy honor and blow the scene. There's no social signif here. I'm a sickie because it's a buck. That's it. I'm whole; I'm not a weirdie, that's just my bit. It goes over.

Sure, Marty. Sure, babe. I understand perfectly.

What'd you call me?

Not a thing, swinger. Not a mumblin' thing.

You'd damned well better not call me yellow, either.

Cool it, man. No one's asking you to cop out. The whole world loves Marty Field. He's a swinger. He's a funny man. He was a funny kid, maybe too, but now he's a funny man. Go on, sweetie, there they are, waiting behind the hurricane fence, waiting to greet the conquering hero. Go on, Attila, say something funny for the people.

The banner was raised by two children, then, and Marty Field's face broke into its calculated good humor at the sight of

WELCOME HOME MARTY FIELD

PRIDE OF LAINESVILLE!!!!

It wasn't such a long ride, but then it never had been. Thirty-one miles, past the Fair Grounds, past the Colony Lumber Company where he had played so long before. Remembering the condemned pond, so deep behind the Colony Lumber Company; remembering his birthday, when he had thought there would be no party and he had stayed all day, miserable and wasting time, only to go home and see the remains of the surprise party, held without him. Remembering the tears for something lost, and never to be regained.

Past Lathrop grade school, where he had broken one of the ornamental lamps over the door. Past Harmon Drive, where he had lived. Down Mentor Avenue, and after a time, into the center of town. The square, and around the square, past what was once the Lyric Theatre, now metamorphosed into an office building. Remembering the tiny theatre, and its ridiculous banner beneath the marquee: *Lake County's Most Intimate Theatre*. Remembering how you had to sit in your neighbor's lap, the movie was so small. Intimate, indeed. Remembering.

Then the hotel, and washing up, and a fresh white shirt with button-down collar, and your Continental suit, so they could stare and say, "He really knows how to dress in style, don't he?"

All that, all so fast, one bit after another. Too many memories, too many attempts to ravel the truth about what really happened. Was it a happy childhood? Was it the way they say it was, and the way you'd like to remember it?

Or was it something else? Something that has made you the man you are . . . the man who climbs into the spotlight every day of his life, takes a scissors and cuts up his fellow man. Which way was it, Marty? Come on, stop stalling.

An honor banquet, and Lord! they never had food like that in Lainesville before. No pasty dry sliver of white chicken meat for Marty Field, no, indeed, not! The best of the best for the man who outTrendexed *Maverick*. And after the meal, a fast tour of the town — kept open, center-stripe on Main Street left rolled out after eight o'clock — just to stir that faulty, foggy memory.

A dance at the Moose lodge . . .

A late-night pizza . . .

A lot of autographs . . .

Too many handshakes . . .

Then let's get some sleep, don't forget the big dedication of the plaque tomorrow, over at the High School, that's a helluvan honor, doncha know.

Sleep. You call *that* a sleep?

"Ladies and gentlemen," the Principal began, "humor is a very delicate thing." He was a big, florid man; his job had been secure for fifteen years, with the exception of the time Champion Junior High had been condemned, torn down, and joined with the new Senior High. Then they had tried to drag in a man from East Cleveland, but the Principal had called on his brother-in-law, whose influence in local politics was considerable. And abruptly, the man from East Cleveland had found his record wanting. The Principal was a big, florid, *well-fed*, and *secure* man.

"And like all delicate things," he went on, "it takes a special sort of green thumb to make it flower. Such a green thumb is possessed by the man I'm privileged to introduce this afternoon.

"I recall the first time I ever saw Marty Field," he pontificated, drawing thumbs down into vest pockets. "I was Principal of the old Champion Junior High, and one September morning, as I left my office, I saw a thin, small boy hurrying late to class. Well, sir, I said to myself . . . "

Marty Field closed off reception. There it was. Again. The small, short, sickly bit again. Yeah, you were so right, Principal.

I was small, and miserable thin, and that was part of it. But only part. That was the part where I couldn't keep up. But that isn't where it began. It went back much further.

Go back, then, Marty Field. For the first time since they contacted you about the honors Lainesville wanted to bestow on you, go back and conjure it up as it really was.

Tell it true, Marty. No gags, no punch lines, no *shticks* . . . just the way it was.

All things are as they were then, except . . .

YOU ARE THERE . . .

Your name is Morrie Feldman. Your father's name is Lew Feldman, your mother is Sarah Feldman. You are the only Jew on your street, the only Jewish kid in your grade school. There are seven Jewish familiesin town. You go to Lathrop grade school and you are a little kid. At recess time they get you out on the ball diamond, and one of them picks a fight with you. Usually it's Jack Wheeldon, whose head is square and whose hair is cut in a butch, and whose father is a somethingorother at the Diamond Alkali plant. Jack Wheeldon is big and laughs like a jackass and you don't like him because he looks with a terrible strangeness out of his cruel eyes.

You stand there while Jack Wheeldon calls you a dirty kike, and your mother is a dirty kike, and you pee your pants because all kikes do that, don't they, you frigging little kike? And when you swing and hit him on the side of the head, the circle of kids magically grows about you, and while you're locked in an adolescent grapple with Jack Wheeldon (who is all the things in this life that you despise because they are bigger than you and slower-witted and frightening), someone kicks you from behind. Hard. At the base of your spine. With a Thom McAn shoe. And then you can't help it and you start to cry.

You fall down, and they begin kicking you. They all kick you very hard, and you aren't old enough or smart enough to pull your arms and legs around you. So after a while everything goes sandy and fuzzy and you know you are unconscious. There's a special sort of pleasure in that, because that's what happens to the good guys in the movies on Saturday afternoons, when they're being attacked by the bad guys. And after a while Miss Dexter with the pointy nose, from the fifth grade upstairs, comes out on the playground, and sees what is happening, and goes back inside to tell someone else. Then, later, the faceless teacher from the third grade, who likes you, comes running out, and lifts you in her arms and tenderly carries you inside.

The first thing you hear when you wake up is one of the kids saying; ". . . dirty Jewish elephant." And you wonder with childish logic why he calls you an elephant. You don't have a long trunk. That is the first time they let you know you have a *shonikker* apple between your eyes and your mouth.

Your name is Morrie Feldman, and you live at 89 Harmon Drive. You have been away at camp all summer, and now you are back, and your father is telling you that your dog Puddles was gassed while you were away. Mrs. Shanks, next door, called the pound while your father and mother were in Cleveland for the afternoon, and had them take Puddles down and gas him. Your father tells you he is sorry, and doesn't know why Mrs. Shanks would do such a thing, but you run out of the house and hide under the side porch all day and cry, anyhow. Later, you steal Mrs. Shanks's rug-beater from her garage. You bury it very deep in the soft, amber dirt behind the garage.

Your name is Morrie Feldman, and you are in junior high school. You hear something heavy hit the front of your house late one night, and then something else, and then a half-eaten grapefruit comes crashing through your front window, and out on the lawn — here in Ohio, and who'd ever think it — you see a huge cross burning. The next day you learn about the Anti-Defamation League. You don't tell anyone that you saw Mr. Evan Dennis from Dennis's Florists, with soot on his face and hands, running down the street to a car with its headlights out.

The name is the same, and it's later, and somehow you have a girl named Peggy Mantle, who has blond hair and blue eyes and Anglo-Saxon features, and you love her very much. Until you catch her doing things she never did with you. She's doing them in the bushes behind her house after the Halloween party. She's doing them with Leon Potter from across the street, whose mother always slams the door when you come on the porch. You don't say anything. You can't. You're afraid.

You've been afraid for a long time now. When you were smaller, once in a while you could beat Jack Wheeldon, or convince Leon that he should play with you. But they've continued to get bigger, and you've stayed small and frail, and they can beat you with their fists.

So you've learned to cut them up with your tongue.

You've learned how to tear them and shred them and slice them with your mouth. That's how it started. That's where it came from. That's why you leave town in a fruit truck, and go to Buffalo, and from there New York. That's why you go to a plastic surgeon when you've saved the money, and have your nose molded to look like another nose . . . Leon Potter's nose, or as close to it as the surgeon's samples came, but you don't realize that till much later.

That's why you decide to change your name.

Your name is not Morrie Feldman.

Your name is Marty Field.

You're a funny, funny man.

*

" . . . and so it is my extreme pleasure to introduce the boy we watched grow into a national celebrity . . . Marty Field!"

The auditorium caught up the frantic applause and flung it back and forth between the walls. The tumult was like nothing else Marty Field had ever heard. It caught in his eyes and ears and mouth like a great tidal wave, and drenched him with adoration. He rose and walked to the Principal, extending his hand automatically, receiving the embossed bronze plaque and the handshake simultaneously.

Then the wave subsided, leaving him washed up on the shore of expectancy, a sea of eyes beyond, waiting to bathe him in love and fame once more.

Fritz, it's cold; throw another Jew on the fire.

"Th-thank you . . . thank you very much . . . "

Tell them. Tell them, Morrie Feldman. Tell them what it was like. Tell them you know them for what they are. Make them realize that you've never forgotten. Show them the never-healed wounds; open the sores for them. Let them taste the filth of their own natures. Don't let them get away with it. That's why you came, isn't it? That was why the conquering hero returned! Don't let them lie to their children about all the good times, the fine times, the wonderful wonderful Marty Field they all loved and helped and admired. Don't let them spew their subtle poisons to their children while using you as an example of what a good non-you-know-what is like.

Let them wallow in their own scum, Marty Field.

So Abie says, "Business is business."

" . . . I don't know quite what to say . . . "

Don't let him Jew-you-down . . .

" . . . after all these years, to return home to such a warm and sincere . . . "

Kike!

" . . . I want you to know I'll always cherish this handsome bronze . . . "

Yid!

" . . . means more to me than all the awards I'll ever . . . "

Dirty little Christ-killer!

" . . . so thank you very much, again."

You walk off the stage, Marty Field. You hold your thirty pieces of silver (or is that one piece of bronze?) and you leave the high school, and get in the car that will take you back to the airport, and the world that loves you. You had your chance, and you didn't take it. Of course, you didn't, Marty. Because you're a coward. Strike your blow for truth and freedom? Hardly. It's your life, and you handle it for the guffaw, for the belly-buster, for the big exit.

But that's okay. Don't let it wig you, kid. And stop crying; you're not entitled to those tears. Stick with the sick shticks, buddy-boy.

Want a tag line? Want a punch line? How's this:

Have you seen the Do-It-Yourself Easter Kit? Two boards, three nails, and a Jew.

Author signifies audience reaction of laughter, applause, and sounds of scissors.

Yeah, you're a scream, Marty.

Gentleman Junkie

He looked down from the fourth-floor window of the Professional Building, watching an old man in a junk wagon pulled by a spavined horse.

Even from the window he could see the milky white blindness of the horse's left eye. It seemed fitting, somehow.

Walter Caulder turned away from the window, tasting the steel wool in his mouth. It was getting worse. A vagrant shiver flowed up from somewhere deep inside and he locked his arms about his body, trembling.

It was not going to get better, despite what Enid said. Triphammer pressures within his skull pistoned horizontally, threatening to cave his temples outward. A low, canine moan slid between his teeth, oily and hungry and lost in an instant.

"Did you say something, Doctor?" Rita Berg turned her blond head against the couch.

Caulder, an intense, short man with a heavy floss of prematurely grey hair, started abruptly at the sound of the woman's voice.

"What?"

"I asked if you'd said something, Doctor Caulder?" she repeated, sitting up on one elbow.

Caulder lay his head against the cool window frame. "No, nothing. Go ahead, Mrs. Berg. Please, it's getting late."

The tone of incipient annoyance brought her to a sitting position on the consultation couch, animosity in the line of her body, the tilt of her chin. "Well, I'm sorry I asked you to see me this evening, Doctor, but after all, I did have a committee meeting all day at Mt. Sinai, and that is public service work, and . . ."

Wearily he broke in, "Yes, yes, I know, Mrs. Berg. I'm sorry. I'm terribly sorry I snapped. Please go on."

"... and I am! paying you considerably more than your usual rate, there's no need to be snippy, Doctor," she concluded.

The wealthy woman: a tone.

Walter Caulder, who was a psychiatrist, who was a man of deep sensitivity and deeper perception, who was a drug addict desperately in need of a firestream shot in his body, turned away from the window with weariness.

"Mrs. Berg. I'm terribly sorry; I've been working very hard of late, and . . . and really. I'm very tired. Perhaps we had best conclude for this evening."

Rita Berg smoothed the expensive shantung skirt over her hips and stood up. The chill that had descended over her interrupted stream of consciousness persisted as she gathered her bolero jacket and handbag, and cursorily said goodnight to the small psychiatrist.

He walked her to the office door, through the darkened reception room and said meaningless mouthings —"Please call Enid for your next appointment . . . We'll add an extra twenty minutes to the next session . . . You've been very kind, thank . . . " — then she was gone, and he locked the door.

Oh, God, God, rotten God in Heaven or Hell . . . it *hurts*!

He doubled over and lay on the deep pile rug, clutching his stomach. Oh, God.

The shakes took him then.

Flinging him up and bending him terribly, a wild stallion, invisible and fire-snorting, tossing him, sending him down, shaking him with brutal ferocity.

Abruptly, it passed, and his mouth was pumice-filled. He rolled over and lay there, panting. He needed a fix!

After a long time, and it might have been a second, he climbed unsteadily to his feet and weaved to the heavy leather chair behind the desk. For a moment he thought he was through it (how like labor pains, spaced, growing closer together, more passionate) as he fell into the seat; then the black breakers hurled over him and he reached into the wastebasket.

There was water in the desk pitcher, but he could not take it. The effort was too great.

I've got to have a fix!

Night had settled slowly from above, like a great dusty radioactive curtain, filled with a million motes whose staggering numbers melted together to produce a sheet of dark. Now neons came alive outside and below the fourth floor window of the Professional Building.

Walter Caulder lifted the receiver of the phone and dialed a number from memory.

After a short space, during which beads of sickly, greasy perspiration had sprung to his upper lip and temples, he spoke into the mouthpiece.

"Nancy, that's you?"

The familiar voice he had not heard for several months reversed his words.

"I — I want to see you," he said.

"About what?" she inquired. There was calculated hardness in the way the words were spoken.

"I — I think I'd like to see you — I — I need a . . . a fix."

There was silence on the other end.

Then: "What's a'matter, Doc, the boys from Shakesville got to ya?"

His voice became urgent, violently demanding. "Nancy! Don't *do* this. I'm sick, Nancy. What can you do for me?"

"You been makin' yourself a stranger lately, Doc. Been almost two months since I saw ya." There was more than spite in her voice. There was hurt, and desire, and the need to hurt.

"Enid found out I was seeing you after she took my narcotics license, she — "

The girl's voice spat, even across the wires. "Enid! That goddam bitch! You still gonna marry her?"

"Nancy, she's my nurse, we've known each other a long time — I, Nancy, I need a *fix* — "

"Yeah, sure. When ya want a fix, it's Nancy, good old Nancy, but when ya wanna — aw, *crap!* All right. I'll meet you at Puffy's Diner on East 50th, you know where it is?"

He said he didn't, but he hastened to add he would find it.

She said nine o'clock; his agreement was quick. It was now seven thirty-seven.

*

At ten o'clock, hunched into a booth at the far end of Puffy's Diner, 50th and the waterfront, Walter Caulder saw his life flaking to pieces. She had not come, and it was so bad, so terribly, so ohithurts*here* bad.

A dozen cups of steaming, black coffee had gone down his tortured throat while he had waited, from eight o'clock till now. But she had not come.

She was punishing him.

He had known it was madness to involve himself with this girl, this acknowledged junkie, but when Enid had stumbled on the truth, that he was using his narcotics license to obtain drugs to feed his own habit, she had taken steps. Drastic steps. She had confiscated the license proper, and threatened to leave him if he did not turn himself over for medical aid.

Caulder remembered the night at her apartment when he had cried, and crawled on hands and knees to beg her. "Let me do it myself," he had pleaded. "Let me do it cold turkey," and her nostrils had flared, and contempt had shown in her eyes for a split instant.

"You're even using the *language* of a dope addict," she had observed, and it had cut worse than the knowledge that he was, *yes, hooked!*

But he had convinced her: it hadn't taken much — merely a complete renunciation of his manhood. So he had started to "cold turkey" a cure. It had gone badly from the first. At least she had been nearby. He had called her many nights, and she had come to help him. But then, one night she had not been there, and he had needed it, and he had gone where he could find it — where he had found Nancy.

For a while she had sold him what he needed, and Enid had known nothing of it. But she had found out. The strange bird tracks that ran up the insides of his arms. Then he had stopped seeing Nancy.

It had taken more talking, more crying, more begging, and this was his last chance with Enid. She was too good, really, too sensitive, too understanding. She had given him his second, his last chance to "cold turkey" himself back to respectability.

Tonight.

Enid visiting her sister in Minnesota. The chills, the pains, the visions, and Rita Berg describing her inane frigidity. If she had not demanded a late appointment, if he had been allowed to go home, where he would have locked himself in and sunk into a hot bath — perhaps.

But he had been alive, electric, and hungry.

Now he sat in a diner, and she had not come.

He clutched himself and rocked back and forth, like an old Hebrew praying, *dovening* for deliverance. That was the word . . . deliverance.

The tremors passed, and before fresh ones could replace, he slid out of the booth and paid the fat man who must be Puffy, of Puffy's Diner.

The cab deposited him in front of Nancy's leprous-faced brownstone. Inside. The dark hall, the odor of dead rodents, peculiarly the smell of cosmoline, wetted burned paper. Nancy.

The door was locked. He knocked then knocked louder then called then screamed and there was no answer. He took two steps backward long-legged and hit the door with his shoulder. He was a small man; the door hung on years-rusted hinges, silent and discolored. He was thrown back.

His shoulder was bruised raw when the door finally flew open inward and banged against the inner wall. The building was quiet, had no one heard? It was possible; this was a neighborhood of fear. Many things can not be heard if the incentive is great enough.

The smell of sweetness. She had been tooting pot.

More. The mugginess of bedsheets. The closed dry of dust settled in gloom.

He raced through the railroad flat and she was there, in the bed with a man. His tousled hair was all that showed from under the sheet. Caulder pulled back the filthy covering. They were both fully dressed. So it had been a shoot-up session, no sex. It had never been that way with him, he mused. Nancy felt gratified to have a well-known, respectable psychiatrist making love to her; that had been something else. Desire was killed by the drug.

He had to have a fix!

He pulled her out of the bed by her hair and dragged her across the room, into the hall, down to the bathroom. There he propped her on the toilet, and threw great handfuls of water in her face. It seemed to have no effect on her. He slapped her wrists, massaged pressure points at her neck and shoulders.

Finally, the girl's eyes opened to thin slits.

The pupils had a message. The message was simple: I'm gone. "How many caps?" he demanded. "How many, Nancy! I waited for you . . . you *knew* I needed a shot, and you — "

He was speechless. She had shot up with a customer, leaving him to withdraw and suffer.

"H-hi, Pops," she mumbled. Her eyes closed.

"Nancy! Nancy, I need a fix, *now!* I've got pain, Nancy."

Eyes closed, the thirsty lips opened. "Tough, Pops."

"Nancy, where is it, where's the stuff, Nancy! I've *got* to — Nancy, I've got to have a fix, Nancy!" His hands were busy, his terror rising as the pains shot through his stomach, as the lost Arctic chill came to him again. She laughed lightly and lolled against the tiled wall.

There was nothing he could do. So he searched. With the frantic wildness of a man who is dying painfully, he searched. The man in the bed did not stir. He was far out on a cloud of goldspun and nothing. When Caulder finally came back to the bathroom, he was convinced that if she had a boodle somewhere —

He would never find it.

"Tough, Pops," she said, softly, nastily. "Guess you'll have t'tough it out solo." Her eyes closed again, and she rolled her forehead against the chill tile of the bathroom wall.

Then Walter Caulder was slumped on the rim of the bathtub, crying. Holding his head in his feverish hands, his grey, floss hair falling over the fingers, he wept softly, because it hurt and it hurt so much he could not help himself.

From far away he heard her say, "Oh, Doc, don't do that, for

Chrissakes! I — I ain't got any more snow here . . . I'm — I'm sorry, s-sorry . . . he came over at the last minute . . . *Doc! Please!* Look, why don't we go inna other room an' get together, we can — "

He grabbed her by the shoulders, his hands biting into her flesh: "Where can I get a fix? Where can I get a shot, damn you!"

He shook her; her blond hair swirled about her like amputated bird's wings, and she gasped, "I d-don't kn-know, I d-don't know, maybe Spadesville, there's u-usually a g-game going in one of the garages on Ardmore Boule-boulevard."

He pressed her, and she came up with a number, an approximation of a remembrance, and he left her, slumped on the toilet, her head hanging, her senses plastered to the ceiling, whispering to them high above, "You was nice, Doc, so n-nice, stay with m-me . . . "

7103 was wrong.

It was 7003, and the garage was silent when they saw his white skin. They held the dice, bleached squarenesses on black flesh, the ebony of the dice-eyes matching their own hues.

"What you want?" the bearded one asked, settling back on his haunches.

Walter Caulder took three steps into the garage, and the pains hit with mule-kick ferocity. He staggered, clutching his belly, and stumbled clangingly up against the side of the Oldsmobile. He squealed in anguish, and the dice players stared with open wonder.

"Hey, Andus," the bearded one rib-elbowed the man beside him, "close them damn doors before we got the whole damn neighb'hood in heah." Andus rose and, catlike, glided around Walter Caulder, aswim in a sea of pain.

"Who is he, Beard?" asked a little yellow-skinned Negro on the far side of the craps circle.

Beard turned abruptly and gave the little man a hard glance. "Now how the hell am I supposed'ta know who he is? You think I know ev'body in this yeer city?"

Walter Caulder's mouth was filled with alkali dust.

"H-help m-me . . . " he mouthed the words with rubber lips and splintered tongue.

The Beard jerked a thumb in signal and two of the gamblers went to Caulder. They lowered him to the cement and one of them pulled a flask from an inner coat pocket. He unscrewed the jigger cap and offered it to Caulder's mouth.

"N-not th-that . . . " Caulder whimpered. "Shot, I need a . . . a . . . "

He did not finish the sentence, and there was no need for him to finish the sentence, because the sentence had been finished years before by another mouth and by many mouths down through the hungry, devastated years.

They stared at one another.

"Who ah you, Tom?" The Beard asked.

"I'm a guy who, who c-can p-pay for a shot, I n-need a, I'm *dying* please PLEASE!"

The sweat was cold as crystal tombstones on his face. His skin crawled. His belly heaved. His legs ached. His eyes burned. There were rivets in his nerve ends.

"I think you with the nabs, Tom," The Beard ventured, huskily.

"Damn you, d-damn you black — "

The line had been drawn, the chip had been put to the shoulder, the name of the Mother had been defiled, the war between the worlds had begun. "You don't call things down here'n Spadesville, ofay Tom. You don't call, 'cause we beat you futzin' head in."

And the little yellow-skinned gambler took a sharp, short step across the circle. The sharp Italian point of his highly polished black shoe caught Walter Caulder high on the right cheek, tearing a raw gash in his chilled flesh.

Caulder did not feel the blow.

Yet there was a basic embarrassment in him: he had no hatred of Negroes. He was not prejudiced. It had been the aching driving gimme hunger of the shot he had wanted, and it had conditioned a reflex he had never known he possessed.

"Listen to me, l-listen, I — I — "

How to explain to black men that you don't hate black men.

When the wrong impression has exploded, how do you cover it, send it away like spring mist?

They beat him terribly, cut him with small knives that left tearing hurts on the surface of him, and threw him into a gutter.

Someone urinated on him.

When the army ants had feasted on his corroded flesh; when the hobnailed boot of the moon had ceased to step and step on the exposed grey of his brain; when the spoon had quit its rhythmic clink-clink-clink in the coffee cup, he saw the red light.

His eyes were frosted, winter glass on an opaque sea-surface. They showed things that were not. He tried closing them, then opening them again.

It was the revolving angry red eye of a police growler.

"No!"

Then two men, burly and coats smelling of rain that had dried on them and perspiration that had not, lifted him —"Drunken bastard, book him and throw him inna tank with the other winos" — and tossed him into the back of a showroom-new smelling car.

He remembered answering a name. It was his name, so he did not worry about it. (I hurt . . . *here.*)

Here. Everywhere.

Then the hard, unyielding, hard cold, hard surface of a trough. A cell trough, and the ripe, fetid smell that was on him, and that had come from someone else before he had known this cell. There was wetness in the trough. He looked across and there was another man in the cell.

Walter Caulder's God was a madman. Walter Caulder's God had grown diseased and become warped. Yet Walter Caulder's God made miracles; insane, unplanned miracles coming at the wrong times, brought about for all the wrong reasons; gibbering miracles, neurotic miracles, damned miracles.

The other man in the cell was a junkie.

He was withdrawing a bent spoon, a pack of matches, and a safety pin from the inside lining of his pants cuff. As Caulder watched, eyes burning and mouth swollen, the man opposite withdrew several small paper packets from a slit cut on the inside of his shirt collar flap.

He was about to bake down a shot: he was ready for a fix.

Enid, where are you? Walter Caulder bleated in the lost valley of his mind. Faraway echoes reverberated the same cry; no answer, only the same cry.

Aloud he said: "Hey . . . h-hey, l-listen . . . "

The man turned his Irish face toward Walter Caulder and freckles danced before the psychiatrist's eyes. The wide, brown eyes of the Irishman blinked at him rapidly.

"I n-need a f-f-fix," he mouthed, his face stretched taut and painful under the bandages. "Please help me . . . I don't . . . I'll die if you d-d-don't — "

The Irishman's smile was a peculiar thing. He held it a moment longer than was necessary, and then said: "Okay, man, don't sweat. I got some extra Horse for you. I'll putcha up in the saddle . . . I get out inna morning. I don't need the extra boom."

So it was, less than ten minutes later, a ragged, jagged fissure ripped in the soft flesh of his inner arm — a rip made by a dirty safety pin — that Walter Caulder got his fix that night.

A long fix.

A good fix.

A satisfying fix.

As he lay back down in the urine-smeared trough, hands folded across his chest, his mind and senses eased for the first time that day, in many days, Walter Caulder had a singular thought.

As his senses raced out to infinity, as his mind began to experience the multicolored gems of color and sound that only "high" could bring, Walter Caulder sank into his swoon, and thought:

Physician, heal thyself.

But that was just silly.

May We Also Speak?

Four Statements from the Hung-Up Generation

1. NOW *YOU'RE* IN THE BOX!

The pain of it was not knowing what they were thinking. Hank had tried writing it from many angles, including such exotic views as first person present and omnipotent author intrusive, but the book would not jell.

The title was perfect: "Now You're in the Box!" and he had a vague idea what the title meant to him; it was intended to show that everyone is born boxed-in, and the hero had to realize that before he could truly become a man.

But somehow, it wasn't true. It wasn't *right*.

He shoved back from the kitchen table and slammed his palm against the stack of originals and carbons. "Oh, damn," he muttered, and snubbed the fortieth cigarette of the day. He stood up and rubbed the grainy feeling from his eyes.

He had started writing at five-thirty that morning, hoping to cork off a solid five thousand words that day, but the problems had been the same ones of the past month: restlessness, anger at himself, frustration. He just could not get inside his people. It was painful.

He walked about the tiny apartment, picking up dust on his fingertips from first this piece of furniture, then that. The image of the caged animal came to him and he chucked it away forcibly, grimacing at his own cliché.

He wandered back to the kitchen table and the silently accusing strange face of the portable, the unsullied stack of white bond, the jaundiced stack of second sheets. "Henry Willits Jefferson," he spoke to the stove, "you are not doing one damned thing to justify the title of Great White Hope of American Letters. No, you are not."

He reached for another cigarette. Number forty-one.

But there were only two packs available that morning, twenty to a pack, and he had smoked them all. *That's right*, he said to himself, *stunt the creative process with a nicotine fit*.

He chuckled and walked through the apartment to the front door. The hall smelled even worse today; Mrs. Killingsworth was cooking something even more vile than her beans and sauerkraut of the day before. A miasma of cloying proportions hung in the dim second-floor hall. He fled down the stairs quickly.

Mr. Brenner was behind the meat counter when Hank walked into the little one-arm grocery, and the heavy-bodied grocer wiped his big, wide, blocky hands free of blood when he saw Hank.

"What'll it be, Mr. Jefferson?" Brenner asked, strolling quickly around the checkout counter where Hank waited.

The words *Three packs of Marlboros* were ready at his lips, but never made their debut. The Negro came up close beside him and shoved the gun out in front of Hank, almost directly into Brenner's ample stomach.

"Open that registuh and hand me out whut you got in theah," he mouthed with a faint Southern accent.

It was so sudden, Hank did not realize a holdup was taking place. Peculiarly, all he could think at the moment was: *He must have just come from down South somewhere, and can't find work; he's desperate, this is so foolish!*

Brenner was hesitating, staring at the colored boy oddly. Hank shot a long glance at the boy, and the fine, high forehead and alert, dark eyes registered clearly. Still Brenner did not move.

"Ah said *please* open that registuh and hand ovuh what's

there," the boy said again. "Ah'm bein' poh-lite now, Mistuh. Dohn't make me get nasty."

Brenner chuckled, then. It was a rotten, unclean chuckle. "Who the hell you think you're scarin' with that water pistol, kid?" he snapped. His hand shot out.

Gunless, the boy realized he had failed miserably, and suddenly bolted, jarring Hank as he ran away.

"Black sonofabitch!" Mr. Brenner mouthed, his cheeks suffusing with blood. "I'll show that lousy nigger!"

He banged down a button on the cash register and the little bell rang as the drawer slammed open. He pulled the drawer forward and from a compartment behind the change shelf drew a small revolver. No water pistol; real; death.

"No!" Hank heard himself say.

Mr. Brenner gave him a peculiar, lingering glance that took a quarter-instant, before he threw himself around the checkout counter, and pounded out the front door.

Hank stood there only a moment, then followed, feeling foolish, finding himself running also.

The colored boy had cut across the street, dodging cars, and Hank could see Mr. Brenner only fifteen or twenty feet behind him as they raced down the street. Hank barely missed being hit by a car as he gained the opposite sidewalk, and ran after them.

The Negro was throwing his head back and forth wildly, looking for a certain area of escape. No alley or fence presented itself, and in desperation the boy turned into the shallow hallway of an apartment building set close to the sidewalk. He was inside, and Hank could hear him pulling at the door.

It was locked.

The colored boy fell down on his knees, then turned back facing the street. His hands were wide away from his body, and his eyes shined wet-white in his face.

"I'm *unahmed*, I'm *unahmed!*" he screamed as Mr. Brenner ground to a halt before him, aiming the tiny revolver at the boy's head. The boy's mouth was wide-open to scream again when Mr. Brenner pulled the trigger.

It knocked every tooth loose from the Negro's head, and

it tore a gigantic clot from the back of his head as it ripped through his mouth. The boy fell back against the glass door, the locked door, and stained it as he slipped sidewise.

"I worked twelve years in that store," Mr. Brenner said to the corpse, unnecessarily; and abruptly, Hank knew *precisely* what the title of his book meant.

2. THE ROCKS OF GOGROTH

So it had come down to this, finally, as Spence had known it would. All along he had known he would have to make a decision, and every time he thought of it, he went cold inside.

F. J. Gogroth was a man who would find it anathema to accept someone's disliking his beer. "The best goddam malt processing in the game," he often said. Gogroth Beer was more than a firm to F. J. Gogroth; it was a way of life.

And to participate in the rewards of that way of life — even in the secular capacity of advertising account executive — every member of the firm had to *believe*.

So how could Spence tell F. J. Gogroth that his plans for the new advertising campaign were ludicrous, misrepresentative and, worst of all, God forbid, doomed to failure? How could he tell him, when it meant doubting the Way of Life?

That would mean dissatisfaction on Gogroth's part; more, it would mean fury and retaliation. The sort of retaliation that would force Spence's bosses at HHC&M regretfully to release him. Gogroth was too big an account to chance losing. It was easier to dump the blame on Spence and lose *him*.

Spence took another cone of water from the cooler, and eyed the advertising presentation in its leather case, lying on the reception room couch. In that case — the size of a card-table top — was an advertising campaign that had been constructed along the lines F. J. Gogroth had suggested. *Suggested*, in this case, being synonymous with *ordered*. A campaign that would cost his firm hundreds of thousands of dollars in sales losses.

Emotionally annoying; subliminally repugnant; subconsciously negative-thought producing . . . the catchphrases popped into Spence's mind, but he knew they would never fit into Mr. Gogroth's view of the universe.

He sat down, praying the receptionist would not receive that buzz from within. The buzz that would tell her Mr. Gogroth's current supplicator had gone and she could send in the next visitor with his oblation.

How the hell did I ever get into this racket?

It was a demoralizing question he had asked himself, and he put it from himself with a mental wrenching. It was a racket, like any other, and just because he was going to get dumped when Gogroth informed the boss young Spence was not thinking pro-Gogroth, was no reason to damn the entire industry.

Dumped . . .

Then an idea came to him, and he liked it even less than the concept of himself being fired.

The idea remained with him despite his attempts to drown it in a flood of scruples and morality.

There was Jean and her need for worldly possessions. That McCobb sofa and chair suite would run a good fifteen hundred, and a man out of work cannot afford to buy Paul McCobb furniture, or Saarinen chairs, or any of the other fantastic implements of what Jean called "the good life."

Could he afford to lose Jean?

Because that would be one of the resultant consequences of telling old man Gogroth the truth. And if he didn't — what then?

Why then, I'm compromising, he told himself acidly, and all the good nonfiction books on the subject say that is a moral sin for the thinking man in our time, as well as bad for the soul, the talent, and the complexion.

He didn't give a damn about compromising, not really. It was something he could not *afford* to give a damn about. That was for guys with other problems, in other rackets. It was a tough life. All the similes about the Madison Avenue jungle. Other guys with other problems.

Not the problem of Mr. Gogroth and his rocks.

So there was another way out.

There was the simple way out of sharking someone else. Making someone else guilty. If the campaign went as it was planned — and there was no question it was a really bad, insulting campaign — Gogroth would lose a mint, and he was going to demand a head be chopped.

Again, Spence did not care if Gogroth lost his shirt, uppers, and lowers entirely. It might do the fat bastard some good at that to taste poverty.

But what about me?

He had known poverty, and Jean had left him nine times in three years. Okay, so she was mercenary, and the good life appealed more than the poverty. Was that a crime? He knew only that he could not live without her, and if it took lying a little, compromising a little, setting someone else up for the kill a little . . . that was the price one had to pay. Or make someone else pay.

So the idea clung like a porous plaster.

Make it Gerry Coogan's idea, Gerry Coogan's baby all the way. It was in the way you phrased it: "Our boy Gerry Coogan did all the prep work on this, F. J." and "Remember that name, F. J.; Gerry Coogan's the boy who set this up so beautifully for you."

Sure it was a rat trick. That was the law of the jungle. Eat or — oh hell!

He knew he couldn't do it. Coogan needed the job as badly as he did. He had two kids, and that extra after-hours work as a commercial artist wasn't helping out as much as a man in Coogan's position needed. Not with one of the kids being eaten by a tumor.

No, he decided, he couldn't do it. Jean would just have to take their life together as he was able to provide it, or they'd have to part the ways. It was that simple.

The buzz startled him, and for a second after the receptionist's dulcet tones advised him, "You may go in now, Mr. Spence," he sat there.

Then, rising, he tucked the case under his arm and strode up to F. J. Gogroth's door. That man could really throw the rocks . . .

"Good morning, F. J.," he chirped gaily, marching into the presence. "Say, this is one helluva wild promotion we've got shored up for you. One of our best men was the real brain behind it. A guy we're really proud to have on the team . . . "

3. PAYMENT RETURNED, UNOPENED

For her it had been Halley's Comet in her closed hand, sharp pinwheels of light and fire whirling. For him it had been a fast lay on a chick with a harelip. And from this union there came three: a sorrow burning steadily, a hag-riding guilt, and a foetus.

Claude Hammel was a first-year dental student; he waited tables at the ZBT house to make expenses (though working for all those yids bothered him), and he *knew* he could not marry her.

So, logically enough, he went to a fortuneteller.

"Why do I have to tell you all that?" he asked, already firmly convinced she was a charlatan — so why the hell had he come here in the first place?

"I have to know what you consider the truth of it, so that I may more correctly interpret the future as it will affect you." Her hair was caught up under a brightly colored *babushka* and the color of the cloth was challenged by the crimson that chain-reactioned in her wrinkled cheeks and her pipe-bowl nose. She drank, it was there in the wreckage of her face.

"But if I tell you why I came, what good can you do me . . . tell me that, will you?"

She spread her hands, and he felt trapped, somehow. "You came because you were walking and saw this place, and wanted an answer. Do you want the answer . . . or *any* answer?" So he told her about the rooming house where he lived, and about Ann. How she had been crying in her basement room and how he had taken advantage of it, telling her he loved her.

"I don't know, it was just, it was, hell, I don't know. I just did it!"

She stared at him levelly. "And now she is with child and the idea of marrying a harelipped girl repulses you. I can understand that." Her gaze was cynical, mocking.

"That isn't it at all," he jumped to defend himself. "I just can't, I mean, I can't marry *anyone* right now. Not Princess Grace if I'd knocked her, I mean, excuse me, if she was available. I've got to finish school."

The gypsy stared at him for a terrible moment.

"She might kill herself," she ventured.

"Oh, come *on!*" he derided the idea. No one took their life these days over something like that.

"All right, then," she said, clasping her wrinkled fingers. He noticed her joints were arthritically swollen and somehow it disturbed him more than her gaze or words. "Here's the answer to your problem . . ."

He leaned forward. Oddly, he believed she *might* have a solution. It was cockeyed, but that was the way with life, and he was desperate.

"There is safety in numbers," she said softly.

He waited expectantly, but she was finished.

"And?" he asked.

"Pay me now, then go away." Her voice was very cool and businesslike. The conference was concluded.

"Hey, what the hell kind of a fortune is *that?*" he demanded angrily. He felt cheated.

"Pay me and then go," she repeated. There was something deadly in her tone. He reached into his pocket and brought out a dollar bill, almost without realizing he was doing it. Her eyes held him fascinated: cobra and mongoose.

When he was outside, walking the foggy night back toward the campus, he pondered what she had said. At first it made no sense whatever. Then it made a great deal of sense, and it frightened him so much he stopped and swallowed with difficulty.

It was a terrible thing to consider.

He stopped at the first liquor store he could find and bought a fifth of Black & White. He knew she would be at home; she lived alone and no one called her for dates.

She was pleased to see him, timorous at first, fearing her news of earlier that day would have driven him away.

Her hair was very soft, and brown, and reminded him in an obscure way of the robin's wings. She wore it long, in a forties-style pageboy that flattered the long planes of her face. Her eyes were also very brown and moist. It was a nice face.

Except for the harelip, which he stared at in fascination. A fascination she took to be unconcern born of attraction for her as a whole. She thought he did not notice. She was wrong.

It took him only an hour and forty minutes to get her drunk enough where his watery explanation of why he had to leave for a few minutes seemed logical to her. "I'll be right back," he said in her ear. She was staring dimly at the ceiling from her position on the couch with eyes that saw very little.

"I'll turn out the lights," he said.

"You'll be back, won't you?" she begged him.

"I'll be back," he said, cold and wooden inside.

He found ten guys he knew at the Double-Decker, having malts and salamiburgers, and he clued them in. It wasn't quite as he told it, but they accepted his story. He led them back to the rooming house, and sent the first guy down into the darkness of the basement room with a slap on the back.

Her passionate moan sounded final, and while he waited with others, smoking, he recalled what the gypsy had said. Somehow, he could not bring himself to chuckle.

4. THE TRUTH

I'd spent the whole day down at the Union Hall, trying to pick up a good horn, but anybody who'd have fitted in was either out on the cultural exchange bit or blowing on the Coast.

There were half a dozen fat lips lying around, there always are, but I wouldn't have spit on the best of them. Which left me right where I'd started when Cookie had come down with a bad case of holding and the fuzz had carted him away to Lexington. I could've told them they were flapping their wings out-of-rhythm; Cookie'd rather die than lose his monkey.

But he'd been the best horn in town.

Which left us an important side short, going into the most impressive gig of our career. Saul Maxim wasn't paying us for a four-man quintet, and I was about to call one of the numbers I'd taken from those dogs at the Hall, when this kid came into Maxim's, with a horn case tucked tight under his wing.

He looked around, mostly at us on the stand, and finally gave it the leg. He was tall, with a sort of loose-limbed Mulligan look about him, crewcut, nice face, and the white muscle ridge on his upper lip that was his membership badge in the trumpeter's club. Looked like a nice-enough kid, and the boys stopped screwing around as he walked up to the stand.

"You Art Staff, 'round here?" he asked.

I nodded and stuck out my hand. "The same. Something I can do for you?"

He took the hand and looked me cold in the eyes with, "The word's been goin' around you need a horn. I was on the loose, so I figured I'd come over, give it a try. You still needing?"

"We're still needing," I said, "if you can do the work. It's five sets a night, and you'll get scale. That sound okay?"

He shrugged. It didn't seem to matter. "Fine by me. Want I should audition now?"

I was about to say go ahead but Arville Dreiser, our drummer, whistled loud behind me. "Want to hold it a minute, Art? Call of nature."

I gave him the go-ahead and he cut for the sandbox. I invited the kid to sit down and jaw with me for a couple minutes. He set the case right beside himself, and slumped onto the stand beside me. "What's your name?" I asked.

Deliberately, he wiped the corners of his mouth where little sticky clots of saliva-dirt had gathered. "Del Matthews," he answered, coolly. It seemed to fit.

"You don't look like you need this gig too bad," I made small talk. "Who've you played with?"

He made a small wave in the general direction of nowheresville. "Around," he said. "Nobody you'd know. A few rhythm-and-blues outfits. I been in the city a couple months, haven't been able to make too much of a connection."

That sounded bad. If the kid had been any good, with the shortage the way it was, he'd have been bound to pick up at least something. "You, uh, you got a card?" He nodded, reached into his hip pocket, and brought up an empty, weathered wallet. He flashed the card. It was current. It looked bad.

"What'd'ya blow?" I inquired, as politely as I could, trying not to let him know I was spooked.

"Anything, mostly. Makes no difference. You call 'em, I can play it. Just as long as I can blow, that's all I'm looking for. Just work."

There was something peculiar in his eyes. I'd have laughed at myself if I'd recognized that look at the time, but I didn't. It was only lots later that I dug it was the same expression I'd seen in paintings of the big man, Christ. Strange how things like that hang with you. I didn't dig, then, but later it came to me.

All he seemed to want to do, apparently, was work.

So I was game to try. We had to work that night, and I was backed to the wall. We needed the gig bad.

*

About that time Dreiser came out of the KINGS room and hopped up onto the stand. He sat down behind the traps and gave me the nod. I heaved a sigh, stood up (wondering which number I should ring up for a horn when this kid blew out), and moved to the piano. The kid took his horn.

I figured we ought to give him every possible, so I asked him if he knew the Giuffre "Four Brothers." He said he did, without hesitation, so I gave it a three-bar intro, and Rog came on with the bass the way we'd rehearsed it; Dreiser hit the drums down soft and Frilly Epperson joined at the same instant with his sax. We were all swinging, and waiting for that first note, when the kid came on.

Now I want to tell this just so. He could blow, that was the first thing. I don't mean he copied: he wasn't Farmer, and he wasn't Miles; he wasn't Nat Adderley or Diz, either. He was all himself.

He was fingering a Selmer that looked as though it had seen a few hock shops, and hadn't been shined very often, but he could blow. He came on like the west wind and for a second we all stumbled, listening to him.

Then when we hit the solo spot where Cookie'd usually ride out —"Four Brothers" was a virtuoso piece any time — the kid went on ahead like Hurricane Hilda. He caught the repetitive riffs and whanged on each one till it said "Uncle!" Frankly, I was impressed as hell.

The kid wasn't any finger-poppin' Daddy, either. He knew his sounds. There was — *what was it?* — there was like *truth* in what he blew. It was really, honest to God, *saying* something. I looked over and Frilly was staring at the kid with eyes like pizzas. I heard Arville Dreiser drop the beat for a second, which he *never*, so I knew they were all pretty high on the kid.

When he had expended his conversation, we went into a restatement of the theme and finished it up faster than even Cookie had been able to gun it. I didn't say anything for a minute, then said, "Let's try 'Laura.'"

He nodded, and Frilly opened it so quick I gave him a long look. But he didn't give a damn; he wanted to hear more of that horn, he couldn't wait.

Well.

He blew "Laura" like it would have made Gene Tierney bawl. And this time I was sure. The kid was blowing the truth. It was the kind of sound Monk has in his piano, the kind of thing Bird had, and the thing Bix had right up to the end. It was the kind of thing Louis had for a while till he found the tomming routine paid better. It was simply the truth.

"Laura" finished and the sound still hung. When it had gone to its velvet rest, I realized the kid had finished the piece alone, we'd sunk to silence digging.

The kid didn't say anything. He just banged out the spittle and settled onto one hip, waiting for the word.

I swung around on the stool and pulled out a butt. I lit it, and didn't look at him as I said, "Sorry, kid, don't think you're exactly what we want. We play a little too hard bop for you, I guess. Maybe some other time. No hard — "

He cut me off with a flat sweep of his hand. He'd heard it all before. He holstered the Selmer and mumbled a cool, "Thanks. Yeah, later," and was gone.

Nobody said anything to me.

But nobody argued with me — either.

Hell, it was obvious. I got up and dropped off the stand, making for the phone booth. I didn't feel so good. But it was obvious:

Nobody likes to hear the truth. Makes you realize how not-so-good you *really* are. The truth hurts.

That was when I recognized the look in the kid's eyes.

I finally got my hornman, that night.

He sounded like hell.

Daniel White for the Greater Good

Begin with absolute blackness. The sort of absolute blackness that does not exist in reality. A black as deep and profound as the space directly under a heel pressed to the ground; a black as all-encompassing as blindness from birth; a black *that* black. The black of a hallway devoid of light, and a black — advancing down that hallway — going away from you. At the end of a hallway so black as this, a square of light painfully white. A doorway through which can be seen a window, pouring dawn sunlight in a torrent into the room, through the doorway, and causing a sunspot of light at the end of the pitch-black hallway.

If this were a motion picture, it would be starkly impressive, the black so deep, and the body moving away from the camera, down the hall toward the square of superhuman white. The body clinging to the right-hand wall, moving down the tunnel of ebony, slowly, painstakingly, almost spastically. The body is a form, merely a form, not quite as black as the hallway mouth that contains it, but still without sufficient contrast to break what would be superlative camera work, were this a motion picture. But it is not a motion picture. It is a story of some truth.

It is a story, and for that reason, the effect of superlative cinematography must be broken as the body pulls itself to the door, lurches through, and stumbles to grasp at the edge of a chest-high wooden counter. The camera angles (were this a motion picture) would suddenly shift and alter, bringing into immediate focus the soft yet hard face of a police desk sergeant, his collar open and sweat beading his neck and upper lip. We might study the raised bushy eyebrows and the quickly horrified expression just before the lips go rigid. Then the camera would track around the squad room, we would see the Georgia sunrise outside that streaming window, and finally our gaze would settle on the face of a girl.

A white girl.

With a smear of blood at the edge of her mouth, with one eye swollen shut and blue-black, with her hair disarrayed and matted with blood, leaves and dirt . . . and an expression of pain that says one thing:

"Help . . . me . . . "

The camera would follow that face as it sinks slowly to the floor.

Then, if this were a movie and not reality, in a town without a name in central Georgia, the camera would cut to black. Sharp cut, and wait for the next scene.

It might have been simpler, had he been a good man. At least underneath; but he wasn't. He was, very simply, a dirty nigger. When he could not cadge a free meal by intimidation, he stole. He smelled bad, he had the morals of a swamp pig, and as if that were not enough to exclude him from practically every strata of society, he had bad teeth, worse breath, and a foul mouth. Fittingly, his name was Daniel White.

They had no difficulty arresting him, and even less difficulty proving he was the man who had raped and beaten Marion Gore. He was found sleeping exhausted in a corner of the hobo jungle at the side of the railroad tracks on the verge of the town. There was blood on his hands and hair under his fingernails. Police lab analysis confirmed that the blood type and follicles of hair matched those of Marion Gore.

Far from circumstantial, these facts merely verified the confession Daniel White made when arrested. He was not even granted the saving grace of having been drunk. He was surly, obscene, and thoroughly pleased with what he had done. The fact that Marion Gore had been sixteen, a virgin, and had gone into a coma after making her way from the field where she had been attacked to the police station, seemed to make no impression on Daniel White.

The local papers tagged him — and they were conservative at best — a conscienceless beast. He was that. At least.

It was not unexpected, then, to find a growing wave of mass hatred in the town. A hatred that continually emerged in the words "Lynch the bastard."

At first, the word *black* was not even inserted between *the* and *bastard*. It wasn't needed. It came later, when the concept of lynching gave way to a peculiar itch in the palms of many white hands. An itch that might well be scratched by a length of hemp rope.

It had to happen quickly, or it would not happen at all. The chief of police would call the mayor, the mayor would get in touch with the governor, and in a matter of hours the National Guard would be in. So it had to happen quickly, or not at all.

And it was bound to happen. There was no doubt of that. There had been seeds planted — the school trouble, darkie rabble-rousers from New Jersey and Illinois down talking to the nigras in Littletown, that business at the Woolworth's counter — and now the crop was coming in.

Daniel White was safe behind bars, but outside, it was getting bad:

. . . the big-mouth crowd that hung out in Peerson's Bowling and Billiard Center caught Phil the clean-up boy, and badgered him into a fight. They took him out back and worked him over with eight-inch lengths of bicycle chain; the diagnosis was double concussion and internal hemorrhaging.

. . . a caravan of heavies from the new development near the furniture factory motored down into Littletown and set fire to The Place, where thirty-five or forty of the town's more responsible Negro leaders had gathered for a few drinks and a discussion of what their position might be in this matter. Result: fifteen burned, and the bar scorched to the ground.

. . . Willa Ambrose, who washed and kept house for the Porters, was fired after a slight misunderstanding with Diane Porter; Willa had admitted to once taking in a movie with Daniel White.

. . . the Jesus Baptist Church was bombed the same night Daniel White made his confession. The remains of the building gave up evidence that the job had been done with homemade Molotov cocktails and sticks of dynamite stolen from the road construction shed on the highway. Pastor Neville lost the use of his right eye: a piece of flying glass from the imported stained glass windows.

So the chief of police called the mayor, and the mayor called the governor, and the governor alerted his staff, and they discussed it, and decided to wait till morning to mobilize the National Guard (which was made up of Georgia boys who didn't much care for the idea of Daniel White, in any case). At best, ten hours.

A long, hot, dangerous ten hours.

Daniel White slept peacefully. He knew he wasn't going to be lynched. He also knew he was going to become a *cause célèbre* and might easily get off with a light sentence, this being an election year, and the eyes of the world on his little central Georgia town.

After all, the NAACP hadn't even made an appearance yet. Daniel White slept peacefully.

He knew he didn't deserve to die for Marion Gore.

She hadn't really been a virgin.

The NAACP man's name was U. J. Peregrin and he was out of the Savannah office. He was tall, and exceedingly slim in his tailored Ivy League suit. He was nut-brown and had deep-set eyes that seemed veiled like a cobra's. He spoke in a soft, cultivated voice totally free of drawl and slur. He had been born in Tenafly, New Jersey, had attended college at the University of Chicago, and had gone into social work out of a mixture of emotions. This assignment had come to him chiefly because of his native familiarity with the sort of culture that spawned Daniel White — and a lynch mob.

He sat across from Henry Roblee (who had been picked by the terror-stricken Negro residents of that little central Georgia town as their spokesman) and conversed in three A.M. tones. Seven hours until the National Guard might come, seven hours in which anything might happen, seven hours that had forced the inhabitants of Littletown to douse their lights and crouch behind windows with 12-gauges ready.

"We've never had anything like this here," Henry Roblee admitted, his square face cut with worry. He rubbed his blocky hands over the moist glass. A thin film of whiskey colored the bottom of the glass. A bottle stood between them on the table.

Peregrin drew deeply on his cigarette and stared into Roblee's frightened eyes. "Mr. Roblee," he said softly, "you may never have had anything like this before, but you've certainly got it now, and the question is, 'What do we intend to do about it?'" He waited. Not so much for an answer as for a realization on the other man's part of just what the situation meant.

"It's not White we're worried about," Roblee added hastily. "That jail is strong enough, and I don't suppose the Chief is going to let them come by without doing something to stop them. It's what's happening all over town that's got us frightened. We never seen the people round here act this way. Why, they in a killing frame of mind!"

Peregrin nodded slowly.

"How is your Pastor?" he asked.

Roblee shrugged. "He's gone be blind in the one eye, maybe both, but that's what I *mean*. That man was respected by everybody 'round here. They thought most highly of him. We got to protect ourselves."

"What do you propose?" Peregrin asked.

Roblee looked up from the empty glass suddenly. "What do *we* propose? Why, man, that's why we asked for help from the N-double A-CP. Don't you under*stand*? Something terrible's gone happen in this town unless we decide what to do to stop it. Even the sensible folks 'round here are crazy mad with wanting to lynch that Daniel White."

"I can only make suggestions; that's my job. I can't *tell* you what to do."

Roblee fondled the glass, then filled it half full with uneven movements. He tipped it up and drank heavily. "What about if we just all moved on out for a few days?"

Peregrin shook his head.

Roblee looked away, said softly, ironically, "I didn't think

so." He moved his tongue over his thick, moist lips. "Man, I am
scared!"

Peregrin said, "Do you think the Chief would let me in to
speak to White tonight?"

The other man shrugged. "You can try. Want me to give him
a call?" Peregrin nodded agreement, and added, "Let me speak
to him. The organization might carry a little weight."

It was decided, after the call, that Peregrin and Roblee would
both go to see Daniel White. The chief of police advised them to
come by way of the police emergency alley, where the chance of
their being seen and stopped would be less.

In the cell block, Peregrin stood for several minutes watching
Daniel White through the bars. He studied the face, the attitude
of relaxation, the clothing the man wore.

He mumbled something lightly. Roblee moved up next to him,
asked, "What did you say?"

Peregrin repeated the words, only slightly louder, yet distinctly.
"Sometimes I wonder if it's worth it. Sometimes I think there are
too many fifth columnists."

Roblee shook his head without understanding what Peregrin
had said.

"Should we talk to him?" the Georgia Negro said to the Ivy-
tailored visitor.

Peregrin nodded resignedly. "Not much bother, but we might
as well. We're here."

Roblee stepped up to the bars. He called in to Daniel White.
The man woke suddenly, but without apprehension. He sat up
on the striped tick mattress and looked at his two callers. He
smiled, a gap-toothed grin that was at once charming, disarming,
frightful, and painful. "Hey there, y'all." He stood up and walked
to the bars with a lazy, rolling strut.

"You the man from the N-double A-CP I bet," he said, the
words twisted Georgia-style. Peregrin nodded.

"Glad t'meetcha. You gone keep them sonofabitches from
hangin' me?" He continued to grin, a self-assured, cocky grin
that rankled Peregrin.

The tall Negro moved his face very close to the bars. "You
think I should?"

Daniel White made a wry face. "Why, man, you and me is brothers. We the same, fellah. You can't let them string up no brother of yours. Got to show them damn ofay we as good as them any day."

Peregrin's face momentarily wrenched with distaste. "*Are* we the same, White? You and me. You and Mr. Roblee here? Are we all the same." He paused, and leaned his forehead against the bars.

"Perhaps we are, perhaps we are," he murmured.

Daniel White stared at him for some time, without speaking. But he grinned. Finally, "I gone beat this thing, Mister NAACP, you just wait an' see. I gone get outta this."

Peregrin raised his eyes slowly. "You don't even feel any remorse, do you?"

White stared at him uncomprehending. "Whatch'ou mean?"

Peregrin's face raised to the ceiling, helplessly, as though drawn on invisible wires. "You really don't know, do you?" he said to himself.

Daniel White grunted and bared rotten teeth. "Listen to me, Mister NAACP you. I gone tell you somethin'. That little white bitch, that Gore child, she a bum from a long way back: man, I seen her in the woods with half a dozen boys from time on time. She not such a hot piece, I tell you that."

Peregrin turned to Roblee. "Let's go," he said, slowly. "We've done all we can here."

They moved back down the cell block: the empty cell block from which the three drunks and the vag had been removed when the first rumors of lynch had begun circulating.

Outside, it was not so quiet. There were mutterings from dark corners of the central Georgia town. Murmurings, unrests, fear, and rising voices.

In his cell, Daniel White returned to sleep. *He* knew what was going to happen. He had it locked. He was a poor darkie who was going to get all the benefits so long overdue his people.

The man from the NAACP would tend to all that . . . even if he was a fruity-looking cat in a funny suit.

"What the hell you mean, for the greater good? Are you crazy or something, mister? You can't let that mob take him and lynch him?" Roblee's face was a mask of horror. "Are you crazy or *what?*"

Peregrin's forehead was a crisscross of weaving shadow, caught in the flickering light of the candle. They sat at the table once more, joined by five others, all hidden in the grey and black of the room. The shades were drawn, and behind the shades, curtains had been pulled. And they sat staring at the man from the NAACP, Peregrin, who had just told them, without preamble, that they must not only let the whites lynch Daniel White, but they must do everything in their power to aid the act.

"Say, listen, Mister Peregrin, I think you out of your mind. That's *murder*, man!" The speaker was a stout, balding man with coffee-colored skin and a wart at the side of his wide nose.

"Just what do you mean, 'for the greater good?'" Roblee sank a hand heavily on Peregrin's sleeve. Peregrin continued to sit silently, having said what he felt he must say.

Roblee shook him. "Dammit, fella, you gone answer me! What'd you mean by that?"

Peregrin looked up at them, then. His eyes caught the candlelight and threw it back in two bright lines. His face was shattered; there was conflict and fear and desperation in it. But determination. "All right," he said, finally.

They stared at him as he dry-washed his cheekbones and temples with moist hands. "Daniel White is sleeping up in that jail, and he doesn't care *what* happens to any of you. He had his fun, and now he wants to capitalize on all the work we've done for so long, to escape punishment. He's banking on everyone making such a hue and cry that no one will dare hurt the poor nigger being taken advantage of, down in rotten Georgia."

Roblee continued to watch the tall man, impassively, waiting. There was confusion in the cant of his head, in the frozen hand on Peregrin's sleeve.

"Those people out there," Peregrin waved a fist at the shaded window, "they're stretched as tight as piano wires. They've been told that everything they've believed for hundreds of years is a lie. They've been told the Negro is as good as them, they've been told their white sons and daughters are going to have to move over and share five-and-ten-cent store seats with them, and schools with them, and buses with them, and movies with them . . ."

His breath came labored. He ground his teeth together and went on with difficulty.

"They've had the rug pulled out from under them, and they're still falling. They'll *be* falling for a long time. Done slowly, they could adjust to it. But then Daniel White rapes a sixteen-year-old girl and they've got a reason to hate, they've got something to focus their hate on. So they start taking out their fear and confusion in any way they can.

"Look what has happened in just the few hours since the girl was found. Your church has been bombed. Negroes have been fired and ostracized, some have been beaten up and perhaps that boy they stomped will die. Your homes and that bar have been burned. This isn't going to stop here. It's going to get worse. And it's not even going to stop with your town. It's going to march like a wave to the beach, washing all the work we've done before it.

"If Daniel White goes free."

He paused.

Roblee made to interrupt, "But to let them haul him out of there and lynch him, that's . . ."

"Don't you *understand*, man," Peregrin turned on Roblee with fury. "Don't you hear what I'm telling you? That man up there isn't merely a poor sonofabitch who got loaded and pawed a white girl. He's a cold-blooded miserable animal, and if anyone deserved to die, it's him. But that has nothing to do with it. I'm talking to you about the need for that man to die. I'm telling you, Roblee, and all of you, that if you don't take their minds off the Negro community as a whole, you're going to set back the cause of equality in this country fifty years. And if you think I'm making this up you better realize that it's already happened once before, just this way."

They stared at him.

"Yes, dammit, it happened once before. And though we didn't have anything to do with the way it turned out — and thank

God it turned out as it did — we would have told them to do it just the way they did."

They stared, and suddenly, one of them knew.

"Emmett Till," he breathed, softly.

Peregrin turned on the speaker. "That's right. They didn't even know for sure what the circumstances had been but the trouble was starting up — not even as bad as here — and they hauled Till out and killed him. And it stopped the trouble like *that*!" he snapped his fingers.

"But *lynching* . . . " Roblee said, horrified.

"Don't you understand? Are you stupid or something, like they say we are? Monkeys? Can't you see that Daniel White dead can be more valuable than a hundred Daniel Whites alive? Don't you see the horror that Northerners will feel, the repercussions internationally, the demands for justice, the swift advance of the program . . . can't you see that Daniel White can serve the greater good. The good of all his people?

"What he never was in life, that miserable bastard up there can be in death!"

Roblee sank away from Peregrin. The taller man had not spoken with fanaticism, had only delivered with desperate and impassioned tones what he knew to be true. They had heard him, and now each of them, where there was no room for anyone else's opinions, was thinking about it. It meant murder . . . or rather, the toleration of murder. What they were deliberating was the necessity of lynching. There was no doubt that the trouble could be much worse in the town, that more homes would be burned and more people hurt, perhaps killed. But was it enough to know that to sacrifice up a man to the mob madness, to the lynch rope? Was it enough to know that you might be saving hundreds of lives in the long run by sacrificing one life hardly worth saving to begin with?

It might have been easier, had Daniel White been a man with some qualities of decency. But he wasn't. He was just what the White Press had called him, a beast. That made it the more difficult; for had he been easier to identify with, they could have said no. But this way . . .

There were murmurs from around the room, and the murmurs were, "I . . . don't . . . know . . . I just don't know . . . "

It meant more than just saving the skins of the people in Littletown — though men had been sacrificed to save fewer lives — it meant saving generations of children to come, from sitting in the backs of movie houses, of allowing them to grow up without the necessity of knowing squalor and prejudice and the words "shine," "nigger," "Jim Crow."

It meant a lot of things, that thin thread of life that was Daniel White. That thin thread that might be stretched around Daniel White's neck.

It meant a lot.

It was a double-edged sword that slicing one way would tame the wrath of the mob beast, and slicing the other would make a path for more understanding, by use of shame and example.

But could they do it . . . ?

Were this a motion picture, and not a story of some truth, the camera might play about the darkened room, candlelit and oppressive. It might play about the gaunt, hardening faces of the men, and mirror their decisions. If this were a motion picture. And the emphasis on good camera studies. But it is not a motion picture, and when they threw up their hands saying they could not decide, Peregrin had to say, "Let's go talk to someone who knows this mob."

So they agreed, because the decision was not one that men could make about another man.

When they opened the door of the house on the edge of Littletown, and stepped out, they did not see the mass of moving dark shadows. The first warning they had was the heat-laden voice snarling, "You goin' tuh save that nigger rape bastard, Savannah man? Like *hell* you are!"

Then they jumped.

At first they used the lead pipes and the hammers, but after the first flurry they spent their fury and went on to fists and boots. Peregrin caught a blow in the face that spun him around, sent him crashing into the wall of the house. Off in the darkness he could hear Roblee screaming and the wet, regular syncopation of someone kicking at bloody flesh.

Later, much later, when all the lights had stopped whirling, and all the strange new colors had become merely reds and greens and blues, they dragged themselves to their feet

Roblee's face looked like a pound of moist hamburger. He daubed at the ruined expanse of skin and said very defiantly, "It's that White's fault. All this. All this, it's *his* fault. We don't hafta take it for him."

Peregrin said nothing. It hurt too much merely to breathe. His rib cage had been crushed. He lay against the house, listening, hearing what they had to say.

The others joined in, between sobs and rasps of breath. "*Let them lynch him. Let them do it.*"

They knew who to see . . . they knew the men with the ropes . . . the men who would start to hit them when they appeared, but who would listen when they said they had come to give up Daniel White. They knew who to see.

They told Peregrin: "We'll be back. You rest there. We'll do it." And they moved off into the night, to make their vengeance.

Peregrin lay up against the building, and he began to cry. His voice was soft, and deep as he said to the sky, "Oh God, they're doing it, but they're doing it for the wrong reasons. They're hating, and that isn't right. They'll give him up, and that's what we need, Lord, but why do they have to do it this way?"

Then after a while, when he had fainted several times, and had the visions of the men storming the jail, and striking the guards and dragging the snarling, defiant Daniel White from his cell, his thoughts became clearer.

It was worth it. It had to be worth it. What they did, what they allowed, it had to be worth something in the final analysis. For the greater good, he had said. It had to be that. Because if it wasn't, surely there could be no hell deep enough to receive him.

If it was worth it, the end had to be in sight.

And had this been a motion picture, with a happy ending desirable — instead of a grubby little story out of central Georgia — then the man called Peregrin would have considered the inscription they must carve on the statue of the martyr, Daniel White.

Lady Bug, Lady Bug

Ivor Balmi found the party already in progress when he arrived back at his studio. "Studio" was a lofty coloring for a colorless loft, but in the New York of that season, so vastly in flux with all the *right* people either just returning and unsettled, or moving to the Coast, to Europe, especially to the Maritime Alps — Ivor Balmi's "studio" was one of the few places to go for stimulation. For all to go, that is, but Ivor Balmi; to him, the parties — the interminable, dull-gaudy brawls with rising laughter and empty tears — were hunting sessions.

For tall Ivor Balmi, whose eyes had a caked look of European deprivation and a glistening look of American hunger, the parties not only served to pay his rent, but furnished him with fresh prey. It was simply too much trouble, the barbaric dating and picking-up, the ritualistic fencing and prancing so necessary to get a girl within reach.

Ivor Balmi was very much a self-contained man, and his interest in women was on an elementary level: they were sex. He felt no warmth for them, felt no desire to do for them or give *to* them or have them around when they became complicated. It was a very transitory warmth Ivor Balmi sought.

He came through the hall, ignoring the two college students in madras Bermuda shorts, propped against the wall sharing a rope-bound bottle of Chianti and some Jeremy Bentham philosophy. It was the usual crowd. The ones who had come to pick up someone clean and not too clinging, others who needed the heat and pulse of a party . . . a get-together . . . a something-outside-loneliness; and the ones who needed to watch. Ivor hated them the most, the watchers. Self-styled Isherwoods. "We are cameras," they proclaimed, seeing superficialities, lacking the perceptivity to understand or apply what they had seen. They were, to the frozen soul of Ivor Balmi, voyeurs in the game of life. Unable to detach themselves as he did, unable to novocaine their emotional umbilicus, they sought halfway answers in subjective inadequacy. Too many knothole-peepers. Seekers after clichés.

Someone had turned up the hi-fi and, of all things, Bobby Short, mi*God!* It was a bedlam; not as bad as three weeks ago but still fetid with wearing-off under-arm deodorant, frantic perfume, and the stink of slowly disintegrating egos — the smell of clothing caught in the rain. Tight. Hot. Desperate. Nasty. He stumbled over a girl who had passed out, her pearls caught up under her nose and over her forehead. He looked at her for a passing-overhead instant and went on through the crowd.

Someone shouted "Hey, Ivor!" and it was Jeff who had thrown the party (who would donate half the two-bucks-per-head door charge to Ivor's rent fund); Ivor Balmi waved a hand in his direction. Another shout, and it was one of the girls he had kept overnight several weeks before. She had called four times; he had ignored her.

With the intense purpose of an animal streaking for safety in the bush, he wanted the sanctuary of his bedroom, and struck toward it shouldering them aside one after another.

He saw her leaning against the wall, being talked at.

Grover was talking at her, in his coming-on-strong way. She was letting her eyes wander. To anyone but Grover it would have been a signal that he was not getting through. Yet Grover continued to come on.

She wasn't young, but there was youth about her. She was not beautiful, but she had known beauty of several kinds. Her hair was caught up in an auburn bun at the nape of her neck, held in place by a tortoise-shell clip. Her face was long and the chin spade-shaped. The hair and the face were adjuncts to her cheekbones, wondrously attractive, high and round features that commanded attention particularly when (as now, gratuitously) she smiled (Grover welcomed it, took it as a go-ahead) and inclined her head (in boredom), catching a sheen of light across them, shadowing the eyes.

The eyes caught Ivor Balmi and she let them widen.

She broke into Grover's explanations of inconsequentialities to murmur something. Grover turned and tracked the crowd with his dull little brown marmoset eyes, finally picking out Ivor. "You, Ivor, c'mere a minute, baby, I want you to meet someone."

He continued walking, side-stepping. When he reached the bedroom he went in, slammed the door behind himself, and tossed the books littering the bed onto the bureau. Then he tossed himself onto the bed, and fell asleep immediately.

The door opened very quietly, the woman stood looking down at him with a particular peculiar expression on her planed light-and-shadow face, then just as quietly closed the door behind her, and went back to the party.

There was an air of resigned boredom about her: she was determined to wait out this charade. More important things were coming.

Ivor Balmi, wrapped in the security of his aloneness, slept the sleep of the lazyweary. Later, he would paint. Badly, but that was as he wanted it. Always; badly.

In the dream, there was a newspaper caught by the breeze, lifted from the sidewalk and slapped across his face. In the dream, he pulled it free and stared at it: the newspaper was blank. In the dream, he smiled, then awoke.

Awake, he saw her leaning against the closed door, her legs crossed, the cigarette just coming away from her lips.

"Do I know you?" he asked, half-rising.

She gave him a smile totally unlike the smile she had given Grover, and did not answer.

Ivor Balmi swung his legs off the bed, and rose. His hair was mussed, his shirt wrinkled and tacky from sleeping in it. The time seemed to be much older than any time he had known before. He felt something was wrong.

Then he recognized it.

The party was over. There was no sound from the other rooms. Silence in the land of Ivor Balmi. Silence, and this woman who stared at him, her lips saying he was — what? A fool? A wastrel? A sex-symbol, *the* Ivor Balmi? What?

"They've gone," he said. There was no fear in him, in fact, no determined interest. His observations were one and the same with reality. If the woman was here, it was for one reason, essentially. If he felt like one that night, if he felt like *that* one that night, then he would include her in the worldview. If not . . .

He moved to the door and she stepped aside, letting him open it. In the huge living room, lights still burned, and a couple had fallen asleep, still joined, on the big battered sofa by the window.

Ivor Balmi's loft had been a bare box when he had moved in, and through the device of liberating old furniture placed out for the rubbish collectors in front of the more expensive apartment buildings, he had been able to furnish it, if not in style and luxuriance, at least in moderate comfort.

That comfort was now being enjoyed by half a dozen dozing drunks — one on the homemade window seats, one on the long table, and four on the floor — and of course, the couple on the sofa. Ivor walked to them, and nudged the man with his knee.

"Jeff, you got my rent?" He looked down at the nude figure, his hand extended. The figure mumbled something.

"Sleep like hell," he said quickly, "either get it up or get out of here." Jeff struggled free of the girl, who mewed sensitively, rolled over, and exposed a pimpled backside.

"Jeesus, Ivor, you coulda let me sleep, couldn'tcha? I'd of given it to ya in the morning . . . " He tapered off embarrassedly. Balmi stood with hand outstretched, his face turned elsewhere. He simply was not interested.

Jeff went to his pants, thrown carelessly over a beaded lamp, and fished some bills from a side pocket. He gave them to Ivor Balmi, who counted them twice. Then the naked figure returned to the sofa.

The girl had sprawled, would not move. Jeff slipped to the floor and fell asleep once more, his head propped against the front of the sofa. They snored in the same key.

Ivor Balmi returned to his room, closed the door tightly, and turned to his bed. The woman was sitting on the side, still smoking, her legs crossed, her skirt primly over her knees.

"I'm going to sleep," he said. "Get out."

"I want to talk to you," the woman said. She had very grey eyes. They were constantly being lost in the shadows.

"Out," he said, slipping past her on the bed. He lay down, removed his sandals, and placed his street-dirty feet well within range of her.

"I'm Meg's mother. I want to talk to you."

For a long time he lay there staring at the water scum on the ceiling. Then he remembered who Meg was. "She isn't here, go away, I'm tired, I've got a painting to finish tomorrow. Scram."

The woman snubbed out the cigarette on the orange crate serving Ivor Balmi as an end table, and said, very softly, "Either we talk, or I go to the police tomorrow. Meg is only sixteen."

Ivor Balmi shut his eyes very tightly. The woman did not go away, the evening did not get cooler, the faint smell of kitty litter somewhere in the room did not disperse. "You don't really think I give a damn, do you?" he said.

"Jail?" the woman offered. An hors d'oeuvre.

Balmi shrugged. "I've been there."

The woman turned halfway on the bed, looking down at him now. "Mr. Balmi, when my husband died, he left me a great deal of money. I've been unable to find things to do with it except to indulge myself and my daughter." Balmi saw that was so: her suntan was the sort enjoyed only by wealthy women able to afford the time and locale for sun-reflectors behind the ears; an all-over tan; it fitted her like a golden warmth. "I would consider it in the nature of a public service to hire the sort of men who would forever put you out of Meg's — and anyone else's — way. Do I make myself clear, Mr. Balmi? I will have you killed.

"Without compunction, Mr. Balmi." He considered what she said, weighed it against the expression on her face, and decided it would do no harm to listen. Still, nothing more than a desire to go back to sleep suffused Ivor Balmi.

The ennobling capacity for not caring is one that must be nurtured in Man (the caring animal), and once full-grown, like milkweed, is hard to kill.

"All right, Meg's mother," Ivor said, sitting up, "we'll talk. You talk first."

"I want you to stop seeing Meg, I want her to stop coming here, I want — "

Ivor Balmi threw up a hand. Exceedingly flamboyant, Alfred Drake-poised, the hand silenced the woman instantly. "You want, you want, you want," he chided her severely. "Meg's mother, you are a pain in my royal rumper room. Your precious daughter Meg — sixteen and all of her — came jouncing in here one night, made a sloppy mess of herself and proceeded to deposit her can in my bed. While I am not known far and wide as a lofty example to young womanhood of the contemporary knight in shining armor, I am not that depraved that I rob cradles.

"Your daughter, lady, had me. I was filled, and still am filled, if you must know, with a monumental disinterest in your daughter, her rutting habits, and such nonsense as her continued appearance at my door. She wakes me when I want to sleep.

"Very much like her mother.

"Good night." He rolled over, sliding down, and closed his eyes.

"You are unbe*lieva*ble!" the woman cried. She hit him in the back with her fist. Ivor Balmi leaped up and grabbed her wrists before she had a chance to strike again.

"I don't want to have to heave you down six flights of stairs on your ass, lady, so please get off my bed, out of my studio, and split!" His voice was still even, unruffled, carrying the message with a tinge of ennui.

"Balmi!" She almost spat the word, watching him with a peculiar coldness. "You are the most amoral animal I have ever met."

Ivor Balmi released her wrists.

"Do you love Meg?" she asked.

He stared at her amazed. "You're kidding," he said simply. "You've got to be kidding." She stared back at him. A tiny tableau, with nuances of deepness. "You don't seem to get the message. Your daughter paraded herself around here, I was horny and laid her and that, *believe me*, was that. The half a dozen times she's been back, I've almost had to boot her. I don't need her, I'm not interested in her and, frankly, the role of enraged parent doesn't suit you.

"You're better-looking than your daughter. Probably a better lay, too."

The woman's face went white. His words had been delivered as a necrologist would gather details for his obituary column — dispassionately, analytically. She slapped his face. He hauled back after a moment and rammed his fist into her jaw. The woman sprawled off the bed.

"Lady, *one* you get for free, the second has to cost."

She lay at the side of the bed, her skirt disarrayed about her thighs, and as the red spot began to swell, she began to cry. Ivor Balmi, cursing softly, stepped over her, marched into the living room, through it, and into the plywood-partitioned studio beyond. He snapped on the light over the easel and stood staring at the painting in progress.

Black rocks flew up into a mourning sky. Birds, whose eyes had seen the ash of solemn hopelessness, age and despair wrought, wheeled in that mourning sky. The world was a mass of turquoise pulsation, bordering and verging on the assimilation of air by darkness. A stricken man, arms flung Earthward with crying need, carried a hump of peat guilt on his warped back. He made for a city whose structure was Mondrian-as-a-psychopath. It was a very bad painting.

For twenty minutes he worked at it, striking it as a desert wanderer strikes a snake, smiting it with color in broad, insensitive strokes. He worked with a fervor, a fury of touching brush to canvas that was more gymnastic than artistic. He lunged at the painting, he deployed his strength and hurled it shotlike at the work already there. Sweat glinted brightly across his upper lip, caught up by the light over the easel, by the insane reds, the deranged oranges, the lunatic yellows of the fire raging in his city-there-in-paint.

After twenty minutes, he threw down the palette, let the brushes sink exhausted into their jelly jar of turpentine.

When he turned, he realized at once that she had been watching him. He had no idea how long she had been there. For the first time since he had struck his father in the face with the volume of Spinoza, that forenoon so long ago, his fury built, stoked, flamed, blazed, consumed him. "You dizzy *bitch*," he

snarled, starting for her, "what the hell do you *mean* watching
me — "

"Are all your paintings as bad as that?"

It stopped him frozen tight cold hard empty *there.*

What was this woman? Some sort of Punch-and-Judy clown
half-filled with idiocies ("Do you love Meg?"), half-filled with
ice-water realities too true, too penetrating to be expressed? He
was stopped, and she knew it. There, at that point, his observation
of her altered.

He nodded slowly, with resignation. "Yes, they're all that
bad. I'm a very bad artist . . . consequently all my paintings are
worthless."

She came into the room, studied the canvas. "That isn't so. It
isn't worthless."

Her jaw was swollen where he had hit her. It would soon
turn black and blue. But the outside beauty was still present.
He wanted to say something to her, but had said it all in silence
many times before.

He turned away from her and went back to the bedroom. She
followed him, and now there was not the disinterested, bothered
detachment that was Ivor Balmi, but a feeling of becoming
terribly, inextricably involved with her. Meg's mother, who are
you? What do you want from me . . .

(My name is Ivor Balmi, I have black dead eyes. My soul is
a heap of autumn leaves ready to be burned. I await only the
coming of the burner's long match, on the Night of the Long
Matches. I am alone, I have always been alone, I like being alone.
Once I loved a girl, for a very short time, and when I no longer
loved her, or she no longer loved me — what does it matter, it's
all the same, really — I looked again at her face and saw only a
shadow of someone I had once known. It was easy to walk away
from this stranger. Strangers, I decided then, can never hurt you.
So I know only strangers, and care nothing for them. My name
is Ivor Balmi, I am alone, I live with my sadness and my self-
pity and I like them, love them, adore them for they give me the
way to go, the way to see, the way to work. They are the status
quo and with that bland, egocentric sameness I can never feel
pain, can never feel the frustration and inadequacy, the terror

of wanting to do things but not being quite good enough to know them as they should be known, but always flawed, error-filled like reject socks sold by a greasy man on a street corner in bundles of eight packed with a butcher's paper band. I am Ivor Balmi and you *will* let me cling tightly, cuddling, to my ways. No one will touch me, and I will paint badly if I want to paint badly, and that way I do not have to struggle.)

(My name is Ivor Balmi. *Let me sleep!*)

She sat down on the edge of the bed again, and looked at the mass of black hair that hid his expressions by cast of unneeded shadow. "When I learned from Meg who she had been seeing, when I learned that she had slept with you, I knew I had to do something." She twisted the air in nervous hands.

Then she went on. "When I saw you — I managed to get your address, this party tonight, from Meg — I couldn't see what she saw in you. You have many women here, don't you?"

He did not answer. He stared at the wall as if unable to tear his eyes away.

"Yes, of course you do. They must bother you terribly. It's the distance you put between yourself and everyone. It's the farawayness of you. That's very appealing. I can see why Meg — you're right, I know she's wild, I didn't want anyone capitalizing on that, she's all I've got since Bert died — I can see why she came here. Your painting . . . why do you do it? You really aren't very good, but the way you do it, the way . . . I watched. It was frightening. I had to watch."

Ivor Balmi turned to her, lipped hesitatingly at his words, then said desperately, "Please. Go away. Go now. I don't want you here. I want . . . "

Then he reached for her, she came to him, and from that moment their affair began its downhill slide.

At first, she came irregularly, once, perhaps twice a week. But as her intensity of feeling mounted for him, she found it more and more difficult to stay away. Then came the difficulties, the subterfuges, the guilt — for Meg knew something was afoot. Just what, she was unable to tell, but to Meg's mother — whose name, Ivor Balmi learned almost a week later, was Christina — it was apparent that her daughter might soon begin to suspect the truth.

She mentioned it to Ivor one night, as they sat at his chipped, wobble-legged kitchen table.

"So what if she finds out?" he said, taking a bite from the fried chicken leg. She pursed her lips and shrugged her shoulders; there was a great deal of Ivor Balmi in the expression, the movement.

"Meg would be very hurt. I really think she loves you, Ivor." She arched her eyebrows at him. He continued eating. "You're so alone, Ivor. You're always alone . . . and you don't *have* to be that way. There are people who care about you, who love you, who just wait for a little return of that love . . . "

He had been listening imperiously, still eating. Now he threw down the chicken leg and glared at her. Once more she had spoken an unpleasant, piercing truth.

"*Love;* that's just fine, just fine; love, is it?" Ivor Balmi chuckled. "You use that word like it was a dust mop — it'll clean everything up. *Love!* You've got the wrong guy for that. Hate is more in my line. I know *all* about hate. Really I do. But I don't know a damn thing about love.

"Love is some kind of pigeonhole label; you feel need, you feel lust, you feel the boost to your ego, you feel lonely — call it love. Lump it all together; none of it makes the word. The word's a label, a phoney, like 'middle class' or 'beatnik' or 'the right way to do things.' It doesn't exist, except for people with clichés for synapses.

"But if you want to know about hate, *that* I can tell you. I can expound for hours. I had a father who was simple; no, I mean *really* simple. He got into the Communist Party *after* the Depression, so you can't even rationalize him on grounds of pie in the sky. He was pure and simple a humanitarian; he gave a damn about his fellow man. There's room enough in the world for everyone, good or bad, he used to tell me, and he thought the Commies could do it. Maybe that's one reason why I don't want to get involved with people: you care too much, you'll always get your throat stepped on. Yeah, he cared. What an ass. So when McCarthy cut loose, there was my old man, sitting in a chair in front of the committee, playing God. 'What is your occupation?' McCarthy asked him, and you know what he answered? 'I'm a pedagogue.' That was brilliant. It made all the eggheads watching the witch hunts on TV very happy. It also lost my old man his job. Hate? I know it inside and out. Hate was what I breathed on my block. No one talked to us. The grocer stopped giving credit, and that was that. Every night the ice cream man came by with his bells ringing, and I stood watching the other kids getting theirs; we couldn't afford a five-cent ice cream sucker. Have you any idea what it is to be shunned? We were those Red Balmis. I used to have to fight my way home for lunch every day. It was lovely.

"Hate? You bet your ass I know it. So don't talk to me about love. I hated my old man — you had to hate anyone that stupid — and I hated the world and I hated myself most of all. So don't come sucking around me looking for little bird-leavings of love. They've all been gobbled by the vultures.

"And that's what I'll do to you if you hang around. Fair warning. Hate is a kind of dry rot; it's catching." He had been talking so fast, so intensely, his face had grown red, and around the jawbones quite white. His eyes were heavy and frosted over. He looked inward, seeing things.

After that discussion, she avoided making mental demands on him, in ways he might construe to mean attachments. She was in love with him — she needed no more involved diagnosis than that — and though she knew he was an incomplete man, in many ways a hollow man, she felt the need to be near him, even when he reverted to his former manner and excluded her completely from his world.

But there was change in Ivor Balmi. It showed in unsuspected ways, but most obviously in his painting:

A scene of intense light. Distantly the golden-belled trumpets blare heralding the appearance of the Straight Man, his hair almost paper-white. Columns of marauding starshine pour down, lighting the plain across which he walks. Gates within gates within gates open to him and the look on his face as he advances (four behind him, watching to see if he gets through, joyful to

see he will) transfigures his basic homeliness. The apotheosis of
simple man. The deification of groundlings.

Ivor Balmi sold the painting for two hundred and fifty dollars
to the third person who viewed it at the Kulten Galleries, where
Christina had taken it. It had taken her three days to convince
Ivor that she should take it for display. He acquiesced to her
wishes with a shy smile, finally.

The night they celebrated receipt of the check for the sale of
the painting, Meg came to call.

It was a bad scene, filled with the sort of true-confession
bathos that Ivor Balmi reviled with all his heart, yet was drawn
into like a maelstrom. When it was over, and Meg had called her
mother a whore and had steamed out of the loft ("Never to be
seen again, good *God!*" said Christina), they sat staring at one
another emptily.

This is ridiculous, thought Ivor Balmi.

"Get out," he said to her. She jerked her head up as though
stabbed with an electrically charged wire. Her grey eyes were
filled with ash, and the youthful look of her face aged in an
instant. Old, old, old as Nineveh and Babylon; old as the first
woman who had ever been sent away. Old, that old, very old,
terror-old.

"Ivor . . . " she said.

"I don't want it. I don't want it at all," he cried. His face was
falling back into those lines they had held when first she had
met him. He was independent, lonely Ivor Balmi; she saw him
slip away as she watched.

"Go back to your daughter, lady. Go back and tell her what
a bastard I am. That way you can both nurse the same images,
you'll cleave together, have something to belong to: The Society of
Ivor Balmi Haters. Go on. Beat it, I don't want all this feeling and
needing and being one with one. That's too much responsibility
for me, it's too much worry, too much anguish every day, caring
what happens to someone else. I don't want it. You're making me
fight, you're throwing me into the struggle in the streets. I have
to paint now . . . I have to be good . . . I have to succeed . . . I
don't need it . . . let me *alone* . . . !"

"You've started painting with meaning, Ivor; what you do now has quality, it's *good* . . . " she argued.

"Yeah, yeah, it's good and that's bad. I was content before. I did it, it was stinking, and I knew it. I didn't have to struggle. Now it's too much . . . too much . . . get out!"

But she would not go. So he forced her to go.

He used those subtle instruments of torture known only to men and women who have lived with each other for a time. Those weapons of word and inflection and facial expression that cut so much deeper than knives. He used them, and he used them ruthlessly for this was his survival he fought to retain, slashing at her, calling her names he tasted like salt as he spoke them.

"Stop playing with me, Meg's mother," he ordered. "You came here to play at love, and now you've had your game, so get out of my life. I don't need you, or what you want, or what you offer.

"Lady bug, lady bug, fly away home," he said, "your children are losers, your house is on fire."

And when the heavy fire door on the first floor had slammed behind her with a metallic clang, Ivor Balmi went to the window and stared out at the street.

The grey patina of dust and city soot that covered the glass lent everything a ghostly pallor.

The city had died once more. A cadaver stretched out at his feet, beginning to smell bad, as it once had, now that all the spring flowers were ash.

Once more he was alone. He *needed* to be alone. It was the only way he could live. Secure. Untroubled. He was whole once more, settled into a life that promised the security of poverty, mediocrity, loneliness. There were no surprises, but there were also no threats. It was — a life.

He stood staring at nothing for a long while, then went into the kitchen and found a bread knife, rusting on the sideboard. Fortunately, he was able to slash every painting in the loft, even while crying.

Free with this Box!

His name was David Thomas Cooper. His mother called him Davey, and his teachers called him David, but he was old enough now to be called the way the guys called him: Dave. After all, eight years old was no longer a child. He was big enough to walk to school himself, and he was big enough to stay up till eight-thirty any weeknight.

Mommy had said last year, "For every birthday, we will let you stay up a half hour later," and she had kept her word. The way he figured it, a few more years, and he could stay up all night, almost.

He was a slim boy, with unruly black hair that cowlicked up in the back, and slipped over his forehead in the front. He had an angular face, and wide deep eyes of black, and he sucked his thumb when he was sure no one was watching.

And right now, right this very minute, the thing he wanted most in all the world was a complete set of the buttons.

Davey reached into his pants pocket, and brought out the little cloth bag with the drawstring. Originally it had held his marbles, but now they were back home in his room, in an empty Red Goose shoebox. Now the little bag held the buttons. He turned sidewise on the car seat, and pried open the bag with two fingers. The buttons clinked metallically. There were twenty-four of them in there. He had taken the pins off them, because he wasn't a gook like Leon, who wore *his* on his beanie. Davey liked to lay the buttons out on the table, and arrange them in different designs. It wasn't so much that they had terrific pictures on them, though each one contained the face of a familiar comic character, but it was just *having* them.

He felt so good when he thought that there were only eight more to get.

Just Skeezix, Little Orphan Annie, Andy Gump, the Little King, B. O. Plenty, Mandrake the Magician, Harold Teen — and the scarcest one of them all — Dick Tracy. Then he would have the entire set, and he would beat out Roger and Hobby and even Leon across the street.

Then he would have the whole set offered by the cereal company. And it wasn't just the competition with the other kids; he couldn't quite explain it, but it was a feeling of *accomplishment* every time he got a button he did not already have. When he had them all, just those last eight, he would be the happiest boy in the world.

But it was dangerous, and Davey knew it.

It wasn't that Mommy wouldn't buy him the boxes of Pep. They were only 23¢ a box, and Mommy bought one each week but that was only one comic character button a week! Not hardly enough to get the full set before they stopped putting the buttons in and offered something new. Because there was always so much *duplication*, and Davey had three Superman buttons (they were the easiest to get) while Hobby only had one Dick Tracy. And Hobby wouldn't trade. So Davey had had to figure out a way to get more buttons.

There were thirty-two glossy, colored buttons in the set. Each one in a cellophane packet at the bottom of every box of Pep.

One day, when he had gone shopping with Mommy, he had detached himself from her, and wandered to the cereal shelves. There he had taken one of the boxes down, and before he had quite known what he was doing, had shoved his forefinger through the cardboard, where the wall and bottom joined. He could still remember his wild elation at feeling the edge of the packet. He had stuck in another finger, widening the rip in the box, and scissored out the button.

That had been the time he had gotten Annie's dog Sandy.

That had been the time he had known he could not wait for Mommy to buy his box a week. Because that was the time he got Sandy, and no one, not *anybody* in the whole neighborhood, had ever seen that button. That had been the time.

So Davey had carefully and assiduously cajoled Mommy every week, when she went to the A&P. It had seemed surprising at first, but Mommy loved Davey, and there was no trouble about it.

That first week, when he had gotten Sandy, he had learned that it was not wise to be in the A&P with Mommy, because she might discover what he was doing. And though he felt no guilt about it, he knew he was doing wrong . . . and he would just die if Mommy knew about it. She might wander down the aisle where he stood pretending to read the print on the back of the box, but actually fishing about in the side for the cellophane packet — and see him. Or they might catch him, and hold him, and she would be called to identify this naughty boy who was stealing.

So he had learned the trick of waiting in the car, playing with the buttons in the bag, till Mommy came from the A&P with the boy, and they loaded the bags in, and then she would kiss him and tell him he was such a good boy for waiting quietly, and she would be right back after she had gone to the Polish Bakery across the street, and stopped into the Woolworth's.

Davey knew how long that took. Almost half an hour.

More than long enough to punch holes in ten or twelve boxes, and drag out the buttons that lay within. He usually found at least two new ones. At first — that second week he had gone with Mommy to do the shopping — he had gotten more than that. Five or six. But with the eventual increase in duplication, he was overjoyed to find even one new button.

Now there were only eight left, and he emptied the little cloth bag onto the car seat, making certain no buttons slipped between the cushions.

He turned them all up, so their rounded tops were full toward him. He rotated them so that Phantom and Secret Agent X-9 were not upside-down. Then he put them in rows of fours; six rows with four in a row. Then he put them in rows of eight. Then he just scooted them back into the bag and jingled them hollowly at his ear.

It was the *having*, that was all.

"How long have I been?" Mommy asked from outside the

window. Behind at her right a fat, sweating boy with pimples on his forehead held a big box, high to his chest.

He didn't answer her, because the question had never really been asked. Mommy had that habit. She asked him questions, and was always a little surprised when he answered. Davey had learned to distinguish between questions like, "Where did you put your bedroom slippers?" and "Isn't this a lovely hat Mommy's bought?"

So he did not answer, but watched with the interest of a conspirator waiting for the coast to clear, as Mommy opened the front door, and pushed the seat far forward so the boy could put the box in the back seat. Davey had to scrunch far forward against the dashboard when she did that, but he liked the pressure of the seat on his back.

Then she leaned over and kissed him, which he liked, but which made his hair fall over his forehead, and Mommy's eyes crinkled up the nice way, and she smoothed back his hair. Then she slammed the door, and walked across the street, to the bakery.

Then, when Mommy had gone into the bakery, he got out of the car, and walked across the summer sidewalk to the A&P. It was simple getting in, and he knew where the cereals were brightly stacked. Down one aisle, and into a second, and there, halfway down, he saw the boxes.

A new supply! A new batch of boxes since last week, and for an instant he was cold and terrified that they had stopped packing the comic buttons, that they were offering something worthless like towels or cut-outs or something.

But as he came nearer, his heart jumped brightly in him, and he saw the words FREE WITH THIS BOX! on them.

Yes, those were the boxes with the comic buttons.

Oh, it was going to be a wonderful day, and he hummed the little tune he had made up that went:

"Got a nickel in my pocket,
"Gonna spend it all today.
"Got my buttons in my pocket,
"Gonna get the rest today."

Then he was in front of them, and he had the first one in his hands. He held the front of the box toward himself, hands at the bottom on the sides, and he was pressing, pressing his fingers into the cardboard joint. It was sometimes difficult, and the skin between his first and second fingers was raw and cracked from rubbing against the boxes. This time, however, the seam split, and he had his fingers inside.

The packet was far over, and he had to grope, tearing the box a little more. His fingers split the waxpaper liner that held the cereal away from the box, but in a moment he had his finger down on the packet, and was dragging it out.

It was another Sandy.

He felt an unhappiness like no other he had ever known except the day he got his new trike and scratched it taking it out the driveway. It was an all-consuming thing, and he would have cried right there, except he knew there were more boxes. He shoved the button back in, because that wouldn't be the right thing to do — to take a button he already had. That would be waste, and dishonest.

He took a second box. Then a third, then a fourth, then a fifth.

By the time he had opened eight boxes, he had not found a new one, and was getting desperate, because Mommy would be back soon, and he had to be there when she came to the car. He was starting his ninth box, the others all put back where they had come from, but all crooked, because the ripped part on their bottom made them sit oddly, when the man in the white A&P jacket came by.

He had been careful to stop pushing and dragging when anyone came by . . . had pretended to be just reading what the boxes said . . . but he did not see the A&P man.

"Hey! What're you doin' there?"

The man's voice was heavy and gruff, and Davey felt himself get cold all the way from his stomach to his head. Then the man had a hand around Davey's shoulder, and was turning him roughly. Davey's hand was still inside the box. The man stared for an instant, then his eyes widened.

"So *you're* the one's been costin' us so much dough!"

Davey was sure he would never forget that face if he lived to be a thousand or a million or forever.

The man had eyebrows that were bushy and grew together in the middle, with long hairs that flopped out all over. He had a mole on his chin, and a big pencil behind one ear. The man was staring down at Davey with so much anger, Davey was certain he would wither under the glance in a moment.

"Come on, you, I'm takin' you to the office."

Then he took Davey to a little cubicle behind the meat counter, and sat Davey down, and asked him, "What's your name?"

Davey would not answer.

The worst thing, the most worst thing in the world, would be if Mommy found out about this. Then she would tell Daddy when he came home from the store, and Daddy would be even madder, and spank him with his strap.

So Davey would not tell the man a thing, and when the man looked through Davey's pockets and found the bag with the buttons, he said, "Oh, ho. Now I *know* you're the one!" and he looked some more.

Finally he said, "You got no wallet. Now either you tell me who you are, who your parents are, or I take you down to the police station."

Still Davey would say nothing, though he felt tears starting to urge themselves from his eyes. And the man pushed a button on a thing on his desk, and when a woman came in — she had on a white jacket belted at the waist — the moley man said, "Mert, I want you to take over for me for a little while. I've just discovered the thief who has been breaking open all those boxes of cereal. I'm taking him," and the moley man gave a big wink to the woman named Mert, "down to the police station. That's where all bad thieves go, and I'll let *them* throw him into a cell for years and years, since he won't tell me his name."

So Mert nodded and clucked her tongue and said what a shame it was that such a little boy was such a big thief, and even, "Ooyay onday ontway ootay airscay the idkay ootay uchmay."

Davey knew that was pig Latin, but he didn't know it as well as Hobby or Leon, so he didn't know what they were saying, even when the moley man answered, "Onay. I ustjay ontway ootay ootpay the earfay of odgay in ishay edhay."

Then he thought that it was all a joke, and they would let him go, but even if they didn't, it wasn't anything to be frightened of, because Mommy had told him lots of times that the policemen were his friends, and they would protect him. He *liked* policemen, so he didn't care.

Except that if they took him to the policemen, when Mommy came back from the Woolworth's, he would be gone, and then he would be in trouble.

But he could not say anything. It was just not right to speak to this moley man. So he walked beside the man from the A&P when he took Davey by the arm and walked him out the back door, and over to a pickup truck with a big A&P lettered on the side. He even sat silently when they drove through town, and turned in at the police station.

And he was silent as the moley man said to the big, fat, red-faced policeman with the sweat-soaked shirt, "This is a little thief I found in the store today, Al. He has been breaking into our boxes, and I thought you would want to throw him in a cell."

Then he winked at the big beefy policeman, and the policeman winked back, and grinned, and then his face got very stern and hard, and he leaned across the desk, staring at Davey.

"What's your name, boy?"

His voice was like a lot of mushy stuff swirling around in Mommy's washer. But even so, Davey would have told him his name was David Thomas Cooper and that he lived at 744 Terrace Drive, Mayfair, Ohio . . . if the moley man had not been there.

So he was silent, and the policeman looked up at the moley man, and said very loudly, looking at Davey from the corner of his brown eyes, "Well, Ben, it looks like I'll have to take harsher methods with this criminal. I'll have to show him what happens to people who steal!"

He got up, and Davey saw he was big and fat, and not at all the way Mommy had described policemen. The beefy man took him by the hand, and led him down a corridor, with the moley man coming along too, saying, "Say, ya know, I never been through your drunk tank, Chief. Mind if I tag along?" and the beefy man answered no.

Then came a time of horror for Davey.

They took him to a room where a man lay on a dirty bunk, and he stank and there were summer flies all over him, and he had been sick all over the floor and the mattress and he was lying in it, and Davey wanted to throw up. There was a place with bars on it where a man tried to grab at them as they went past, and the policeman hit his hand through the bars with a big stick on a cord. There were lots of people cooped up and unhappy, and the place was all stinky, and in a little while, Davey was awfully frightened, and started to cry, and wanted to go hide himself, or go home.

Finally, they came back to the first place they had been, and the policeman crouched down next to Davey and shook him as hard as he could by the shoulders, and screamed at him never, never, never to do anything illegal again, or they would throw him in with the man who had clawed out, and throw away the key, and let the man eat Davey alive.

And that made Davey cry more.

Which seemed to make the policeman and the moley man happy, because Davey overheard the policeman say to the moley man named Ben from the A&P, "That'll straighten him out. He's so young, making the right kind of impression on 'em now is what counts. He won't bother ya again, Ben. Leave him here, and he'll ask for his folks soon enough. Then we can take him home."

The moley man shook hands with the policeman, and thanked him, and said he could get any cut of meat he wanted at the store whenever he came in, and thanks again for the help.

Then, just as the moley man was leaving, he stooped down, and looked straight at Davey with his piercing eyes.

"You ever gonna steal anything from cereal boxes again?"

Davey was so frightened, he shook his head no, and the tear lines on his face felt sticky as he moved.

The moley man stood up, and grinned at the policeman, and walked out, leaving Davey behind, in that place that scared him so.

And it was true.

Davey never *would* steal from the cereal boxes again, he knew.
As a matter of fact, he hated cereal now.

And he didn't much care for cops, either.

There's One on Every Campus

As he watched Sylvia undress, Cal Jacobs felt the unease of the evening mount to a high pitch. It wasn't that she was ugly, nor that she was overly pretty; in point of fact, Sylvia . . . he abruptly realized he didn't even know her last name . . . was just ordinary looking.

But, as he watched her roll down one nylon stocking, he realized something else.

No one actually *looked* at Sylvia.

There was always one on every campus like her. It wasn't a business with her, she didn't charge; all she wanted was that a boy be decent to her, treat her like a human being, and she'd sleep with him — if she wasn't booked up. She didn't go to State, but lived in town, yet every college man, from freshman get-acquainted luncheon to graduation day, knew Sylvia.

But no one actually *looked* at Sylvia.

They never really saw her, because her reputation was a film that covered her. Those who saw her only saw the legend, not the girl, and that was what made Cal feel so odd. He felt uneasy about sleeping with that film. He took a very close look at her as she rolled down the other stocking, then lifted his eyes to her face. A plain face, not an extraordinary face.

Yet it was the first time he had seen her, though he'd slept with her a dozen times.

He was thankful he'd gotten her up here to the hotel room rented for this night only, before anybody he knew had seen him. Because if they had seen him, they wouldn't have said anything; they would have just snickered. Though each of them had spent a night with Sylvia at one time or another, they'd have snickered.

That was the way of it; had *he* seen Sylvia with a guy he knew, the snickering would be from him. But tonight he was sleeping with Sylvia, and he didn't want to be seen with her.

Not because she was ugly, but because she was what she was, and that was more legend than life.

"Aren't you gonna get undressed?" Sylvia asked with interest. Nothing seemed to faze her, except roughness, which she would not tolerate. Passion was one thing, brutality another.

She was a simple girl, working downtown during the days, usually spending the night with a college boy. Her parents (if they really *were* her parents) didn't seem to give a damn, even if she stayed out all night.

Cal dragged his thoughts from the private life of this girl. He had to stop thinking about what went on in her head — probably nothing at all, actually. Just a stupid broad, that's all she was.

"Yeah . . . yeah, sure. I'll be with you in a minute."

Cal found it rugged, throwing off these thoughts. He pulled a cigarette from the crumpled pack in his shirt, and went to the window seat by the dirty hotel window. He sat down and struck the match on the sole of his shoe, looking down into the street, across to the campus buildings rising in the dark.

The evening was tainted for him, and he couldn't figure why; it wasn't what *he* thought of her — hell no! It was, well, the way the campus thought of her. There were girls who did, and girls who didn't, and one way or another the word got around.

Oh nuts! Cal thought, snubbing the butt on the window ledge with viciousness. *Why all this deep intellectual worrying? Why this social consciousness all of a sudden? What's eating me now?*

He drew himself away from the dark pictures, and turned to face Sylvia, determined to bury all these useless, morbid thoughts.

She was standing there shivering slightly in the cold of the hotel room; after ten they shut off the heat, figuring anyone who wasn't in bed by now wouldn't be in any condition to know the difference. The hotel was makeout heaven, and the management knew it.

Her blond hair held a flat, painted look in the light that shone through the transom. She had said, "I don't know. I just kinda don't like gettin' undressed in the light, you know." Cal hadn't realized, in all the time he'd known her, that she was sensitive even to *that* extent.

Her body wasn't voluptuous, nor even full-fleshed. She wasn't thin either. It was a state somewhere between bones-sticking-out and firmness. She was just a girl . . . and Cal felt an alarming urge to hold her tightly. So he went to her.

He pressed close to her, and felt the warmth of her. Her hair tickled under his chin, and he felt a vague annoyance that her face was crushing the half-pack of cigarettes in his pocket.

"Sylvia . . . " he heard himself whispering into her ear, and it was more than a physical thing . . . more than desire . . . He had the instant thought that it rang through with loneliness.

Now why that? If anyone wasn't lonely it was him! With all the women on the campus, Cal Jacobs was the *last* man to be lonely.

She was talking to him, softly, like a mother to a child, and yet with the odd transposition of personalities; as of the mother asking the child for affection:

"Cal, oh Cal, you *do* love me, don't you? You're not like all the rest of them, are you? You do, I mean, you *do* care for me a little?"

And his mood snapped. He felt it leave him, throwing him back into the play-actor's role of answering what she wanted to hear, not what he wanted to say.

Not saying she was a girl with a film around her so that he had never really seen *her* till tonight.

Not saying she was a fleshly outlet for everything in him.

Not saying there was an unnamed need in him he couldn't describe.

Just, instead, feeding her the manure she heard from every other faceless body on the campus, and that she'd hear till the day she was too old and ugly for the boys.

"Yeah, sure, sure, I like you a helluva lot, Sylvia. I wouldn't be here with you if I didn't. I wouldn't have rented this room, it's not cheap, y'know."

She giggled then, and bounced onto the bed. "Hurry up, slowpoke!"

He made certain he didn't touch the dirty carpet, made sure
his socks were between him and ringworm or athlete's foot, or
whatever the hell you picked up in these joints, and sat down on
the bed. He pulled off the socks as though they were the last ties
that bound him to an island he was leaving.

Minutes later, next to her, he caught himself wondering
crazily:

What color are her eyes?

Hazily, as he sat smoking on the window ledge and she
straightened the collar of her blouse, Cal felt the energy circling
the room anxious to leave, and he opened the window an inch,
feeling it whizz out, leaving him forever, taking with it something
he could not name.

This was an evening of mix-up.

Then she said something utterly unbelievable, utterly out of
the question.

"Cal, take me downstairs for a milk shake?"

He sat stunned. If he was seen with her in the street, why
miGod! that would be the end. What if a girl he dated from one
of the sororities saw them? What if the guys from the frat were
walking the street? What could he say? Here he was, Cal Jacobs,
out having a soda with the campus slut. He shuddered inwardly
at the idea.

"Well, uh, I've, uh, got to get back to the House, Sylvia, and
you know, sort of, uh . . . "

"I want a milk shake, Cal," she said, and there was a strength
in her voice he knew was resignation, determination. He hadn't
credited it to her.

She was about to say something like, "Ain't I good enough to
be seen in public with you? Only good enough to lay, but not to
eat with, huh?" and he knew he would say something imbecilic
like, "Your idea, not mine, Sylvia, but you're right," and that
would louse up a steady thing.

So in the end, after a second that stretched to the tension
level of time, he said all right, and they left the hotel room —
leaving it unlocked.

When they walked through the small, seedy lobby, the bellboy and the clerk snickered. He wanted to brain them. She held his hand, and it felt like dirt on him. Like filth he'd never wash off.

In the Isaly's dairy store they took a booth near the back, though she could tell — he saw in her eyes that she knew he was hiding them — he didn't want to be seen from the street. They sat for a moment, and the waiter — a boy who worked in his off-study hours — took their order.

Sylvia: milk shake.

Cal: nothing but whirling thoughts.

She sat silently for a moment, studying the glass of water and the rectangular fold of the paper napkin, and finally looked up at Cal. The mouth in the face on the body in front of Cal spoke, and said something, and he answered, but the face relaxed and smiled, and he assumed he'd said the right thing, and if not, so what?

Then the horror, the slow horror began.

The waiter brought her so-smooth milk shake; he stood by the table for a minute, as though a landmark for what was to sweep over them next.

The guys came in, with their girls. Five guys and five girls, they came in. And as though they had been briefed by the Devil, as though they had known he would die and wither within himself if they saw him, they all called out, "Hey, look who's here! It's Cal!"

And then one of the girls, a honey blonde with a pretty Boston name like Clarice or Maude or Pamela added, "And look who he's with . . . isn't that that, uh, what's her name? That Sylvia?"

Then the wave of them washed across him with the greeting and the snide hellos, and before he knew it they were all packed in the booth, with Sylvia across from him, and both of them jammed against the wall where there was no escape, and extra chairs, drawn up so everyone could sit.

Then the horror went full into itself.

"How's studies, Cal? Making a four-point this quarter?"

Cal tried, God how he tried, but he couldn't get his eyes to come up from staring at his own water glass, half filled now with tiny bubbles clinging to the sides. "No. No four-point."

Then the chatter turned to other things, and none of it was

addressed to Sylvia. As if they had not quite realized she was
there, yet he *knew* they were aware of her, that it was all a
ribbing session to make him feel ridiculous, and to make her feel
left out.

Finally, one of the girls said, "Hey, Cal, the prom's day after
tomorrow. Who're you taking?"

And Cal could not answer, for the weight in him dragged him
down and down . . .

The silence grew and one of the boys, urging, added, "Yeah,
who, Cal? I'm taking Patty here. Who're you taking?"

Another said, "I'm going with Marlene. You got a date yet,
Cal?"

Answer. Go on and answer. Answer them that you have a
date with a girl in dorm number seven, a girl with clean hands
and a straight body and a mother and a father and hours to be in
at night. Go ahead and answer.

While they stared at Sylvia, to see her expression.

Go ahead.

"I'm, uh, not, uh, going, I don't think. No dough. And lot of,
uh, lots of studying. Midterms soon. No, I don't really think I'll
be . . ."

He trailed off. It was hollow. It was worthless. It was meant
to degrade *her,* and she's done nothing to deserve it. Nothing.
They didn't know here was a woman, they only knew here was a
shadow and they never saw the girl behind it. They didn't know
she was gentle and good to him when he needed somebody who
was warm and gentle. None of that, and they'd made him carry
all his own rottenness into the light, where it stood stinking for
all to smell.

They stared at Sylvia, not at him.

She moved, and they moved away from her. She reached up
to grasp the back of the booth, and they slid out, letting her
get up. Then they sat down, and she stood all alone, watching
nothing, staring at him but not seeing him. Or, perhaps, seeing
him for the first time, and seeing all of them, and realizing what
they were.

Then she reached into her pocket and brought up a quarter;

she carefully set it down beside the still-full milk shake glass. To pay for it. To pay for it.

She walked away from them, to the front door, and no one said goodbye. The prophet Elijah had come and gone, and they had known he was there, but there was no acknowledging it.

She walked through the door, and they watched as she crossed the street. She passed across the street with her head lowered. The wide pool of a streetlight caught her as she stopped on the opposite curb. A bus wheezed to a stop, invited her with air-puffed open doors, then shrugged away down the street. She didn't turn around, but they saw her head sink even lower, then abruptly rise, with some obscure growing pride. Then she walked away into the night's smothering darkness, and was gone to them always.

They sat, and their stares riveted back on Cal.

He knew it, knew the pattern of it, knew they were staring at him.

What?

What could he say? Was there anything? He knew he had to say *something* to show them he was with them, but not of them, that he knew her and that they were rotten, and he was ashamed, God how ashamed. So he said it, and knew it wasn't right, but said it just the same.

"Oh hell, she wouldn't have wanted to go anyhow."

But they knew what he meant.

Because there was one like her on every campus.

At the Mountains of Blindness

While waiting, there were nine things Porky was able to watch, in the alley. The first was a bloated rat, the upper half of its cadaverous-grey body thrust through a gnawed hole in a rusty garbage can, gorging itself on refuse. The second was a clarinetist in the building across the alley, running changes, practicing scales. The third was the traffic that ran past the mouth of the alley; the fourth was the winking neon sign DENNY'S JAZZ CLUB in red and gold that had no reason for existence, back here near the stage door of Denny's.

The remaining five were the nails of his right hand, methodically chewed to the quick. These he studied best of all. Porky was a pusher. He was waiting for his mark to come and make the connection. Porky was also a philosopher of sorts. A phlegmatic philosopher whose ethical view of the Universe, simply stated, was, *Them as strikes first don't get struck.*

It was a sultry night, mid-August, a good night to make the connection and then go back to the apartment for beer and Beethoven. The steel fire door of Denny's shuddered open and a thick slash of light erupted from the doorway, ran up the brick wall opposite.

A snatch of crowd noise and rattling glasses followed, then was sliced off as the door closed.

"Porky?"

The pusher shoved away from the wall and turned toward the raised platform with its metal guardrail. The thin, dark-suited man stood against Denny's door, back pressed tightly to the metal, staring down into the shadows of the alley. His voice was soft and tremulous. Porky — had he been more the suckblood pushers are characterized to be — might have smiled, knowing that tone in the other's voice. It was the sound of need, the hunger of want, the stomach-drying, lip-wrenching desire for junk . . . the last stages of withdrawal before the junkie would start crying, thrashing, cursing, dying a little, then a great deal. Had Porky not been a phlegmatic philosopher and a good businessman, had he been a succubus as the vice squad typified him, he would have gloated. It meant the market was prepared to stand as much as he could lay on. He would have no trouble wringing the last cent tonight.

"Hey, uh, you out there, Porky?"

Porky stepped into the feeble light cast by the street lamp at the mouth of the alley. "I'm here, Tómas."

The Latin cast of the young man's face eased with the passing of apprehension. Porky was here. A fix. It was all right. The sweat — bottled inside — burst forth. "Hey, mon, like I thought you wasn't gonna make it."

Softly, Porky made his point, then dismissed it: "I'm here, Tómas."

The Puerto Rican came down the three steps to the moist stones of the alley. He two-fingered a cigarette from his shirt pocket and stuck it in his mouth, hand shaking. Porky watched. Phlegmatically.

"Nice night, leetle hot, maybe, but a nice night," Tómas said, staring up into the sky. The sky was filled with nothing. It was that sort of night.

"You got the money, Tómas? I've got an appointment." There was quiet, measured impatience in Porky's voice. The business at hand, then away.

"Yeah, mon, nice night," Tómas said. He was sweating like a pig, too much, now.

Porky didn't speak. He turned to go. It was a bust connection. The mark couldn't raise the bread; no dough, no H.

"Hey!" Tómas laughed lightly, "Take it easy, mon. I got the goods. I was just take'n it light, you know."

The pusher paused. "I've got an appointment, Tómas, let's get this over with," he said. Gentle. Nothing but soft. A businessman doesn't argue with his customers. He merely sets up the supply, to match the demand.

The Puerto Rican reached into his inner jacket and brought out a wallet. He began counting bills. Then he handed the sheaf to Porky. The look of expectancy was on the Puerto Rican's face; Porky didn't bother counting.

"You're short, Tómas."

The Puerto Rican wiped a hand across his mouth, his cigarette down-to-filter between two fingers, yellowed from cigarettes long-gone.

"I'm not bad, Porky. Listen, we got a gig uptown at some deb brawl tomorrow night, mon, I get you the rest. I'm only down a few bills. Stake me, Porky. I breeng you the rest . . . "

Porky had laid the money gently on the concrete platform, and was walking away. Tómas lunged for him, grabbed his arm. "Hey, listen, mon, you don't do thees to me — "

Porky neither struggled nor fought back. He merely said (gently), "Tómas, you lay a hand on me, you'll never get fixed again." No blow to the stomach could have worked more effectively. The Puerto Rican backed off.

"I-I got to have the stuff, Porky. You g-got to take care of me, mon. I'm dead cat if you don't." His Spanish accent — submerged since his arrival in Nueva York seven years before — became stronger with his frenzy.

Porky spread his hands. "Sorry, Tómas. You know how I carry on my business. If you can't pay, I can't take care of you."

The Puerto Rican slumped down on the steps. A moan and soft sob. "I tried ever'ting. I bugged my seester lives up on 82nd Street, I hocked my fiddle case, mon I deed ever'ting. I can't get it up till tomorra'."

Porky shrugged. "I'll come back tomorrow then."

Tómas clutched at the air in front of Porky. "No, mon, I can't stand eet. I can't stand the pain, they comin' close together now, they gone toss me off this gig if I don't steady. Some of the other guys they hooked but they make other gigs, mon, they can get the bread — "

Porky knew. He dealt with half a dozen musicians on this street. Two of them from this group. He knew they had Sutton

Place broads keeping them in junk, or money from home, or ex-wives' wealthy parents, or . . .

He preferred not to think about where some of them got it.

"Sorry, Tómas," Porky said. Again, this time with no pretense to draw out the market dealings, he strode off. The shriek came from nowhere, from Tómas, from everywhere, and ricocheted off the brick walls of the alley; the clarinet player slammed the window. Tómas leaped off the stairs, his jacket flying behind him.

His hands locked around Porky's throat, dragged him backward. Porky gagged, flailed the air, kicked back and missed Tómas's shin. The steel door to Denny's slammed open. A heavy voice yelled, "*Tómas!* Get off him!"

The sound of a body hurling the guardrail, the slap of soles hitting the alley. Three running steps, and rough hands grabbed the Puerto Rican by the ears, as Porky slumped to his knees.

Tómas thrashed as he was dragged by the ears, and the attacker hurled him against the wall. The Puerto Rican — lost, lost, fogged and lost with no way to go — came off the wall, rebounded — and caught the fist in the mouth. The attacker knew where to hit him: not a horn man, hit him in the mouth. Tómas slapped the walking bass, get him anywhere but the hands, the back.

Tómas settled in a heap.

The attacker lifted Porky and stood him against the wall, still holding his throat. "Didn't he have the scratch, Porky?"

Porky looked up and saw another of his customers.

Norman Eney, leader of the group in which Tómas played bass, stared at the little pusher. His eyes were giveaways: he was just coming down off a high. Yet he had overcome his depression, his withdrawal (light now, but soon to get worse), to aid . . . who? Porky? Or Tómas?

"That's my business, Eney. Do you want to buy?" Norman Eney shook his head slowly. He stood away from Porky, not moving, watching him out of cool, grey eyes that said nothing. He was a tall crew-cut man, the natural conception of a trombone player.

Finally, he murmured, "He's not one of the good ones, Porky."

You shouldn't deal with him: he can't defend himself the way we can."

They stared across a knowing abyss at one another. Buyer and seller, both knowing how the system worked. Both knowing Porky was a dealer, but not a decider.

"Everybody's got the right to go to hell in his own way, Eney," the pusher said. "Nobody ruins anybody else. They only open doors. No one forces them through: that's each man's decision, whether to walk through the door or not."

"You open doors for too many people, Porky."

The pusher shrugged. He was a businessman. The ethics of the thing didn't enter. He turned and left the alley. Tómas stirred feebly as Norman Eney lifted him under the shoulders, carried him back into Denny's.

The rat continued feeding. There was hunger, and a way to assuage that hunger. Traffic moved. So did the night.

They came for Porky in his apartment.

The pusher's apartment was uptown, and insulated from the world in which he conducted his business affairs by sight and sound and frame of mind. With the door closed New York was a mythical kingdom, far away. A Babylon not to be confused with realities, as this apartment was a reality. With the door closed, and the draperies pulled, with the air conditioning making an atmosphere all his own, and the stereo handling its Scarlatti, its Bach, its Orff — he was where he wanted to be. In a world not of that other world, in a world he made for himself, with no taints or remembrances from beyond. The sanctity of Porky's world was a matter of custom-fitted bookshelves, well-stocked larders, and full turntables.

The sanctity was shattered by the ringing of the doorbell. Four-thirty A.M. The jazz joints were closed, the cops in the subways slipped their pennies into the candy machines and received their coated peanuts for the long beat, up and down the platform, looking for mashers, smokers. The cabbies lounged against steering wheels reading the finals. Somewhere the Pulmotor squad raced, siren-screaming, through the night streets. Gutter-cleaning machines with massive brushes churning marched up the cross streets. It was too late for visitors, here in the private universe of Porky's.

He opened the peephole and stared out.

Norman Eney stood there, sweat-white pearls of hope and need and want on his face. He had come to the Man for his junk. Porky was annoyed; this was the first time — though his address was no great secret — one of his customers had come here to make a connection. He was annoyed —

But the loss of the expected revenue from Tómas had made him fall behind in receipts this week, so he opened.

Norman Eney was not alone.

Out of sight on either side of the apartment door, below the peephole level, they hung at ready. When the door swung inward, they leaped. There were five and Eney. They slammed the door behind themselves, and Porky was afraid, quickly.

But they made no move to hurt him. He knew them: all were junkies, all were customers. What was happening? Who . . . ?

"Get your soul together, Porky," one of them said. He was a thin-lipped pianist, hooked through the bag and out the other end with a need and a monkey so big it played King Kong to an SRO audience. He knew them all. They were all jazzmen. Some the good, others the screamhorn, but all played that sound. He knew them, knew they could not afford to hurt him. There were other Men on the turf, but none so steady, none so honest, none so businesslike as Porky. He knew they would not hurt him.

"I don't keep my cache here, boys," he assured them. "I'm not taking a fall for holding. So if it's need you got, you'll have to wait till business hours tomorrow." He tried to usher up a smile, but it wouldn't leave where it cowered, down there inside him.

"Let's do that thing, man," said Orville Grande, who played piano at the Concourse Inn. "You need a hat?" It was rhetorical: mid-August, hot, Porky was a nonhatter. They moved him (the center of that group) out the door, closing it softly behind, and down the back stairs to a car. Ralph Shetland (trumpet, The Jazz Lab) drove, and they took Porky back downtown, to the street.

Denny's was a dark waiting place. Chairs lay up on the tables like so many dead animals, feet rigor mortis in the air. The still-moist hush of dead smoke, weak booze, loud voices, bad jazz. It was still there, a million smells and sounds and scrabbling touches imbedded in the whatcolor? walls. Porky was apprehensive, not frightened, merely apprehensive:

(I'm not a crook. I'm a businessman. I only take care of a need. If they didn't want it, I wouldn't push it. Take away the bottom of the pyramid of hungers and the top collapses. I'm a link, not a totem. There's no need for violence here . . .)

(Can you hear me?)

But he was silent, and they were silent. Even when they pulled the slat-back chair off the bandstand and tied him to it with their belts and silk rep ties. Even then they were nothing but silent. So cool.

It was not important before, but it is now. This is what Porky seemed to be, looking from the outside. He was short, perhaps five six and, except for the roll of baby fat about his middle, not particularly porcine. His face however, was that peculiar combination of stubble and sallowness that melded with pudge and pinpoint eye, immediately conjuring the impression of a hog. Hence, Porky. His hair was short, thinned across the temples and forehead, and the nose pugged back revealing two hair-overgrown nostrils. Despite this, he was not an unpleasant-looking man. He was clean, almost to a fault, and carried himself very straight. In other circumstances in some other walk of life, he might easily have been thought of as a credit and a caller. It was not important what Porky seemed to be, before, but it was now. The change was in the offing.

Norman Eney was the first to reach the bandstand. The others followed him, and from the darkness came three more. Nine jazzmen. All in a row. See how they blow. *Go!*

Porky watched, and tried to devise a rationale. There was a theme here, a statement, a meaning, they were trying to do, say, convince, something. What it was . . . well, perhaps there would be an explanation. Porky was phlegmatic, and his worldview contained the unquenchable belief that whether or not the questions get asked (how many neon bulbs, flickering on Times Square, to make the riddle high enough and bright enough for the right people to see it?), the answers are always given.

"Do you know what you do, Porky?" Norman Eney asked.

"Do you know what you're killing? Every time you let us feed ourselves, you take something. You take it and you bury it, man, and not only we miss it, because it's us, but everybody, all of them, they lose it. We're going to let you know. Tonight."

Porky grasped for a handle. "Why tonight?"

Orville Grande, the pianist, turned on the stool: "Tómas got busted by the fuzz tonight. He was trying to hold up the deli on the corner so he could buy his stock from you." He paused and saw something in the darkness, something nothing, then went on, "He was so sick, man, he tried to split, and they burned him down."

A sax man — a customer named Eli — added, "He's got the last sign on him, man. He's got that big toe tag in the morgue."

"So we're going to show you, Porky," Eney explained. "All these years you been living at the mountains of blindness, not knowing, not caring, just selling, man. Now we're going to show you what you take from us, what we've got."

And they played.

What did they play? They made their sounds in the dark moist cavern of the jazz club, and some of it said things and some of it didn't, but it was them. All of them, from the shallowest part to the deepest niche, and the wail was first lonely then blaring and demanding, driven on a pastel breeze from a corner of the universe where the ones-who-hear-things-always lived. Porky listened, and knew he had *better* listen, because this was a credo for him, there was a test coming and notes should be taken, because this was the final exam. He was not a punk, nor was he a stupid man . . . he had thought himself a businessman, and his morality, his living, was a separateness, not to be confused with what he sold these damned ones. But it now seemed he was wrong. They wailed, they blew, these creatures who had drawn themselves on elbows and knees into his light-life. Now he could not ignore them. He had been thrust into Bedlam with them, and to survive, to ken their meanings, he must pay close attention.

Willow weep for me in the still of the night when the world was young . . .

That was it. But not all of it. Men who had done their living without mamas and without papas, in a half-light legend of junk and sound. These were the things they said:

I don't sleep nights; I hear the rhythms.

There ain't no good women for me because they don't see me, they see an image, a jazz musician and that's a false bit. I'm lonely, where's a good broad in all this?

You got to have roots to sink, a place to go. I'm thirty-seven, man, and it's been a long time since I had a place to lay my head.

Take this from me and I'm hollow.

If I had a son, I'd want him to be a horn man, it's God right in the stomach, the way to go.

This is my truth, all of it. All I want. All I need.

That was what they played, and that was what they said. So Porky listened, and knew what they wanted. They did not want him to stop pushing, because they would only need it from someone else. They did not want to hurt him for denying Tómas, because that had been the kid's gig, and not Porky's. But they wanted him to *know*. It wasn't the punishment, or whether anything happened, it was merely being aware, of knowing what was reality, and what was blindness.

How long can you live in that thatch hut without windows, without cracks of light at the foot of the mountains of blindness? How long? Forever, unless you're shown.

He was trapped, and they were trapped, one by the other — him by demand, and them by supply. But now he could not turn his *non sequitur* eyes on them, without knowing what things boiled in them. Porky listened, and they restated their theme.

The sax lifted the dusky night and slid it out on a wave of tired but struggling. Horn came up, trumpet from the sea, and with eyes closed, hunkered down into his shoulders, a man told of the freight cars left on the sidings, still rank from pig and cow, where the army blanket spread lumpy for a needed sleep. The sound of the country, of a hundred million nameless bad ones and bedouins, tramping away from Louisiana graves with a fast jog time-step funeral chant. The wails of lonely and depressed and sick and hungry and down at the socks guys who needed what was roiling and tumbling and kicking in the gut. That was the theme, softly snaggingly bangwham repeated. That was it, for all the world (who was Porky only) to hear and put down just right.

Yeah, even Lawrence Welk.

In there somewhere.

And when the sound had flown off, an almost extinct bird with plumage that crumbled to dust motes if touched too harshly, they stared down at Porky from the bandstand, their eyes cat and bird and snake intent. To see if he had seen. To hear if he had heard. To find out if they had written their primer so that even a pusher could dig.

Porky nodded his head. He still lived at the mountains of blindness, but it was different. He could not move, because home is where the home is, where you've been, and where you can exist, and for Porky this was the only way to make it.

But the difference was the greatest difference in the whole wide world. Now he knew.

Nothing would change.

The pyramid of hungers still existed, because it was the way the scene was run, and who changes it? Not a damned soul. Especially not the damned souls.

Porky knew and said with eyes that were mouths of sense: I'm one of you. I'm not the preying animal, I'm the preyed upon. By life, by need, by circumstance. I'm one with you, and though I can't help you, I understand.

And that, in its own way, was the worst punishment of all.

This is Jackie Spinning

Hi, y'all, this is Jackie spinning. That's right, it's 7:00, Eastern Standard Time, and this is Jackie Whalen spinning the hot ones, the cool ones, the bop and the rock ones, and all for you, just you, little old you. And tonight's show is a real joy-popper! Be sure to stick right by that radio, kids, because as our special guest tonight Jackie has got the lovely, luscious Kristene Long, singing star of Sapphire Records, as his guest. We'll be playing Kris's new smash, "Mocking Love," as well as her hit parade topper, "Shagtown Is My Town," a little later; and we'll be talking to that living doll, Miss Long, as well. But right now — right now — let's hear a little of Ricky Nelson's new one.

(Fade music up)

(Jackie Whalen, a short man with a great deal of curly hair tumbling onto his forehead, almost to the eyebrow line, cues the next record and stands up behind the consoles. He stretches out of his severely Ivy League sports jacket and hangs it on the back of his chair. He unbuttons the cuffs of his piqué buttondown shirt and, scratching a wrist, rolls the sleeves up to the biceps. He pulls down the small four-in-hand knot of his conservative challis tie and unbuttons the collar of the shirt. Then, pouring a glass of water from the carafe at his left, he takes two small pink pills from the neat pile on the edge of the right-hand turntable, and tosses them off, with the water in close pursuit. His dark, angry eyes track across the control room and light on the sheer nylon-encased legs of the tall blonde sitting expectantly in the metal chair near the control booth's big picture window. He smiles at her legs, and the smile travels up carefully, slowly, till it reaches her blue eyes, where the smile has magically been transformed into a leer. She smiles back insinuatingly. "Later, baby," he tells her, licking his lips. She moves languidly in the chair, revealing a knee. Jackie Whalen reluctantly looks away from her, to the record that is almost ending. He sits down and flips a toggle switch.)

(Music up and out)

Well, that was Ricky's new one, and there's no doubt about it being number seventeen on your Top Sixty list this week. And speaking of the Top Sixty, all you tough teens, when you want a record to while away those hours, make sure you do your shopping at The Spindle, 6720 Seventeenth Street. All the boys out there, especially Bernie Glass the manager, they'll take good care of you. Just tell 'em Jackie sent you, and you can expect that *big* Jackie Whalen discount.

But right now here's one that your "disc Jackie" thinks will be in number-one spot real soon. In fact, if I can make a prediction, this *will* be number one. It's that new star, the voice of Rod Conlan, singing and swinging his smash hit . . . "I Shouldn't Have Loved You So Much!"

(Fade music up)

(He cues the next record and turns to stare at the girl again. She grins at him and says, "Have you told your wife about us yet?" His face darkens momentarily as honest emotion shows through; then the façade of sleek, well-fed humor moves back into place and he replies, "Don't worry about it, baby. When the time comes, she'll find out." The girl stands up, smoothing the tweed skirt over her thighs, and walks to him at the console. "Gimme a cigarette," she says. As he shakes a filter-tip cigarette free of its pack, she adds, "Florey made some pretty broad hints in his column this morning. Won't she read it and wonder where you were last night?" He lights the cigarette for her with a slim sterling-silver lighter, and the affected, boyish grin spreads up his face once more. "She's not too bright, Kris. You forget I married her when I was with that dinky two-hundred-and-fifty-watter upstate. She's a farm girl . . . she may have read it, but it won't dawn on her that Florey meant me. She thinks I was at a retail record distributor's convention last night. Don't let it bug you; when I want her to know, she'll know. Right now I've got bigger things to worry about." The girl recrosses to her chair and sits down. "You mean things like Camel Ehrhardt and the Syndicate?" His face once more loses its sheen of camouflage and naked fear shines wetly out of his eyes. "You've been pushing that Conlan dog for over a week now. They're not going to like it, Jackie. They covered Patti Page's version with their own boy, and every other jockey's fallen in line to give it the big play. You're cutting your throat by pushing Conlan." Jackie Whalen pulls at his petulant lower lip and replies, "To hell with those hoods. I've got dough in Conlan, and this could be the big one for him. They won't press their luck. They're afraid I'll go to the Rackets Committee if they push me too hard. Besides, I'm working an angle. The Conlan gets the big shove from *this* jock!" The girl grins wisely and adds, softly, "Jackie, baby, I'd hate to have to lose you so soon. Those guys don't play games. You know what they did to Fred Brennaman when he refused their stuff for his jukeboxes." Visions of a man being fished from the river, hair matted with scum and plant life, flesh white, eyes huge and watery, skitter across Jackie Whalen's mind. He sits in the comfortable foam-bottom chair, and his thoughts consume him to such a depth that only the shushing of the needle repeating in the final groove of the spinning record brings him to attention.)

(Music down and out)

And that was the big one for Rod Conlan, kids. "I Shouldn't Have Loved You So Much," and it's going right to the top. I've heard 'em all for a good many years, but Rod has got it locked this time, if I'm any judge.

So I hope you'll all drop over to The Spindle, 6720 Seventeenth, and pick up a copy of Rod Conlan's big new one, "I Shouldn't Have Loved You So Much."

And it's time right now to run down the top five of the Top Sixty, kids, so here they are:

In first place is Kris Long's "Shagtown Is My Town" — and don't forget, in just a few minutes we'll be talking it up with Kristene Long herself. In second place Fats Domino's "When the Saints Go Marching in" is still holding its own, and third place this week is occupied by Sam Cooke and "Nobody Could Hate the Cha-Cha-Cha." Fourth spot goes to Steve Don and the DonBeats with "Foolin' Around Too Long" and that big fifth place goes to Rod Conlan's "I Shouldn't Have Loved You So Much." So let's catch Rod again with that smash, because we think it's bound for the million mark.

(Music up)

("You're really digging your grave, Jackie," the girl says, worry lines marring the ivory perfection of her forehead. "Oh, don't get on my back, Kris," he says, cueing the next record. "Sybil does the same damned thing, and I can't stand *her*." The girl winces at the comparison between herself and Whalen's wife, and settles back with the stub of her cigarette. Whalen leans over in the console chair and pulls at his lower lip, mumbling to himself. "What?" the girl asks him. "I forgot to bring that damned revolver with me today," he says. "I left it in the nightstand." The girl rises once more, walks to the console and snubs the cigarette in the large ceramic ashtray. "You might need it today," she says. Her face is unmarked by lines of annoyance or worry. It is obvious she thinks no harm can come to Whalen; it is obvious in her carriage, in her looks, in her voice. "What the hell," he says, "I'll pick it up when I go back to the apartment to change. It's safe where it is." "But are you?" the blonde demands. He ignores her, and watches the black disc spinning under the rapier tip of the diamond needle. As it reaches the final grooves, he flips a switch.)

(Music under, Announcer voice superimpose)

. . . your cool lips have told me . . .

. . . I shouldn't have loved you . . . so-o-o mu-uch.

And that was Rod Conlan again, kids, swinging his big new one, "I Shouldn't Have Loved You So Much." After this word about Blim, the miracle cream that will rid you of unsightly pimples and blackheads in just one week, we'll be back to have that talk with the lovely Kris Long.

(E.T. Commercial up)

(He riffles through a sheaf of after-commercial comments written by the continuity department and tosses over the console, "This Blim crap couldn't remove dirt from a sand pile," to the girl. She laughs lightly, and examines a fingernail with its polish chipped. She bites at the nail absently.)

(Commercial out, segue to Announcer)

That's the straight stuff, kids. Blim is guaranteed to do the job, guaranteed to leave your skin fresh and clear and clean, or your money will be refunded. Don't miss going to that hop just because of unsightly blemishes or blackheads. Jump out right after the show tonight, kids, and fall down on a jar of that great Blim.

And now, what you've all been waiting for, let's call over that singing sensation of Sapphire Records, Miss Kristene Long, whose rendition of "Shagtown Is My Town" is holding tight to first place all around the country.

Hi, Kris.

"Hi, Jackie."

We're really thrilled to have you here today, Kris.

"It's a big thrill to be here, Jackie."

Kris, let's get serious for a minute, and find out just how you got into the singing game. You're a lovely girl, and you look to be — oh, about twenty-one.

"Ha-ha-ha. Why, thank you, Jackie. Actually, I'm twenty-five, and I first got my break singing with Earl Pettifore's band in Detroit. It was just a step up to singing on my own, I guess."

Well, that's really tremendous, Kris. Tell me, how do you feel about the success of "Shagtown Is My Town"?

"Jackie, I'm really thrilled. I mean it's such a great thrill to know you've recorded a song so many people like so much. When Al Hackey at Sapphire first showed it to me, I wasn't too hot about it, but Al isn't A&R man at Sapphire for nothing. He certainly — "

— Excuse me, Kris.

For all you kids out there who might not be familiar with the term, A&R means Artist and Repertory, and it's the title used by the man who selects the songs and who'll sing them. Sorry to interrupt, Kris, go on, won't you?

" — well, all I was gonna say was that Al certainly knows a hit when he hears it."

And so do we, Kris. So for all those kids out there who've made "Shagtown Is My Town" the number one song in the nation, here's Kristene Long doing her rocking, socking version of that big sensation.

(Music up)

(Jackie Whalen cues and then draws a cigarette from the pack and lights it. "One for me," the girl says, and he hands her the lit one from his mouth. "Much more of this kind of idiot chatter and I'll be ready for Hysteria House," she says, drawing the smoke into her lungs. He shrugs, "It's what the teenaged morons want, so who am I to argue. It's bought me a Porsche." The girl points a finger at him, "Yeah, and Florey called attention to it in that damned item. Why can't you drive a studio car when you're out with me?" Whalen rubs his lower lip with a manicured fingernail and waves her objection away. "Forget it. There's no surprises left in this life for old Jackie Whalen, baby.")

(Music down and out)

Kris, now that we've heard your number-one hit parade entry, what's new for you these days?

"Well, Jackie, right now I'm in town for the opening of my new movie *Holiday Rock* which opens at the Rialto tomorrow. It's my first big singing role, and working with such great stars as Fats Domino, Tommy Edwards, Joni James, Gene Vincent and the Redcaps, and Bill Haley was a tremendous thrill."

Say, that is news, Kris. I know we'll all be down there for that smash premiere tomorrow at the Rialto. How about you giving us that title again, Kris:

"*Holiday Rock*, Jackie."

Well, Kris, it's about time for some more music, so why don't we spin that new one of yours, "Mocking Love," that has everybody so excited.

"That'd be swell, Jackie, and thanks a million."

(Fade music up)

(Jackie Whalen cues the next record and turns to say something to the girl, who still sits behind the spare microphone at the right-hand turntable. He stops in midturn, for three men are looking into the control room through the huge picture window. He sighs tightly, recognizing one of them. The girl catches the direction of his stare, and turns to look. "What's the matter?" she demands, looking between them. "Ehrhardt," he says simply, staring at the squat man in the camel's hair coat. The man has a brown snap-brim down over his eyes, and a pipe clutched tightly in a corner of his thin-lipped mouth. "I'm getting out of here," the girl cries, starting to rise. He quiets her with a vicious "Sit where the hell you are. I'll handle this. I've been — been waiting for them." He beckons to the men to enter the control room. The red ON THE AIR lights has gone off. One of the taller, silent-faced men with Camel Ehrhardt opens the door to the control booth, and the squat man enters. "How'd you get in, Camel?" Whalen demands in a cheery, false good-humor voice. The squat man draws a metal chair up to the console and sits down. He speaks with difficulty around the pipestem. "We have ways," he says, in a cultured, dulcet tone. "We asked you to cooperate with us, Jackie. You know we have a lot of time and money behind Wally George. We hate to see all that dough going down the drain so you can make a buck off that dog Conlan." Whalen begins to speak, but the record ends. He motions to everyone for silence, noting the half-crazed expression of terror in Kristene Long's blue eyes. He flips a switch.)

(Music out)

That was Kris Long's big new one, "Mocking Love," kids. And here's Mitch Miller and his orchestra on the Columbia label with "The Munich Drinking Song." So, sing along with Mitch!

(Music up, automatic gain reduces volume set too high)

(Camel Ehrhardt draws a large, meaty hand from a patch pocket of the camel's hair coat. A .32 Police Special is clutched in the hand. "Jackie, you're going to make radio history tonight. Your listeners are going to be the first to hear a man actually die on the air." Whalen cues in the next song and settles back in the chair, and the two sidemen of Ehrhardt move around the console toward him. "You can't commit murder while we're broadcasting, Ehrhardt." He laughs at them. "Too many people saw you come in and too many people would see you — " Ehrhardt interrupts rudely, "No one saw us come in, no one sees us go out." He takes the pipe from his mouth. Jackie Whalen's full lower lip trembles and the girl is trying to suck up all the air in the booth through a big wet hole in her face. Whalen puts a flat palm against the air to ward off Camel Ehrhardt's action. "Hold it a minute, Camel. I've been waiting for you to come around to see me. Look, there's no reason why we have to be on opposite sides of this thing." The squat man cocks a heavy eyebrow. "No? Why not? Am I supposed to like penny-ante chiselers who take nicks out of my till?" Whalen leans forward and the bully-boys twitch with readiness to pounce on him. "Listen, Camel, you can make twice as much as you're making now." Camel Ehrhardt's face tilts querulously, and he says, "I'm listening to you." The record rasps as it catches in the last groove, and Jackie motions Ehrhardt to silence for a moment.)

(Music down and out)

Mitch Miller and "The Munich Drinking Song." Looks like another hit to follow "Bridge on the River Kwai March" and "Children's Marching Song." That one is really big this week. As my buddy Ed Sullivan says, "A reeeleee big shewwww." Old Jackie wants to take sixty seconds now to give you the word about Sparkle Toothpaste, kids, so bend your ears around this word from Wayne Marks.

(Commercial record up)

("Go on," Ehrhardt says. Jackie looks at the huge clock on the wall, timing the commercial, and launches quickly into "I've got Rod Conlan and you've got Wally George. So okay, why couldn't the Syndicate — " Ehrhardt snaps, "Don't call us that!" and Whalen pales, then continues, " — why couldn't your group have *both* of them? That way you have *two* moneymakers going for you. And I could make you a mint on both of them, by plugging their hits." Ehrhardt's gun hand wavers, and he stares thoughtfully at Whalen for a long time. "You want to cut us in on Conlan?" Jackie nods. "What percent?" Ehrhardt asks. Jackie motions him to silence, and cuts in over the commercial's fading sound.)

(Commercial out, segue to Announcer)

For teeth that shine like true love, kids, don't get steered onto any brand but Sparkle. It contains the miracle ingredient PAX-60 and it tastes like fresh, clean mint. So when your toothbrush is empty, don't be startled . . . be Sparkled!

Now here's one you've been asking for, and we're sending this one out to Angie and Phil, Marcia and Carl, Dave and Someone

Special, and all the kids out at the Triangle Dairy Hop. Here it is, that big new one for Jerry Lee Lewis . . . "Rip Tide"!

(Music up)

("Goddamit, Whalen, what percent?" Ehrhardt asks again. The gun hand has steadied. "No percent," Jackie Whalen answers, cueing and grinning hugely at the same time. The girl draws a sharp breath, and the two bullyboys cast appreciative glances at her sweater front. "Straight out sale, Camel," Whalen says. "Fifty thousand and he's yours, contract and all, with my personal guarantee that I plug the hell out of his records. As well as Wally George's stuff." The squat man licks his thin lips for a moment, and his face is a mask of imperturbability. "Why the fast change of heart, Jackie?" Ehrhardt asks. Whalen spreads his hands. "You boys don't think I'm going to buck you, with your organization, do you? I bought Conlan's contract so I could sell it to you. I've been waiting for you to come along for a talk. I'm only sorry you waited this long and thought I was crossing you. But now that you can see I've got a good property in Conlan, I know you're businessmen enough not to knock off the goose that can lay the golden eggs for you." Ehrhardt stares solidly at Jackie Whalen. Abruptly, he slips the still-silent weapon back into his coat pocket. With marked slowness he lights his pipe with a kitchen match. He shoves the chair back and stands up. "I'll be talking to you." He nods sharply to the side boys and the three men leave the control booth. As Jackie Whalen reaches for the pickup arm of the turntable the three men pause outside the great control room window, and stare at him.)

(Music down and out)

That was "Rip Tide" and it was Jerry Lee Lewis smashing. Don't forget, The Spindle, 6720 Seventeenth Street, where you can buy all these hits with that big Jackie Whalen discount. Hits like this one: Frankie Avalon and "Sweetlips."

(Music up)

(Jackie Whalen sits in silence, lips pressed tightly closed, eyes also tightly closed, the lids trembling slightly. The girl makes a sound, a half-formed word, but he waves her to silence, then rubs his eyes with his fingertips, fiercely. He waits in darkness for the record to end. When it does, he cuts in abruptly.)

(Music down and out; cut to Announcer)
Well, today has been a big day, kids. Bigger than you know, really. And I see by the big clock on the wall that it's almost 8:00, time for your disc Jackie to close down the old shop and say so long till tomorrow. We've just got time for two more, so I'll lay 'em on together and let 'em run out to close the show. We don't usually hit a platter as hard as we're hitting these two, kids, but today has been a real special day, so we'll break our own rule. Here they are, because *you've* made them your favorites.

Here's Rod Conlan again with that hit you've been phone-bombing us to play more often, "I Shouldn't Have Loved You So Much," and the extra-beautiful Kris Long with "Mocking Love," what I predict will be the two big ones of the season.

(Music up)
(Jackie Whalen stands, scratches at himself, and walks to the chair in which Kristene Long sits, her back very straight, her face very pale. "You lead a real rough life, Mr. Whalen," she says. He leans down, takes her face in his hands and kisses her full on the lips. "You'll find out just *how* rough tonight, baby." He grins. Jackie Whalen straightens, reaches back, and takes the pack of cigarettes from the console. He shakes one out. With the smoke full in his lungs he replies to her unasked questions: "It was a calculated risk, honey. I knew they'd come around to dicker first. The days of the St. Valentine's Massacre may not be gone completely, but these guys are businessmen, even though they're hoods and punks. They won't pass up a chance to get hold of a good property like Conlan. They'll come across; I made a sale today. That was the angle I was playing." The girl shakes her head. "They'll sell him down the river. Lousy songs with big pushes, too many personal appearances, too many bookings for benefits, they'll screw him good, Jackie. They always do." Whalen shrugs and sits on the edge of the console. "That's the way it goes," he says. "It was either him or me. And he'll like working for the Syn — for the group.")

(Segue first record into second)
(The girl stands up and half turns away, tucking a lock of blond hair that has tumbled over her forehead back into place. As she turns, she faces the big control booth window and sees

a short, dark woman in a beret and black coat, standing in the center of the glass, staring at them. A peculiar expression trembles on the woman's face. She is holding a gun out before her, stiffly. "Jackie!" the girl shrieks. Whalen turns and sees the woman. "Sybil!" he gasps, as she brings the gun up an inch. Thoughts pile through Jackie Whalen's head as the gun travels that inch. They are jumbled, disorganized thoughts. One is:

She *did* understand who Florey was talking about in his column.

Another is:

How did she find the revolver in the nightstand?

A third is:

How stupid: to make it past one bunch of killers who make their living knocking guys off, just to get it from a stupid, jerky farm girl. Oh, Jeezus!

And the last thought of all is:

There are no more surprises in this life for Jackie Whalen.

And as the crash of the revolver echoes through the anteroom, into the control booth, as the glass of the picture window magically sprouts three small bull's eyes with millions of radiating lines, as fire and pain and chagrin and cursing fill Jackie Whalen like an empty vessel . . .)

(Music fade up and GONE. EXTREMELY GONE.)

No Game for Children

Herbert Mestman was forty-one years old. He was six feet two inches tall and had suffered from one of the innumerable children's diseases at the age of seven, that had left him with a build decidedly pigeon-chested and slim to the point of emaciation. He had steel-gray hair and wore bifocals. It was his avocation, however, that most distinguished him from all other men: Herbert Mestman knew more about Elizabethan drama than anyone else in the country. Perhaps even in the world.

He knew the prototypes and finest examples of the genre of drama known as the "chronicle history." He knew Marlowe and Shakespeare (and believed firmly the original spelling had been Shexpeer), he was on recitation terms with Dekker and Massinger. His familiarity with "Philaster" and Johnson's "Alchemist" bordered on mania. He was, in essence, the perfect scholar of the drama of Elizabeth's period. No slightest scrap of vague biographical or bibliographical data escaped him; he had written the most complete biography — of what little was known — on the life of John Webster, with a lucid and fantastically brilliant erratum handling all early versions of "The Duchess of Malfi."

Herbert Mestman lived in a handsome residential section in an inexpensive but functional split-level he owned without mortgage. There are cases where erudition pays handsomely. His position with the University was such a case, coupled with his tie-up on the *Britannica's* staff.

He was married, and Margaret was his absolute soulmate. She was slim, with small breasts, naturally curly brown hair, and an accent only vaguely reminiscent of her native Kent. Her legs were long and her wit warmly dry. Her eyes were a moist brown and her mouth full. She was, in every way, a handsome and desirable woman.

Herbert Mestman led a sedentary life, a placid life, a life filled with the good things: Marlowe, Scarlatti, aquavit, Paul McCobb, Peter Van Bleeck, and Margaret.

He was a peaceful man. He had served as a desk adjutant to the staff judge advocate of a smaller southern army post during the Second World War, and had barely managed to put the Korean Conflict from his notice by burying himself in historical tomes. He abhorred violence in any form, despised the lurid moments of television and Walt Disney, and saved his money scrupulously, but not miserly.

He was well liked in the neighborhood.

And —

Frenchie Murrow was seventeen years old. He was five feet eight inches tall and liked premium beer. He didn't know the diff, but he dug premium. He was broad in the shoulders and wasped at the waist. The broads dug him neat. He had brown hair that he wore duck-ass, with a little spit erupting from the front pompadour to fall Tony Curtis-lackadaisical over his forehead. He hit school when there wasn't any scene better to make, and his '51 Stude had a full-race cam coupled to a '55 Caddy engine. He had had to move back the fire wall to do the soup job, and every chromed part was kept free of dust and grease with fanatical care. The dual muffs sounded like a pair of mastiffs clearing their throats when he burned rubber scudding away from the Dairy Mart.

Frenchie dug Paul Anka and Ricky Nelson, Frankie Avalon and Bo Diddley. His idols were Mickey Mantle, Burt Lancaster (and he firmly believed that was the way to treat women), Tom McCahill, and his big brother Ernie who was a Specialist Third Class in Germany with the Third Infantry Division.

Frenchie Murrow lived in a handsome residential section in an inexpensive but functional split-level his old man had a double mortgage on. His old man had been a fullback for Duke many years before, and more green had been shelled out on the glass case in the den — to hold the trophies — than had been put into securities and the bank account.

Frenchie played it cool. He occasionally ran with a clique of rodders known as the Throttle-Boppers, and his slacks were pegged at a fantastic ten inches, so that he had difficulty removing them at night.

He handled a switch with ease, because, like man he knew he could *do* with it.

He was despised and feared in the neighborhood.

Herbert Mestman lived next door to Frenchie Murrow.

HERBERT MESTMAN

He caught the boy peering between the slats of the venetian blind late one Saturday night, and it was only the start of it.

"You, there! What are you doing there?"

The boy had bolted at the sound of his voice, and as his head had come up, Mestman had shone the big flashlight directly into the face. It was that Bruce Murrow, the kid from next door, with his roaring hot rod all the time.

Then Murrow had disappeared around the corner of the house, and Herb Mestman stood on the damp grass peculiarly puzzled and angry.

"Why, the snippy little Peeping Tom," he heard himself exclaim. And, brandishing the big eight-cell-battery flashlight, he strode around the hedge, into Arthur Murrow's front yard.

Margaret had been right there in the bedroom. She had been undressing slowly, after a wonderful evening at the University's Organ Recitals, and had paused nervously, calling to him softly:

"Oh there, Herb."

He had come in from the bathroom, where the water still ran into the sink; he carried a toothbrush spread with paste. "Yes, dear?"

"Herb, you're going to think I'm barmy, but I could swear someone is looking through the window." She stood in the center of the bedroom, her slip in her hand, and made an infinitesimal head movement toward the venetian blind. She made no move to cover herself.

"Out there, Margaret? Someone out there?" A ring of fascinated annoyance sounded in his voice. It was a new conception; who would be peering through his bedroom window? Correction: his and his *wife's* bedroom window. "Stay here a moment, dear. Put on your robe, but don't leave the room."

He went back into the hall, slipped into the guest room and found an old pair of paint-spattered pants in the spare closet. He slipped them on, and made his way through the house to the basement steps. He descended and quickly found the long flashlight.

Upstairs once more, he opened the front door gingerly, and stepped into the darkness. He had made his way through the dew-moistened grass around the home till he had seen the dark, dim form crouched there, face close to the pane of glass, peeking between the blind's slats.

Then he had called, flashed the light, and seen it was Arthur Murrow's boy, the one they called Frenchie. Now he stood rapping conservatively but brusquely on the front door that was identical with his own. From within he could hear the sounds of someone moving about. Murrow's house showed blank, dead windows. *They've either got that television going in the den, or they're in bed*, he thought ruefully. *Which is where I should be. Then he added mentally, That disgusting adolescent!*

A light went on in the living room, and Mestman saw a shape glide behind the draperies through the picture window. Then there was a fumbling at the latch, and Arthur Murrow threw open the door.

He was a big man; big in the shoulders, and big in the hips, with the telltale potbelly of the ex-football star who has not done his seventy sit-ups every day since he graduated.

Murrow looked out blearily, and focused with some difficulty in the dark. Finally, "Uh? Yeah, what's up, Mestman?"

"I caught your son looking into my bedroom window a few minutes ago, Murrow. I'd like to talk to him if he's around."

"What's that? What are you talking about, your bedroom window? Bruce has been in bed for over an hour."

"I'd like to speak to him, Murrow."

"Well, goddamit, you're not going to speak to him! You know

what time it is, Mestman? We don't all keep crazy hours like you professors. Some of us hold down nine-to-five jobs that make us beat! This whole thing is stupid. I saw Bruce go up to bed."

"Now listen to me, Mr. Murrow, I saw — "

Murrow's face grew beefily red. "Get the hell out of here, Mestman. I'm sick up to here," he slashed at his throat with a finger, "with you lousy intellectuals bothering us. I don't know what you're after, but we don't want any part of it. Now scram, before I deck you!"

The door slammed anticlimactically in Herbert Mestman's face. He stood there just long enough to see the shape retreat past the window, and the living room light go off. As he made his way back to his own house, he saw another light go on in Murrow's house.

In the room occupied by Bruce.

The window, at jumping height, was wide-open.

FRENCHIE MURROW

Bruce Murrow tooled the Studelac in to the curb, revved the engine twice to announce his arrival, and cut the ignition. He slid out of the car, pulling down at the too-tight crotch of his chinos, and walked across the sidewalk into the malt shop. The place was a bedlam of noise and moving bodies.

"Hey, Monkey!" he called to a slack-jawed boy in a stud-encrusted black leather jacket. The boy looked up from the comic book. "Like cool it, man. My ears, y'know? Sit." Frenchie slid into the booth opposite Monkey, and reached for the deck of butts lying beside the empty milk shake glass.

Without looking up from the comic book Monkey reached out and slapped the other's hand from the cigarettes. "You old enough to smoke, you're old enough to buy yer own." He jammed the ragged pack into his shirt pocket.

He went back to the comic.

Frenchie's face clouded, then cleared. This wasn't some stud punkie from uptown. This was Monkey, and he was Prez of the Laughing Princes. He had to play it cool with Monkey.

Besides, there was a reason to be nice to this creep. He needed him.

To get that Mestman cat next door.

Frenchie's thoughts returned to this morning. When the old man had accosted him on the way to the breakfast table:

"Were you outside last night?"

"Like when last night, Pop?"

"Don't play cute with me, Bruce. Were you over to Mestman's house, looking in his window?"

"Man, I don't know what you're talkin' about."

"Don't call me 'man'! I'm your father!"

"Okay, so okay. Don't panic. I don't know nothin' about Mr. Mestman."

"You were in bed."

"Like I was in bed. Right."

And that had been that. But can you imagine! That bastard Mestman, coming over and squeaking on him. Making trouble in the brood just when the old man was forgetting the dough he'd had to lay out for that crack-up and the Dodge's busted grille. Well, nobody played the game with Frenchie Murrow and got away with it. He'd show that creep Mestman. So here he was, and there Monkey was, and —

"Hey, man, you wanna fall down on some laughs?"

Monkey did not look up. He turned the page slowly, and his brow furrowed at the challenge of the new set of pictures. "Like what kinda laughs?"

"How'd you like to heist a short?"

"Whose?"

"Does it matter? I mean, like a car's a car, man."

Monkey dropped the comic book. His mongoloid face came up, and his intense little black eyes dug into Frenchie's blue ones. "What's with you, kid? You tryin' ta bust the scene . . . you want in the Princes, that it?"

"Hell, I — "

"Well, blow, jack. We told ya couple times; you don't fit, man. We got our own bunch, we don't dig no cats from the other end of town. Blow, willya, ya bother me."

Frenchie got up and stared down at Monkey. This was part

of it: these slobs. They ran the damned town, and they wouldn't take him in. He was as good as any of them. In fact, he was better.

Didn't he live in a bigger house, didn't he have his own souped short? Didn't he always have bread to spread around on the chicks? He felt like slipping his switch out of his high boot-top and sliding it to Monkey.

But the Laughing Princes were around, and they'd cream him good if he tried.

He left the malt shop. He'd show those slobs. He'd get old busybody Mestman himself. He wouldn't bother with just swiping Mestman's crate either. He'd really give him trouble.

Frenchie coasted around town for an hour, letting the fury build in him.

It was four-thirty by the car's clock, and he knew he couldn't do anything in broad daylight. So he drove across town to Joannie's house. Her old lady was working the late-hour shift at the pants factory, and she was minding her kid brother. He made sure the blinds were drawn.

Joannie thought it was the greatest thing that ever came down the pike. And only sixteen, too.

HERBERT MESTMAN

There was something about orange sherbet that made an evening festive. Despite the fact that no one these days ate real ice cream, that everyone was willing to settle for the imitation Dairy Squish stuff that was too sweet and had no real body, Herbert and his wife had found one small grocery that stocked orange sherbet — in plastic containers — especially for them. They devoured a pint of it every other night. It had become a very important thing to them.

Every other night at seven-thirty, Herbert Mestman left his house and drove the sixteen blocks to the little grocery, just before it closed. There he bought his orange sherbet, and returned in time to catch the evening modern-classics program pulled in on their FM, from New York City.

It was a constant pleasure to them.

This night was no different. He pulled the door closed behind him, walked to the carport, and climbed into the dusty Plymouth. He was not one for washing the car too often. It was to be driven, not to make an impression. He backed out of the drive, and headed down the street.

Behind him, at the curb, two powerful headlamps cut on, and a car moved out of the darkness, following him.

It was not till he had started up the hill leading to that section of town called "The Bluffs" that Herbert realized he was being tailed. Even then he would have disbelieved any such possibility had he not glanced down at his speedometer and realized he was going ten miles over the legal limit on the narrow road. Was the car behind a police vehicle, pacing him? He slowed.

The other car slowed.

He grew worried. A twenty-one-fifty fine was nothing to look forward to. He pulled over, to allow the other car to pass. The car stopped also. Then it was that he knew he was being followed.

The other car started up first, however. And as he ground away from the shoulder, the town spreading out beneath the road, on the right-hand slope, he sensed something terribly wrong.

The other car was gaining.

He speeded up himself, but it seemed as though he was standing still. The other car came up fast in his mirror, and the next thing he knew, the left-hand lane was blocked by a dark shape. He threw a first glance across, and in the dim lights of the other car's dash, he could see the adolescently devilish face of Frenchie Murrow.

So that was it! He could not fathom why the boy was doing this, but for whatever reason, he was endangering both their lives. As they sped up the road, around the blind curves, their headlight shafts shooting out into emptiness as they rounded each turn, Mestman felt the worm of terror begin its journey. They would crash. They would lock fenders and plummet over the side, through the flimsy guardrailing . . . and it was hundreds of feet into the bowl below.

The town's lights winked dimly from black depths.

Or, and he knew it was going to be that, finally, a car would come down the . . .

Two spots of brightness merged with their own lights. A car was on its way down. He tried to speed up. The boy kept alongside.

And then the Studebaker was edging nearer. Coming closer, till he was sure they would scrape. But they did not touch. Mestman threw a glance across and it was as though Hell shone out of Frenchie Murrow's young eyes. Then the road was illuminated by the car coming down, and Frenchie Murrow cut his car hard into Mestman's lane.

Herb Mestman slammed at the brake pedal. The Plymouth heaved and bucked like a live thing, screeched in the lane, and slowed.

Frenchie Murrow cut into the lane, and sped out of sight around the curve.

The bakery truck came down the hill with a gigantic whoosh and passed Mestman where he was stalled.

FRENCHIE MURROW

This wasn't no game for kids, and at least old man Mestman realized that. He hadn't spilled the beans to Pop about that drag on the Bluffs Road. He had kept it under his lid, and if Frenchie had not hated Mestman so much — already identifying him as a symbol of authority and adult obnoxiousness — he would have respected him.

Frenchie held the cat aloft, and withdrew the switchblade from his boot top.

The cat shrieked at the first slash, and writhed maniacally in the boy's grasp. But the third stroke did it, severing the head almost completely from the body.

Frenchie threw the dead cat onto Mestman's breezeway, where he had found it sleeping.

Let the old sonofabitch play with *that* for a while.

He cut out, and wound up downtown.

For a long moment he thought he was being watched, thought he recognized the old green Plymouth that had turned the corner as he paused before the entrance to the malt shop. But he put it from his mind, and went inside. The place was quite empty, except for the jerk. He climbed onto a stool and ordered a chocolate Coke. Just enough to establish an alibi for the time; time enough to let Mestman find his scuddy cat.

He downed the chocoke and realized he wanted a beer real bad. So he walked out without paying, throwing at the jerk a particularly vicious string of curse words.

Who was that in the doorway across the street?

Frenchie saw a group of the Laughing Princes coming down the sidewalk a block away. They were ranged in their usual belligerent formation, strung out across the cement so that anyone walking past had to walk in the gutter. They looked too mean to play with today. He'd cut, and see 'em when they were mellower.

He broke into a hunching run, and rounded the corner. At Rooney's he turned in. Nine beers later he was ready for Mr. Wiseguy Mestman. Darkness lapped at the edge of the town.

He parked the Studebaker in his own folks' garage, and cut through the hedge to Mestman's house.

The French windows at the back of the house were open, and he slipped in without realizing he was doing it. A fog had descended across his thinking. There was a big beat down around his neck someplace, and a snare drummer kept ti-ba-ba-ba-powing it till Frenchie wanted to snap his fingers, or get out the tire jack and belt someone or get that friggin' cat and slice it again.

There was a woman in the living room.

He stood there, just inside the French doors, and watched her, the way her skirt was tight around her legs while she sat watching the TV. The way her dark line of eyebrow rose at something funny there. He watched her and the fog swirled the higher; he felt a great and uncontrollable wrenching in his gut.

He stepped out of the shadows of the dining room, into the half-light of the TV-illuminated living room.

She saw him at once, and her hand flew to her mouth in reflex. "What do you — what . . . "

Her eyes were large and terrified, and her breasts rose and fell in spastic rhythm. He came toward her, only knowing this was a good-lookin' broad, only knowing that he hated that bastard Mestman with all his heart, only knowing what he knew he had to do to make the Princes think he was a rough stud.

He stumbled toward her, and his hand came out and clenched in the fabric of her blouse, and ripped down . . .

She was standing before him, her hands like claws, raking at him, while shriek after shriek after shriek cascaded down the walls.

He was going to rape her, damn her, damn her louse of a big-dome husband, he was going to . . .

Someone was banging at the door, and then he heard, ever so faintly, a key turning in the lock, and it was Mestman, and he bolted away, out the French doors, over the hedge, and into the garage, where he crouched down behind his Stude for a long time, shivering.

HERBERT MESTMAN

He tried to comfort her, though her hysteria was beginning to catch. He had followed the boy after he had come home and found the cat. Sir Epicure had been a fine animal; quick to take dislike, even quicker to be a friend. They had struck it off well, and the cat had been a warmth to Herbert Mestman.

First the peeping, then the trouble on the Bluffs Road, and so terribly this evening, Sir Epicure, and now — now —

This!

He felt his hands clenching into fists.

Herbert Mestman was a calm man, a decent man; but the game had been declared, and it was no game for children. He realized despite his pacifist ways, there were lice that had to be condemned.

He huddled Margaret in her torn blouse closer to him, soothing her senselessly with senseless mouthings, while in his mind, he made his decision.

FRENCHIE MURROW

Mornings had come and gone in a steady, heady stream of white-hot thoughtlessness. After that night, Frenchie had stayed away from Mestman and his wife, from even the casual sight of Mestman's house. Somehow, and he was thankfully frightened about it, Mestman had not reported him.

Not that it would have done any good . . . there was no proof and no way of backing up the story, not really. A stray fingerprint here or there didn't count too much when they lived next door, and it might easily be thought that Bruce Murrow had come over at any time and left them.

So Frenchie settled back into his routine.

Stealing hubcaps for pocket money.

Visiting Joannie when her old lady was swing-shifting it.

And then there were the Laughing Princes:

"Hey, man, you wanna get in the group?"

Frenchie was amazed. Out of a clear field of vision, this afternoon when he had come into the malt shop, Monkey had broached the subject.

"Well, hell, I mean, yeah, *sure!*"

"Okay, daddy, tell you what. You come on out to the chickie-run tonight, and we'll see you got gut enough to be a Prince. You dig?"

"I dig."

And here he was, close to midnight, with the great empty field stretching off before him, rippled with shadows where the lights of the cars did not penetrate.

It had been good bottom land, this field, in the days when the old city reservoir had used water deflected from the now-dry creek. Water deflected through the huge steel culvert pipe that rose up in the center of the field. The culvert was in a ditch ten feet deep, and the pipe still rose up several feet above the flat of the field. The ditch just before the pipe was still a good ten feet deep.

The cars were revving, readying for the chickie-run.

"Hey, you, Frenchie . . . hey, c'mon over here!"

It was Monkey, and Frenchie climbed from his Stude, pulling

at his chinos, wanting to look cool for the debs clustered around the many cars in the field. This was a big chickie-run, and his chance to become one of the Princes.

He walked into the group of young hotrodders, clustered off to one side, near a stunted grove of trees. He could feel everyone's eyes on him. There were perhaps fifteen of them.

"Now here's the rules," Monkey said. "Frenchie and Pooch and Jimmy get out there on either side of the road that runs over the cul. On the road is where I'll be, pacin' ya. And when Gloria — " he indicated a full-chested girl with a blond ponytail, " — when she gives the signal, you race out, and head for that ditch, an' the cul. The last one who turns is the winner, the others are chickie. You dig?"

They all nodded, and Frenchie started to turn, to leave. To get back in his Stude and win this drag.

But the blond girl stopped him, and with a hand on his arm, came over close, saying, "They promised me to the guy wins this run, Frenchie. I'd like to see you bug them other two. Win for me, willya, baby?"

It sounded oddly brassy coming from such a young girl, but she was very close, and obviously wanted to be kissed, so Frenchie pulled her in close, and put his mouth to hers. Her lips opened and she kissed him with the hunger and ferocity of adolescent carnality.

Then he broke away, winking at her, and throwing over his shoulder, "Watch my dust, sweetheart," as he headed for the Stude.

A bunch of boys were milling about the car as he ran up.

"Good luck," one of them said, and a peculiar grin was stuck to his face. Frenchie shrugged. There were some oddballs in this batch, but he could avoid them when he was a full member.

He got in and revved the engine. It sounded good. He knew he could take them. His brakes were fine. He had had them checked and tightened that afternoon.

Then Monkey was driving out onto the road that ran down the center of the old field, over the grade atop the culvert pipe.

His Ford stopped, and he leaned out the window to yell at Gloria. "Okay, baby. Any time!"

The girl ran into the middle of the road, as the three racers gunned their motors, inching at the start mark. They were like hungry beasts, waiting to be unleashed.

Then she leaped in the air, came down waving a yellow bandanna, and they were away, with great gouts of dirt and grass showering behind . . .

Frenchie slapped gears as though they were all one, and the Studelac jumped ahead. He decked the gas pedal and fed all the power he had to the engine.

On either side of him, the wind gibbering past their ears, the other two hunched over their wheels and plunged straight down the field toward the huge steel pipe and the deep trench before it.

Whoever turned was a chicken, that was the rule, and Frenchie was no coward. He knew that. Yet —

A guy could get killed. If he didn't stop in time, he'd rip right into that pipe, smash up completely at the speed they were doing.

The speedometer said eighty-five, and still he held it to the floor. They weren't going to turn. They weren't going . . . to . . . turn . . . damn . . . you . . . *turn!*

Then, abruptly, as the pipe grew huge in the windshield, on either side of him the other cars swerved, as though on a signal.

Frenchie knew he had won.

He slapped his foot onto the brake.

Nothing happened.

The speedometer read past ninety, and he wasn't stopping. He beat it frantically, and then, when he saw there was no time to jump, no place to go, as the Studelac leaped the ditch and plunged out into nothingness, he threw one hand out the window, and his scream followed it.

The car hit with a gigantic whump and smash, and struck the pipe with such drive the entire front end was rammed through the driver's seat. Then it exploded.

HERBERT MESTMAN

It had been most disconcerting. That hand coming out the window. And the noise.

A man stepped out of the banked shadows at the base of the grove of trees. The fire from the culvert, licking toward the sky, lit his face in a mask of serene but satisfied crimson.

Monkey drove to the edge of the shadows, and walked up to the man standing there half-concealed.

"That was fine, son," said the tall man, reaching into his jacket for something. "That was fine."

"Here you are," he said, handing a sheaf of bills to the boy. "I think you will find that according to our agreement. And," he added, withdrawing another bill from the leather billfold, "here is an extra five dollars for that boy who took care of the brakes. You'll see that he gets it, won't you?"

Monkey took the money, saluted sloppily, and went to his Ford. A roar and he was gone, back into the horde of hot-rods tearing away from the field, and the blazing furnace thrust down in the culvert ditch.

But for a long time, till he heard the wail of sirens far off but getting nearer, the most brilliant student of Elizabethan drama in the country, perhaps in the world, stood in the shadows and watched fire eat at the sky.

It certainly was not . . . not at all . . . a game for children.

The Late, Great Arnie Draper

We had all gotten the news by seven o'clock. I'd heard it first on the early news, and rushed to tell the other kids. We somehow wound up at the Campus Malt Shop, about twenty of us, all sitting around gloomy and sick and miserable about it.

Charlie Draper was dead. He had cracked up in his Valiant, on the highway. Charles Arnold Draper, whom some called Charlie and some called Arnie. Funny about that: the girls all called him Arnie, I was one of them, and the guys all called him Charlie. Funny about that, but just typical of Arnie Draper. Friendliest guy in the wide world. Number-one man on campus, with everybody. Not stuck up or self-centered, though God knows he *could* have been, what with being star quarterback on State's Big Ten championship team, a brilliant student, head of the Jazz Committee, president of his fraternity, and a dozen other accomplishments. He could have been the most egotistical slob in the world, but he wasn't. Wanted everybody to call him Arnie, as though he'd known them all his life. Just like that; Arnie. Or Charlie.

Now he was dead. Just like this, he was gone from our lives, and we'd lost a good friend. Not just another kid we were sorry to see die, but a real honest-to-goodness swell fellow, who had figured prominently in our lives.

We sat around the Campus Malt Shop, not ordering anything, just dragging on cigarettes, and staring at each other, as each one of us told what we felt about Arnie. Not that we felt we *had* to say anything, but it seemed as though we were reciting in a class we liked very much, and we wanted very much to be very much a part of it; we had to let out what we felt about Arnie Draper, now that he had been taken from us.

Verna Abernathy, a tall blond English major was talking. "He was so . . . so . . . so damned *refined*. He always seemed to know just what to say at just the right moment. He had a ready action for any situation, you know what I mean?"

Everybody nodded, because we all agreed.

Finley Withers coughed and stared down at the tiny pile of ashes he had been accumulating, chain-smoking since we'd gathered. "It was more than that," he added, "just the knowing what damned movement to make just when.

"What I mean is, he was poised, relaxed, as though he didn't have a worry in the world, even during finals week, when you knew damned well he was worried. It was — " He waved his hand absently, as if to finish the sentence visually.

Everybody nodded, because we all agreed.

Grant Lawson, who had been his roommate at the fraternity house, spoke up. He had a deep voice and a distinctly masculine way about him. "Not only that, but Charlie was a fine person. I saw him pick up a cat that had been struck by some kid's bicycle, and nurse the animal, actually, really *nurse* it back to health. It's still at the House. We call it Satyr. And Charlie wouldn't let anybody help. It was his own good deed, and he wanted it to be that way all the time."

Everybody nodded, because we all agreed.

From the end of the five tables we'd shoved together, Annie Vester, moved I suppose by the honesty everyone had in their voices, and the sorrow of the moment, said, "He was a gentleman, Arnie was. He went steady with me for three months, before he met you, Pauline," she explained unnecessarily to me. I knew Arnie had been going with her before me, but it had just been a slight campus flirtation, like a million others, and there had been no real hard feelings, though I knew Annie had still cared a great deal for him. It hadn't been the real thing with them, as it had been between Arnie and myself. Real love for us, the real thing.

She went on. "Arnie could have taken advantage of me a couple of times. I wouldn't have minded at all, I even, uh, encouraged him slightly," she added, blushing slightly, "but he was a gentleman. We made love the way all girls want to make love before they're married. I'll — I'll never forget him . . . "

She sank into a soulful silence, and we all nodded, because we all agreed.

Brant Pinch, with whom Arnie had collaborated on several group science projects, said, "Not to mention his genius. Charlie would have been a great leader some day. His grasp of science was phenomenal. We never could have gotten in those projects on time if he hadn't done a hell of a lot of the work on them." Everybody nodded, because we all agreed.

"Francine Hasher and I were always amazed at how well-read, how rounded he was," Margie Poole stuck in. "He could talk on any subject from Plato to . . . to Presley. He knew what was going on in the world, and he was seriously interested in what he could do about it.

"And migod, when it came to the arts, Arnie seemed to be able to do anything. We used to go to Iris Pedlang's sculpture classes, at her apartment, you know, and he used to come up with the most *exotic*, I mean exotic forms, you can believe me!" Everybody nodded, because we all agreed.

It went on for over an hour, with everybody chiming in, retelling some little anecdote, spotlighting some feature of his personality, lauding him, and then abruptly, it was my turn.

Silently, it was my turn, because they knew how much I had lost. Charlie and I had been going steady. We were going to be engaged next year, both in our senior year at State. They knew I was crying inside, and shattered, and they turned to me for the capper, the final words that would sum it all up, now that we had lost our Arnie. Our Charlie. He was gone.

"He was so big," I said, trying to explain a concept I hardly had words to explain. "He was a gentleman, and a genius, and a leader, and kind, and good, and everything everybody says, but beyond that," I stumbled for words, "he was . . . he was . . . *big!* Do you, can you, know what I mean?"

Everybody nodded, because we all agreed.

Then — we hadn't even seen her till then, or if we had, we hadn't paid her any attention — a girl in a booth near us spoke.

She couldn't have helped overhearing everything we'd been saying, and she had been there since before we arrived, so we knew it hadn't been contrived, but she said:

"Arnie was a lousy bastard."

We all just sat and looked at her. There wasn't even any violence in us, so calm had she been in saying it. We sat and stared at her, with her pale face and haunted eyes. No one knew her, no one knew her name, though we'd seen her around the campus, of course.

We stared at her silently for a few moments, the quiet of the Campus Malt Shop broken only by the sounds of cars, just like our Arnie's, going by in the street.

Then . . .

Everybody nodded, because we all agreed.

High Dice

I was in the toilet with Kurt, and I was golden.

Every time those dice hit that plywood wall and bounced back on the linoleum, they read heavenly. They couldn't go sour if they'd wanted to go sour. I must have rolled six straight passes at one point, and every time they twinkled up seven, Kurt got meaner and banged his big black fist against the inside of the sink.

And I was getting sicker by the second.

I was starting to see halos around the two naked bulbs in the ceiling, and the pains were starting to come chop! chop! hitting me at regular-spaced intervals like labor pains. My mouth was dry as hell, I was smoking one after another, lighting the new one off the roach of the last, and my skin fairly crawled.

The sonofabitch. He *knew* I needed a fix, otherwise I'd never have got sucked into a crap session with him. He was a cheating sonofabitch to begin with, and when he was down, it was just that much worse.

So I was golden.

I could do no wrong.

And the pains hit me; down on my haunches there in the toilet, tossing those ivories, I doubled and sagged and wrapped my arms around my knees, and it hurt, it really hurt, so help me.

He was into me for about seventy beans, and it didn't show signs of getting any better. All I needed was thirty-five for a pop, but goddam that Kurt, he wouldn't pay me off, kept saying, "Double mah bet, double mah bet," and when I'd say, "C'mon, man, when are you gonna pay up here?" he'd just get a hard shine like the finish off a new car, back in those bloody eyes of his, and give me a little rough nudge with his elbow in my back, and he'd snap, "C'mon, bitch, throw them dice!"

I was trapped. I was sewed up solid. I had to have the bread to get fixed, and my Man was outside that toilet in the restaurant, the Shack, sitting in a corner booth sipping at a chocolate Coke and humming to himself. Man, it was a bee-*itch!* I could feel my skin itching and crawling and wow it was like about a million and a half crab lice all over me. I scratched my thigh and my side, but it came right back.

That Kurt knew. He knew.

Someone banged on the door and rattled the knob, but Kurt didn't even look up. "Hey, man, someone wants into the head," I informed him. His eyes stayed right down there below, and he gave me that damn nudge again, and said, "Roll, guy."

The knob-twister made a helluva ruckus like his bladder was going to pop, because we'd been in there a good twenty-five minutes already, and *everybody's* back teeth were probably floating by this time, but Kurt just nudged me again, and I rolled.

Six was my point.

Thank God it wasn't another pass. I was really getting scared. I mean, how would *you* dig it, being so sick you wanted to puke, and locked in a little bitty dirty toilet with the biggest, strongest, meanest colored cat in the world, who wanted what little loot you had, and wouldn't pay off what he owed? It was bad, very unhappy, is all.

I tossed them and they hit that wall and rattled back an eight. Then a twelve; then a five and a single. Point made. Kurt said something guttural and mean under his breath.

That was a hundred and forty dollars and I *knew* that crook didn't have it! I mean, I *knew* he was shacking with Dotty, the waitress, and he had to give his wife something for the kids, and he was always down in the basement of the Shack's building, shooting high dice or playing poker with the janitor or any of the college kooks he could fish in. I mean, I *knew* he was coming on lying.

Jeezus, did I feel helpless: it was like being strapped into a straightjacket, the way they have to do it sometimes at Lexington when you go into withdrawal and want to smash. I was breathing too deep now, and my face was wet like I'd wee-wee'd all over myself, kind of crawly sweat, moist and sticky and not water at all, but something else. I was really beginning to blow my cool.

Oh, it was getting worse.

Whump! I caught a good one right through the gut, and had to stand up. I got to my feet and the pains in my cramped legs made me totter against Kurt for a second, and that fink just shoved me away.

I mean, I *knew* what that sonofabitch thought of me: he thought I was fay, that I didn't dig Negroes. How wronger could he get? It wasn't his color I hated, it was that slob Kurt himself, I mean, *him* personally.

"C'mon, man, let's go here, I got some burgers to fry."

Why that lyin' sack of —

He was the Shack's cook, all right, but it was just as easy to take strychnine as eat his greaseburgers. And he knew I knew damned well when he disappeared for some craps or cards Dotty would take over at the grill. He *knew* I knew.

He just wanted to keep me locked up in there, with his big foot plastered against the locked door, and his fist all ready-made to belt me up alongside the head if I made any noise to anyone on the other side of that toilet door. I was as salted away in there with him as I'd ever been in the junk farm at Lex, or the Tombs or any other damn slammer. I was fried. He knew it. He knew I was sick and getting worse, and he wasn't about to pay off.

To top it off, Kurt had that gravity knife of his.

That big aluminum-handled shake knife that he could whip out so fast it looked like he didn't have a hand, but some kind of a metal hook at the end of his arm. I was scared of him, all right.

Why, I remember one night when some joker busted on Kurt behind the grill, telling him the eggs were greasy, and dumping the plate down on the breadboard. Kurt didn't even say anything, he just grabbed that muthuh by the neck and dragged him over the counter and beat the crap outta him, and then picked him up by the neck and the seat of his pants and heaved him — I mean he heaved that two hundred pounder — right out of the kitchen and into the second booth down the line.

Kurt was big and muscular and nasty, real nasty, so I wasn't about to fool with him. He'd said the door was locked till we were done, that was *it!*

"One of us gonna leave here broke, man," he'd said when we had entered the toilet. "One of us gonna be Tap City."

My first mistake had been in getting caught short when I needed a fix. That was the first thing. My second mistake was busting on Kurt for the ten bucks he'd owed me for six or seven months. I needed the money, I had twenty-five and that last ten would have made the tariff for my Man waiting out there, but Kurt had gotten a sly look in his eyes — Jeezus, he was a rotten cat — and said, "Tell you what, Teddy, tell you what, man. I'm gonna shoot a little high dice with you, make that bread sing. Howzabout?"

I knew he cheated. Everybody did. He used bombed ivories, loaded down with every kind of BB shot and scrap metal left over from World War II, but I had no choice. I mean, I figured if I had him and had him cold so he couldn't lie or cheat or con his way out of it, he'd come up with the ten. Guys like that feel easier about losing loot in a game than paying back an honest loan. Man, was I snowing *myself!*

So I'd said yes and gone into the toilet at the Shack with the cook, Kurt, and the pains came and the hurt came and I was golden so help me very golden, and I couldn't lose, and Kurt was getting nearer and nearer killing me with his cold, flat eyes and his big aluminum-handled shake knife.

But what could I do?

"Say, look, Kurt." I came on very logical, very pleasant, trying to convince him and me that I wasn't in pain and had to get it *soon* or die. "Now, dig. I've won a hundred and forty bucks from you, this isn't your night, man. Now look, all I want is that ten . . . that's all. Just give me the ten and we'll call it square. Good?"

"Stop jivin' me and fire them dice."

He looked up from where he was hunkered on the dirty floor, and I hope I never see a look like that again. It was killing cold.

And then I dug. Then I realized what I should have known

right in front: that bastard didn't have any money at all. He didn't have a hundred and forty or ten or any other damn thing. He was busted. And he'd been bluffing me, playing me on my own money!

I wanted out then, very bad.

"Okay." I said, "forget it you — " I started to call him a bastard, but stopped, bad move, " — you don't have to pay me now. Just forget it. Just lemme out of here." He didn't budge. He wanted what I had on me. I don't know why, and I don't care, but he was insulted, somehow. He owed me money and he hadn't been able to take me, and he was killing mad because the ofay bastard had him a hundred and forty mythical dollars in the hole. It was suddenly more than a crap game, it was a status thing, the downtown black man and all that. He was a sick guy, putting all that into it, and me just wanting to get the hell out of there and forget the ten, I'll get it off a friend or some damn thing. *Just lemme outta here!*

"I'm gone pay you, man, you just remember that. But we gonna play a bit more. We gonna switch from crap, you been winning too much." He reached into his side pocket and took out that knife, the one I knew he had.

He didn't do a thing with it, just laid it back down in his sock, right tight to the shoetop. He was giving me the word, I'd better not win.

Better not win? Jeezus, what'd I have to do, kill myself to prove I didn't want to win?

"High dice, now," he said succinctly.

He picked up one of the dice and bounced it, so very white, in the center of his palm, so very black. He was really busting on the symbolism. "You throw for roller," he bid me, and my head swam for an instant, everything going furry and grey and I wanted to puke right there.

I threw the cube and it came up six.

Then he threw, and got a three, and I was roller, first.

High dice is played sometimes with two, sometimes with one, but the rule is simple: high man wins. I was his master for a hundred and forty, and this was a quick, frantic way to recoup fast. It's a sucker's game.

"Look, Kurt," I almost pleaded with him, "please, I'm not feeling too well, let me get out of here, will you? You can forget the money, just let me out of here." It was the wrong thing to do; he wanted me to crawl, it was some kind of a thing with him to see me completely hammered and half dead on my feet and the Man still waiting outside there, and me not being able to move, hanging suspended like a fly in a web.

"I think you been cheatin' me, Teddy," he said, rising, towering over me as I crouched down. "I think you been doin' tricks with them dice. Gimme 'em here." He reached down and I gave him my cube. He put them in his side pocket and took a smaller, red plastic pair out of his shirt pocket. They were clear plastic and I could see right through them and I knew as sure as hell they were loaded, the spots painted on with lead paint.

"Well, listen, Kurt," I said righteously, "that other set was yours, too, so where the hell you get this stuff I'm cheating. Now c'mon, for Chrissakes, just get away from that door and let me out of here!"

I was getting a little hysterical now, and even as I raised my voice to him, someone shook the knob and banged half a dozen times quickly with a fist on the door and I heard a voice from the other side of the wood panel yell, "Hey, c'mon you jerks what the hell's going on in there, you a pair of fruits, or what?" and banged again. I was really going out of my mind about then. I started to yell help to whoever was there but Kurt just reached out lightly and slapped me so hard across the mouth I thought my skull would split open. I didn't get rocked back or anything, but it was the hardest I've ever been hit — and it dawned on me that I hadn't had a fight since I was thirteen years old, and how easy it was to avoid violence if you were always afraid, and just never *had* occasion to fight because you didn't want any part of it. But this was real, not the kind of constant wearying violence they have on TV that has no reality because there's such a surfeit of it.

I got hit in the mouth, and I wanted to cry at him.

Then I *did* cry, I really cried, with tears, and my hands were wringing each other and I was begging him, "C'mon, Kurt, please c'mon, let me out of here!" I couldn't give him my twenty-five dollars, I *needed* it, I *needed* that fix, my God, help me please help me God I'm going out of my mind, everything's closing in on me, I'll strangle if I don't get a fix, JeezusJeezus*Jeezus!*

"Man, you really think you gonna do that to me, doncha? You really think ah'm gonna let you outta here with mah money! Now c'mon, damn you, you gone play a little high dice with me, and then . . . when you get straight . . . I'll let you go."

It wasn't real, what was happening. A nightmare, this weird surrealism bit with him saying one thing and meaning another. I didn't have any of his money . . . in fact, he had ten bucks of *mine!* It wasn't the money, it was the whole thing of him being him and me being me and he had to beat me down. I mean, Jeezus, here I was on my knees already crying like a baby, and begging him, what the hell else did he want from me.

I felt everything going strange and wild and brass bands were marching through and outside in the Shack everyone could see through the walls and see how I was getting so sick I wanted to die, and I was seeing things, crawly things that were coming up to bite the hell outta me. I knew the Man was sitting there maybe wiping his hands on his pant leg, or picking his nose, making those tentative first movements that meant he was gonna pick up and split at once, and there would go my fix and I'd just croak, and that would be it. *It!*

That little toilet was the world, right then.

It was the biggest and blackest most angry Negro in the world, all ready to kill me for every white cat that had ever used the word nigger. And I was innocent, so help me God.

The room bulged outward, rubber walls ballooning.

The floor puckered.

I hurt worse and worse. My belly was blasted.

My head throbbed and beat and beat and beat.

Well: it passed, and I was sane again for a second. It had been very bad, all those twisting illusions and strange, dancing colors. I had been out of it completely, but now I was all right (except for the pains) and I had to take very close stock. Now just breathe easily, deeply, and look around. Just forget Kurt there for the moment. What else is there. Well . . .

The toilet has green walls, linoleum halfway up of a deeper

green, and a sort of colorless dirty linoleum floor, and a toilet with the seat up and someone's stuff still there, along with the floating seaweed of a cigarette, and a permanent ochre stain around the bowl. There's a cloth towel rack up there over the sink, with the towel at the end of its tracks and hanging down into the sink. It's very dirty, and some people will wipe their hands *any*where. There's a mirror on the front of that towel rack, but it's too high for me to see myself in it. I'm not too tall and Kurt is so *goddam* big — uh-uh, not Kurt. Analyze the room; what else . . .

Well, there's the sink, without any handles on the faucets, because the jerks who come here would leave the water running if there were. The hot water one is letting down a soft dripping thin stream, just enough to moisten your hands or get some wet on the comb, but since there's no soap, who cares? There's a can of Bab-O on the sink.

They don't have the Gold Dust twins on it any more. Or was it a Dutch girl with a bonnet that hid her face? I don't know.

There's a grille up in the wall that's between the men's and women's johns, but you can't hear much for some reason or other (I know some guys had wanted to hear what their dates were saying after a prom one night, and they could only make out mewling sounds). There is a line wrench with an octagonal socket on the end, leaning against the wall under the sink, so the mains can be turned off completely. Why bother? There isn't enough water coming out to count.

The room is about three-and-a-half feet across.

It is something over nine feet long.

It is very high, maybe ten or eleven feet high.

And all at once, I know it is shaped just exactly like a coffin, a coffin goddamit! A coffin and I'm buried with this no-good sonofabitch Kurt, who wants me dead and now I'm dead with him in the motherin' coffin with me, and that makes *no* sense at *all*, and I get very angry about it when I think about it . . .

"C'mon, throw, double mah bet," Kurt said, and I came up from way down there, angrier than anything, and just stood there watching those two red plastic dice in his hand that I *knew*,

I mean, I *knew* they were ringers, so what the hell did he think I was, a nut or something!

"I don't want to play with those dice," I said.

So I'd opened my big mouth and put down his whole race — that sick bit again — by calling him a cheater. "Teddy, what you doin'?" he asked, and he was so soft it was painful, because I knew he wanted to swing on me, it was that coughing, whispery voice. "What you doin', man? You sayin' I'm not straight . . . that what you sayin' to me?"

Oh jump, oh jump jump jump, he's gonna bust on me any second now, I knew it! "No, listen, hey, I just don't want to shoot any more. I mean, c'mon, you can't keep me in here against my will (he laughed at that, short and sharp). You know damned well Bernie'll wonder where you are."

Bernie ran the Shack, but I guess he was afraid of that mean streak in Kurt, too, because he warned and threatened him with firing and stuff, but he never did anything, and Kurt was about as afraid of him as he was of me, which was not at all.

"*Now, c'mon!*" I shouted. "I'm a free guy and you can't keep me in here, what are you, nuts or something?" Pow! The pain was back, back again from wherever it had been and I learned it hadn't been bad at all before. *Now* it was bad.

I flopped toward him, tried to hug him, show him my love. "Please, please, please, Kurt, *please* lemme outta here, I'm sick, I'm very sick, I'm dying, Kurt. *Please*, he'll leave!"

He shoved me back, and said: "Stop tryin' to whup the game on me, boy. Just shoot."

He pushed me down by the back of my neck and I had one bloody die in my hand, and the shaking was so bad it looked like every last die in the world was right there, in the oily palm of my hand.

I threw it against the wall:

How did you get hooked? How the hell did you stop being a simple-minded college sophomore who went to the Heidelburg for beer and jazzed around at the fraternity house, and dated balling chicks with nice smooth shins above their bobby socks, and became a junior who needed more money for junk than he did for books or tuition? How did you get so screwed up that you wind up on your knees in a toilet, golden, crying like a psycho? Boy, is this ever miserable . . .

It clattered to a stop and lay there very square, very red, and very six.

Kurt called me a dirty name.

He threw his, and it was a five. Ding! Just like that. Two hundred and eighty dollars. Two hundred and eighty punches in the mouth he was going to give me. I had won with his own loaded square cube dice, oh boy that was *it!*

"Sheet, sheet, sheet!" he cursed, drumming at that brown colorless linoleum. Oh, God, was he mad. Mad isn't enough of a word for it. He was so mad he wanted to tear my eyes out. Then he picked up those dice and threw them into the toilet!

I had to vomit.

"Hey, get away from the sink!" I shrilled leaping up about as fast as I could. I tried to elbow past him but he grabbed me and spun me back, and the puke which had started up caught midway in my throat — *God!* — and a little spinnet of dribble hit him on the hand and another on the neck, and that was the end of it. I had spit on him.

You figure it.

The battle of the races was at me all at once.

Why me? I'm innocent I tell you, and he was hitting me, and screaming so loud I knew everyone in the Shack was sitting silent and catching it all, "Who'd you think you are, man, who the eff you think you are you gone spit on me, you — " and he started cursing and hitting me, and so help me God I could barely feel it I was so sick and headachey and vile and wanting to curl up and twitch. He was shrieking and balling and banging on me and I was clattering against those walls like a pea in a pod.

Until he grabbed up that shake knife from his sock and rattled it up into sight, and quiet, so quiet, so very quiet he hissed at me, "You ever been marked, man? You ever been marked?"

And he came on to me. I screamed. I screamed very loud, "Kurt, don't cut me, don't hurt me, don't cut me, Kurt," but he was coming, and I just fainted away and was wide-awake as he stumbled over where I'd been, and I was too scared to do anything at all, so I reached under and grabbed his leg. He came back around so gracefully it was pretty to see, and he did a little movement with his knife hand, and I felt a razor go so smoothly through my face, and then there was blood. I mean, just like that, I was cut, and not lightly either. I was cut real good.

He wanted more. He wanted all of me, every bit of my white skin covered red, and he came again, and I scuttled back on my can, across the floor, and my hand hit that line wrench about two feet long, and I swung it up and hit him someplace private with one movement and then hooray, *he* screamed.

So I got up and belted him again, the sonofabitch.

And then a couple more times.

And I knew my Man was getting quietly up from his table, leaving fifteen cents for a tip, and walking to the front to leave another quarter with his bill, and walking unconcerned out the front door, because he couldn't afford to be around noise and trouble.

So I hit Kurt another one, just because I wasn't going to get my fix and was just going to have to puke and die and that was the last of it. I mean, it was so terrible.

When they finally busted down the door I was just sitting there on the floor with my feet against that other wall, about three feet away, and the line wrench hanging down between my knees, and crying, just crying, like a simp.

But what else could I do? I mean, when you hurt as bad as I did, and there was Kurt all dead and messy and me so ill I couldn't stand it, sitting in my own stuff, it was just hopeless. Just the end of it.

So I wondered all the usual stuff: like why was it I couldn't lose when I wanted to, and couldn't win when I wanted to, and why did they keep saying I was going to jail and maybe a nut house, because *I* knew all that, I knew it, man.

I didn't get my fix.

I even lost when I wanted to win.

Sitting there in the toilet, on the floor, all golden, made of base metals.

Enter the Fanatic, Stage Center

Blown in like a dust-covered September leaf, the bearded man arrived on a Sunday morning. Twisted and whirled like that leaf, he meandered down through the small, Sabbath-silent square, and around it twice, as though seeking an exit from his own personal maze. Then, having found it, he wandered from one side of Pearse Street to the other, heading East toward the Bethany Baptist Church. When he got there, held by the sound of the boys' choir and the organ, he hunkered down on the white cement steps, jacket open, his unclipped tie hanging down between his knees, and waited.

When the service was over, he was the first thing to be seen as the holy-refreshed throng erupted softly through the double doors. He clashed with the Sunday scenery. Everyone stared rudely. He was the only bearded man in the town of Prince.

For a second that backed the crowd into each other as those in front paused in mild shock, the bearded man held the eyes of the people. He held the deep-blue eyes lidded by heavy lashes of Gregg Bancroft, the grey-green eyes of Wilma Foltin, the brown eyes of Guy Earl and the amber eyes of his wife Iris, he held the bloodshot, smoke-stained eyes of old Jerry Dozier. A bond of sight, hurled between the strange, bearded man and five citizens of Prince, then as quickly undone and gone.

The crowd shoved forward and soon everyone was milling about, almost as though afraid to walk down the space between the church and the man; they milled and muttered, waiting (for what?) and asking each other why they were hesitating, who the man was, what was going on.

Then the bearded man slowly rose to his feet, methodically

buttoned his jacket, and walked back down toward the center of town. He did not look back.

Reverend Archer, a stern but receptive man in his late fifties, was deeply disturbed by the bearded man. He was a new factor in Prince, a town distinguished (as he put it in his occasional pieces for the secular bulletins) by sense, sensibility, and system. Reverend Archer called Gregg Bancroft, vice-president of the Prince Better Business Bureau, to his side and suggested, mildly but with a voiced overtone of apprehension, that Gregg find out who the stranger was. How long he planned to stay in Prince. What his affairs might be here. Why there was a tension in the air — product of the bearded man.

The wind had died down. It was very quiet, tremulously so, in the town of Prince. The Reverend stared at the sky: storm?

Again, across that abyss, they stared at one another. Bancroft's eyes fell, and the bearded man said, "Won't you come in, please, Mr. Bancroft."

He stepped aside, allowing the vice-president of the Prince Better Business Bureau passage into the motel room. Bancroft stepped inside, and felt rather than heard the door close behind him. The Gideon bible was huge and black against the white towel covering the dresser. The shower was running.

"I hope I haven't interrupted your shower, Mr. — " He extended it, and the bearded man did not accept. It had been a poor attempt, product of movie clichés, wasted on the strange newcomer. The inquiry about the shower was also fraudulent, for the bearded man still retained his tie and jacket.

"No, certainly not," he replied, "won't you sit down, I'll be with you in a moment." He entered the bathroom, closed the door behind him and for a minute the running water muffled any sounds that might have come from the bathroom. Then, abruptly, the water ceased, and a moment later he returned.

The bearded man hovered over Bancroft — how unnerving he could be without apparently trying — and then settled down in the other chair, hunched over, staring.

Bancroft was for starting the conversation, learning what it was he had to learn, and leaving. But his purpose was thwarted, for at the precise instant that he summoned breath to speak, the bearded man said, "I'm very happy you've come to see me, Mr. Bancroft. I would have had to look you up in any case." Bancroft treaded water in a confusion's span of inarticulateness. Finally, having no grasp of what was happening, really, he smiled. Fatuously.

"As an official of the Better Business Bureau," the bearded man went on, "where would you say the best location might be in Prince for a shop I'm contemplating opening?" He smiled back. It disturbed Bancroft, that smile.

"Well, ha ha," Bancroft squirmed, questioned, not questioning, "that all depends on what sort of shop you had in mind. You know we've got about everything we need in this town. We're small, but comfortable, ha ha."

"An art gallery," the bearded man said softly.

Gregg Bancroft sucked in a breath, then never used it to speak. His face showed a pastel tone of incomprehension. "An art gallery," he said, partially a query.

The bearded man nodded. "An art gallery. The Duvoe Art Gallery. I'm Gunther Duvoe, how do you do, Mr. Bancroft." Gregg Bancroft accepted the extended hand with a maelstrom of confusion spinning him. He was not ordering this interview as he had wanted; he was not a shilly-shally . . . in Prince he was known as a strong man. But this stranger unnerved him. The eyes. They seemed to see more than eyes were meant to see. He did not realize the moment Duvoe had freed his hand.

"I want a small store, something with a rather good front display space, so the paintings may be seen to their best advantage. Do you have such a place for rent, Mr. Bancroft?" Duvoe seemed purposeful, intent. He stared.

Thus, when Gregg Bancroft returned to Reverend Archer, and explained Mr. Duvoe was an artist, in town to open a small gallery, the good Reverend did not find it strange that Gregg had handshake-closed negotiations with Duvoe on the shop that had been the Bon Ton Millinery (now moved to larger quarters in the remodeled Hotel Prince).

He did not even deem it peculiar to see Duvoe quite frequently, thereafter, on the streets, in the shops, even at the services. Even though Mr. Duvoe seemed to be observing rather pointedly. There was even talk that the man took long, late night walks in obscure parts of the town, though he never spoke to anyone.

There was no doubt about it, however, Mr. Duvoe got around quite a bit. He seemed to be everywhere, in fact. And his shop had not yet opened.

But the Reverend Archer did not find that strange, nor did Gregg Bancroft, nor anyone else in Prince. The bearded man was merely feeling out the tenor of the town, sizing it up for this business. That was how they analyzed it.

They could not have been more correct.

Many nights, in the little motel room, the lights glowed. And there was very often the sound of running water. The maid — who had been given instructions not to bother cleaning the room, that it would be done by the tenant — found dirty towels neatly folded outside the door each day. These she replaced with fresh ones, wondering how the laundry would ever get all that paint off the dirty ones. She never tried to peek inside the room: there was no telling when the bearded man was there and when he was not. He came and went so silently, she was afraid she might open the door a crack, and be staring directly into those strange eyes. Duvoe was left quite alone. His rent he paid weekly, his peregrinations about Prince continued. For a while. Until the first paintings appeared in the shop's window.

It was obvious who it was. There was no way to pin it down, no way to bring action legally, because the identity was not so much in what he had painted but in what he had not painted — what he had implied. Yet there was no question who it was. It was Gregg Bancroft, and he was performing some highly intimate acts with Robin Walker, the seventeen-year-old daughter of Mayor Walker. Everyone knew Robin was wild, but Bancroft was over twice her age. That was the first painting. The others, if anything, were worse. Gregg Bancroft was at least a bachelor.

The one in which two women stared at each other with unmistakable passion, in that split-instant before their bodies touched, was terrifying in its clarity. Duvoe (if it had been painted by him) had a rare and remarkable gift. His was an amazing talent, not only the setting down of expression and intent, but the peripheral intangibles that surpassed mere photographic art. One of the women was Wilma Foltin; the grey-green eyes of the painted Wilma cried out in unnatural hunger for the other woman, obviously her love partner. Wilma Foltin was the librarian, a still water that apparently, as Duvoe had indicated, ran very, very deep, and very, very muddy.

There was a painting of Jerry Dozier, the town wino, the town beggar, in his shack at the edge of Prince. He was counting the silver dollars stacked neatly in old socks, hidden under the floorboards. He was laughing cruelly, and indicating with idiocy the townfolk who kept him alive and wealthy.

Guy Earl and his wife Iris were the subjects of two small vignette canvases, set side by side. Theirs were unspeakably frank and alarming. They told in as few lines and tones as a master could demand, that Guy and his wife should never have been married. What can a full-blooded woman do with a husband who cannot have sex?

There were more. Many more. Twenty-six in all; some quite large, others small, but each revealed — without a definite place to point the finger — the innermost personality, the vilest secret, the facet that damned most completely, of everyone Duvoe had met in Prince.

In one morning, the first morning of display, the town of Prince had its soul bared. It recoiled in horror from what it saw.

The gasoline bomb exploded through Duvoe's window shortly after one o'clock. Perhaps it had been thrown by Vern Bressler, whose portrait had revealed that he was half-Negro. Perhaps it had been thrown by Emil or Maxine Lupoff, whose relationships to a local waitress and an intern at the Prince Medical Center were revealed in a long, horizontal canvas, predominantly red.

But no matter; the damage had been done. Everyone who had seen those paintings would remember them. Those who had not seen them learned about them, in grossly exaggerated rumor (needless in the face of Duvoe's art).

Duvoe was accosted on the street by Gregg Bancroft who swung on him, without hello or preamble. Duvoe held his own quite nicely; he looked down on Bancroft, who was nursing the raw, fist-made gash in his cheek, and said: "If you trouble me again, Mr. Bancroft, I will have to unveil a further canvas I've done. Mayor Walker's daughter is seen from a slightly different angle."

Gregg Bancroft limped back to his office. He was shot, later that day, by Mayor Walker, a man known throughout the area for the jealousy and protectiveness he felt toward his daughter, the reigning high school football queen.

Jerry Dozier was robbed and mercilessly beaten by a small but intense group of Negro boys from The Hill, a poorer section of Prince where Jerry Dozier had often cadged meals from those not much better off than he had seemed to be.

Vern Bressler's wife left him. She was so repelled by the concept that the man she had married twenty-two years before was half-Negro, that she attempted to forget in a wild round of drinking and debauchery. She was inevitably placed under custody of the Prince Medical Center, for her own protection. There was some talk of insanity.

Wilma Foltin was summarily dismissed from her librarianship, and Guy Earl sold out his holdings in Prince, left town during the night, and left a note for his wife, Iris, the pith of which seemed to be that half a man was no man at all.

Since Duvoe's shop had been burned out, the front window broken and the canvases destroyed, the reminders were gone, but not the perpetrator. Whatever threat of blackmail through revelation-of-painting he employed to thumb-under Daniel Makepeace (owner of the Prince Hotel) it was sufficient to force Makepeace to display still another, larger painting in the huge front window of the hotel.

This painting, unlike the others, dealt with an entire scene of activity, involving more than essential characters. It was, in fact, a crowd scene. A large crowd scene. It had been done primarily in the shadow colors of blue and dark grey and amber, flashed throughout with angry bursts of violet, stark white, red, and yellow. It was perhaps twelve feet long by four feet high, and its detail-work was both graphic and arresting.

It neatly divided the town of Prince into two armed camps:

The townspeople who were determined *they* would not see their town ruined by the scandal; who were determined even if they had to take the law into their own hands that they would not stand trial with those who had done it; who loathed and despised the perpetrators of that long-forgotten crime they had thought was buried by time and forgetfulness.

And then there was the other group . . .

The townspeople so adroitly pictured in Duvoe's canvas, who had set fire to that house on Fairlawn Boulevard, so many years before, burning alive the old man and his wife.

On one side, the murderers.

On the other, those so frightened, they were the avengers.

It was a matter of defense before the world outside Prince learned of this suddenly uncloseted skeleton and stepped in for retribution. At which point everyone would begin to shout *mea culpa!*

In the rage for justice — an out-of-hand justice with its foundation laid in the quicksand of mob rule — terrible things were done to those beast-eyed residents of Duvoe's canvas. Few managed to escape the noose of insanity and fanatic verve that swept Prince. And in the storm, the eye of that storm moved silently, nearly forgotten. Duvoe packed his easel and brushes, and prepared to leave town.

Till the door of his motel room was kicked inward by one of the few who had escaped.

The bearded man spun from the suitcase lying packed and open on the bed, and confronted his visitor with an air of mixed surprise and horrified fascination.

Reverend Archer seemed quite at home with the pistol in his hand. "Another instance where scripture and science don't conflict?" Duvoe asked.

"What are you, some merchant of evil? A purveyor of miseries? *Who are you!*" The Reverend's face was blotched with emotion. He spoke heavily, each wordsyllable drawn out emphatically, with hatred and bewilderment in the tone. The pistol stayed very level, aimed directly into Duvoe's face.

The bearded man smiled and turned back to the suitcase. He

pulled tight the inside straps and began to close the bag. The Reverend stepped up behind him and spun the artist viciously.

"Answer me, man, because I'm here to wreak vengeance of one kind or another, and nothing will keep me from seeing you dead if you don't talk your way out of it." He was both appealing and condemning. He hated, obviously with an intensity he could not feel for an abstraction: evil. But at the same time he sought an answer, a way out of what he had come to do. He was a man of God, and he could not kill . . . unless it was to kill an abstraction.

"Who *are* you?" His temples throbbed. His voice was vengeful, urging, throaty.

The bearded man smiled again. Wistfully. "I'm a wandering agent of Satan, padre. I'm just a doer of evil because it's my stock in trade. I'm a traveling salesman of sin."

The Reverend's hand lashed out, suddenly. The bearded man's gibes were too much, and the pistol caught Duvoe at the right temple, spun him back against the bedpost and opened a livid wound in the flesh at his hairline. He put a hand up to his face and smeared the warmness down toward his cheek. "Go ahead, Reverend. Go ahead, do it again. It won't stop what's happening in your clean, ordered little town. It wouldn't stop it if you killed me a thousand times over.

"But go ahead anyhow, Reverend. Do your damnedest!"

Archer stood shaking at his own brutality. His hand holding the pistol wavered and trembled, while the holy man's eyes shut tight in an agony of self-examination, consideration of depths till then unknown. He had destroyed himself more than a bit with the action.

"Why have you destroyed my town?" he asked softly, pathetic, almost childlike. "Why? I can't understand how a man could do it. You did it . . . why?"

Duvoe ran a hand across his dry lips. The emotion of the other man drenched him, made him think, made him remember, forced him to consider all that had gone before, what he had done, who had known what was coming, the whys and hows and realities of it, festering till it had had to be lanced.

"Why . . . " he murmured the question softly, half to himself, "why indeed, Reverend. Why indeed."

He slumped down on the bed.

What he said came very gently, as though all the broken glass edges of memory had been sea-smoothed by the wash of emotions.

"They did it in 1942. I was seventeen, away at art school in New York; I didn't learn about it for several weeks. I couldn't understand why my letters never got answered, or why the money stopped coming. Finally, I came home and saw the rubble where my home had been. Do you remember it, Reverend? You were here then; you were tending to the souls of your flock even then. Your flock of bigots and murderers! Do you remember, Reverend?"

Archer's face came up. Comprehension dawned. His mouth worked and he said, "Not Duvoe. Not Duvoe at all. Deutsch! I know . . . *Deutsch!*"

The bearded man's eyes burned steadily, strangely, with a flickering light of inner intensity, "That's *right*, Reverend. That's right! Deutsch. Gunther *Deutsch*, not Gunther Duvoe. Gunther *Deutsch*, son of Cara and Horst Deutsch, who ran the home bakery on Pearse Street for nineteen years, until we went to war with Germany, and the bigots decided old Horst and his *hausfrau* were Nazis, and burned them alive in their house on Fairlawn Boulevard!

"*Now* do you remember, Reverend? *Now* do you know what makes a boy of seventeen run away from even the ashes of his parents, what makes him go mad a little, Reverend, what makes him want to kill something as big as a town? Do you *know* now, my holy father of the guilty ones? Now do you see what warps a boy's life so he doesn't marry, doesn't settle, doesn't *live* till now? Is it clear, at last?"

Archer stared in horror at the warped expression, the burning, desperately *needing* eyes. "You're a fanatic, you've done this, do you know what you've done . . . "

The bearded man stood up, fierce, tense.

"Do I *know*? Reverend, the God you talk about is the only one who knows how *much* and how *well* I know."

"They didn't know what they were doing . . . the war . . . all the talk about saboteurs . . . they were sick people . . . " Archer flailed at nothing, trying to establish a rationale, failing completely.

"So they burned alive an old man and his wife who'd been in this town for almost twenty years. They indulged their patriotic fervor in the defence of their country; old man Deutsch and his wife . . . " he sneered vindictively, " . . . oh, they were dangerous, all right!"

Archer dropped the pistol and turned away. The .45 lay black and huge on the carpet; the Reverend's face (in artistic contrast) was small and milky. Duvoe would not let him retreat, however; he followed him with "And what did *you* do, Reverend? What did you do to set right the wrong? Did you say anything to anyone outside Prince? Or did you let the conspiracy of silence stand? Did you succor them in their hour of need, Reverend? Did you make sure their souls were unblemished?"

The Reverend Archer did not turn. He raised his hands to his face, and soft sobs escaped between the prisoning bars of his fingers. "It was good here, so . . . so ordered . . . "

The bearded man laughed, fur-soft and deeply.

Then he said: "Well, don't let it bother you, Reverend Archer. It doesn't matter."

Then, Archer turned. "What are you talking about? What do you mean?"

And Duvoe said: "It's all a lie, Reverend. My name isn't Deutsch. It isn't Duvoe, either, but it certainly isn't Deutsch. They had no children."

The Reverend Archer's strong chin could not support the wild weight of his slack mouth. His lower jaw dropped open, and he cast about frantically for the reason in this suddenly mad situation. "You're . . . *not*? Then who . . . what did you . . . "

Duvoe's smile was that of the shark. "Everyone has a hobby, Reverend, and when you've done evil for so long it's the only way you know, the only product you can merchandise, well, then I suppose your first guess about me was correct."

"Evil!" the Reverend bellowed, starting forward. "You work for *him* . . . "

"Oh, don't be melodramatic, Mr. Archer. I'm quite as human as you. But all this wearies . . . " and he methodically emptied the .45 into the Reverend Mr. Archer.

Archer fell halfway into the bathroom, and lying there with his face cool against the tile, he smelled the last traces of incense that steam from running shower water was not able to conceal. The cool began to fade, and so did the light as Duvoe wandered about the room carrying his suitcase, murmuring abstractedly, "Now where did I put that road map . . . "

Exit the fanatic, to the smell of sulphur, offstage right.

Someone is Hungrier

Gone to ground, Ricky Darwin — the former Rachel Dowsznski of Appleton, Wisconsin — huddled in her Far North Chicago English basement and tried not to think about acid eating out her eyes.

She could almost feel the biting, fuming liquid. Grey and painful, as though a slim, sadistic man with long, carefully manicured fingernails were gouging the soft stuff out of the sockets: oysters wriggling in their shells.

She could almost feel it. Almost, but not quite. Not yet. They still hadn't found the dingy English cellar where she cowered. But it was only a matter of searching and searching, and the strange magic of tipsters, and then one day —

One day they'd come. God made little green apples . . . and they'd come. Three men with bulky overcoats and narrow-brimmed hats and a small vial of acid, fuming. Courtesy of Marshall Ringler, who was a slim, sadistic man with long, carefully manicured fingernails. A man who hated her and hated her more than even the rackets from which he made his living.

She stared at the flickering grey square of the television in the corner and thought how wise she had been; how clever to have dragged the little 17″ set with her when she had fled 20 East Delaware and being Marshall Ringler's mistress. The phone call from Bernice, warning her that Marshall had found out she'd sold the carbons, telling her Marshall was enraged, had threatened to have her killed. And the flight.

Three pairs of hose and an extra pair of shoes in the black leather beach bag, a carton of cigarettes, some underwear . . . and the TV. She had run out of the glass and chrome building, taken a cab to the elevated, and then changed trains nine times in her flight north. It hadn't been easy finding a place to live . . . she had only come away with the money in her purse; but the English basement was warm, and the TV kept her occupied — though one more afternoon of those insipid guessing games and she'd eat the volume control — so it wasn't too bad.

Just till things quieted down for her, then she could leave town. Hollywood, perhaps, or New York.

The floorboards above her creaked as Mrs. Prokosh in the house upstairs went about her business. Mrs. Prokosh provided the meals by special request and special financial arrangement (on the understanding that Ricky was ducking her ex-husband).

Hollywood, or even New York. They were a long way from Appleton, Wisconsin. A lot longer than Chicago and an English basement. Why had she decided to double-cross Marshall? Had it been the money? She thought about it, and knew that had only been part of it. She had wanted free of him . . . and this seemed a foolproof way of doing it. If he wouldn't let her go, then she would make *him* go from *her.*

So she had agreed to sell the carbons of Marshall's business ledger statements to that shady character known as The Accountant, who in turn would sell them to the police informant — or perhaps to the T-men, since it was a tax matter — and then it was all up for Marshall, and she could be free. But he had found out; it didn't matter how; he had found out. So she had fled the expensive apartment in which Marshall had set her up, and she had gone to ground in a dingy, moist, netherworld basement, waiting. And she would stay this way for —

How long?

Till the money ran out?

Till they found her?

Till she turned white as a maggot in a garbage pail from being out of the light so long? It was a moot point, a senseless series of questions. Here she was, and here she would stay.

She settled back in the dirty, over-stuffed chair Mrs. Prokosh had loaned her from the basement's pile of rubble. Sometime in the recent past the chair had been exposed to water dripping from pipes somewhere, and the arms still retained the mildewed stench of scummy moisture. The TV continued to burble and flicker pompously.

I wanted to hit it big, she thought, and there was pain in her chest at the memory of the loss of dreams. *And this is real big. So big. A basement in nowheresville. Not even where I started was this bad.* Not even Appleton, Wisconsin; chief claim to fame: Edna Ferber was born here. Some big. Some damned big.

You get hungry, she mused, *too hungry*. For life, for success, for *maître d*'s saying, "Right this way, Miss Darwin, we have your table reserved." Hungry for the kind of looks men give you when you can afford the clothes and the jewels and the hairdo that make them look a hundred times. Hungry for big things, for the good things.

Thoughts swirled and she remembered the town with its trees and its small-faced people with their small thoughts *behind* the faces, and the wanting, the needing to be big. To be so hungry to make it you didn't give a damn who you had to chew up to get there. All animals, all hungry, all chewing on each other's personalities to get to the top.

So Chicago was closer to the top, and I was hungry, and it even seemed like making the big time when I got picked up by Marshall in the lounge.

She recalled the day. She had been working as a cocktail waitress in a men's bar. A short tutu skirt, black mesh hose that showed off her long, golden legs, her hair whipped back in a French roll, all auburn and glinting, the bodice of the costume low enough so the cinch-bra pushed her figure up provocatively. And Marshall had seen her, had wanted her, had been hungry for her. *Just as I was hungry for success.*

That was when she had learned: no matter how hungry you are . . . someone else is always hungrier. There are bigger animals trying to chew their way to the top. But Marshall had taken possession of her, and she had become his chattel.

Make it to the top, she thought wryly. And all the little symbols of having made it; the obscure symbols. Like the most expensive nylons — by the dozen. Like signing a name to the check at The Blackhawk or The Pump Room. Like owning a Mexican hairless and walking him on a long golden leash, even though you despised the nipping, shrill insect-like creature. And most personal of all, the symbol that you had dreamed about when you were a hungry high school girl in Appleton, Wisconsin: never carry any change in your purse. Only bills. Change is for suckers, for small timers. When the cab fare is two dollars and fifteen cents, give the hackie three bucks and say, "Keep it, driver." That was the big time; a roll of bills, and *never never* the poverty clink of coins in your purse.

That had been hunger, and that had been on top, and now, now . . . an English basement waiting for three men with acid.

"Would you like some navy bean soup?"

Ricky twitched horribly at the voice, and for a full minute she trembled with shock. Mrs. Prokosh stood in the door-empty doorway of the English basement, holding a blue Limoges soup dish with a spoon handle protruding. Ricky bit the edge of her palm, still gasping in terror — remembered, and tried to speak. She was unable to form the words, and only the dimness of the basement kept Mrs. Prokosh from seeing how drained of life her face, her eyes, had become.

"I didn't startle you, did I?" she asked innocently.

Ricky was finally able to speak, and still feeling the bit-of-death fluttering of fright in her stomach, she replied as kindly as possible, "No, I was just thinking, Mrs. Prokosh. Thank you for the soup."

The young copper-haired girl with the smudges beneath her eyes and the muffin-shaped older woman in her shapeless perhaps-blue perhaps-grey dress stared at one another. There were thoughts of times past, of times to come, of the faces each wore through life. It was a long, silent conversation in a second's time.

Mrs. Prokosh set the bowl of soup down on the straight-backed chair near the overstuffed, and said, "Well, I better be getting back upstairs. Harry's expecting his dinner on time." She moved to the empty doorway. "Oh, by the way," she stopped and turned with calculated hesitancy, "there was a couple of men here this afternoon asking if I had rooms for rent. They . . ."

"*What did they look like?*" Ricky fairly screamed.

Her eyes were very large, surrounded by white. Her breathing was labored; someone had sunk fangs into her throat.

"Oh, they was tall, and they was very polite, y'know, and they just asked if I rented out rooms 'cause they heard I'd taken in a girl, and I told them no, I didn't, and it was my basement I'd rented out."

Ricky was trapped inside Ricky's skull, screaming, beating at the walls of bone, howling at the stupidity of the old woman, who had damned her, doomed her.

"Why didn't you tell me this sooner, *why?*" Ricky pleaded with the old woman. Her face was ruined, desecrated by hobnailed boots of terror.

"Well, honey, I *swear!* I mean, neither of 'em looked anything like what you said your husband looked like; they was real nice gentlemen, and I answered 'em the way I would . . . what're you doing?"

Ricky had risen hurriedly from the chair, was now throwing what few possessions were clean into the leather beach bag. It took no more than a minute.

"I'm leaving, Mrs. Prokosh. I'm getting out of here." She started past the old woman. A meaty hand wrapped around her forearm.

"Now just a minute, Mrs. Darwin. You ate nine meals here this week that you ain't paid for, and that's fifty cents a meal, so that's four-fifty." She stuck out her free hand.

Ricky pulled open the beach bag, reached in to find her wallet, and drew out the sheaf of bills, so thin now. She whispered free a five-dollar bill and gave it to the old woman, started to move away.

"You got half a buck comin' back," Mrs. Prokosh said.

"Keep it," Ricky threw back, over her shoulder. *Change!*

"Well, sorry to see you go, honey; I was gettin' to think you might stay on . . . " But she was talking to herself; Ricky Darwin was on the dark evening street, moving away from the target house and its English basement coffin as quickly as possible.

It might all be imagination. It might have been a couple of Northwestern students needing rooms. Or a zoning action by the rent commission . . . if they still had those things. It might have been nothing.

The headlights erupted out of the bushes.

So it hadn't been her imagination.

It had been Marshall's men. They had found her.

The four headlights bathed her, limning her sharply, poised with mouth open, legs apart ready to spring, the black leather beach bag hanging down like a millstone weight in her hand, the copper hair tangled and dirty after two weeks in the basement.

And the car started up.

She ran, then.

She ran through the bushes at the other side of the street, into a yard, and around the back, through a short alley between garages and down another street. Then she was gasping for breath, and her chest hurt terribly as she ran and ran and looked for a wall to leap over so they could not see her, and then another street, down another street, there's got to be another street. She was hopelessly lost, but ahead the main throughstreet showed cars zipping past occasionally, and she headed for it, hoping to flag someone down.

It was night, the lights were bright and the streetlights were not. She was on the road, and because Chance is what it is, every car that went past her had a man and his wife in it, or a guy and his girl, or two women . . . but no single men, and everybody knows that a lone girl on a highway is picked up by single or hungry men.

And that night, that time, the hungry ones were elsewhere.

All save Ricky Darwin.

And she could smell the melting stench of acid-eaten flesh. She began running hysterically up the highway, crying, dry-heaving. An outside phone booth. A big red and aluminum phone booth, with a light and a phone and a way to call the police.

Police who could not have helped her before, but were able to help her now . . . at least to save her from immediate danger . . . and she ran up to the booth, threw herself into it, slammed the door . . . and opened her beach bag.

Where her symbols lay waiting.

Her symbols of making it to the top, hungrier than the rest.

She slumped back against the glass wall of the phone booth, too tired to run. It was over, it had to be over now. She might have called the police, then stayed in the area, somehow managed to avoid Marshall's men till help arrived. She might have, if she hadn't wanted to make it so big.

If she hadn't wanted to get to the top — so hungry for the good things, the big things — where success was measured by how much money you had. How much money. Not how much small change, just how many bills.

She stared helplessly at the wallet, knowing they would come. Knowing there were worse things than Appleton, Wisconsin, and empty faces. Faces empty, but not burned out.

She stared into the wallet.

Filled with bills. Symbols of hunger.

But the phone took small change.

Memory of a Muted Trumpet

They called the place Valhalla, but it was a loft on Second Street, a wino's-breath from the Bowery, a pub's-crawl from the Village.

It was on the fourth floor of a condemned building, and no one else lived there. Just The Green Hornet and Spoof and Gig-Man. There was Gig-Man's new woman, they called her PattyPeek — because her name was Patty and she looked like she was always peeking around a corner, like that — and half a dozen cats, three of whom were named Shadrach, Meshach, and Boo-*dow*!

The night the girl they later called Irish first showed at Valhalla, they were having a rent party. The Hungarian who owned the rat-trap still made it to their door the first of every month, holding the rope they had nailed up for a banister, and demanding his pound of flesh. So they were having a rent party, and digging.

The Green Hornet was hunkered down in front of the stereo being wigged by Shelly Manne whacking it home on "Man with the Golden Arm" at 180 decibels. The Salamander was sitting in the butterfly chair, combing her hair and trying to rationalize Nietzsche with her harelip. William Arthur Henderson-Kalish was standing in a corner talking to No. 1 and his latest acquisition, a chick named Maureen, who had carrot-colored hair, telling them, "Mencken was a genius, okay. But he had too many blind spots; the Jews, organized religion, isolationism. Genius is no excuse for being so out of it . . ."

Big Walt was sitting like a monarch in the easy chair near the forest of rubber plants. All 314 pounds of him, perspiring freely, making that area *verboten* for anyone with a nose, and drinking from a can of beer on top of a stack of thirty beers. There was an old man nobody knew with a mouthful of gold teeth — so he'd been nicknamed Goldmouth — and he was sitting cross-legged in the middle of the floor, speaking softly in a Vermont dialect about, "Goin' tuh th' barn dance in m'dungies . . . "

In the kitchen six nobodys in button-down shirts and Harris tweed jackets were pouring the contents of a hip flask into the gigantic cooking pot of Sweet Lucy. They had each paid their dollar-fifty for the privilege of attending the party, and they were making certain — through dint of sheer alcohol — that they would each wind up with a weirdie Bohemian chick in their beds that night. Everyone was pointedly ignoring them.

A knock on the door was ignored by everyone except Floormat, a short and exceedingly dumpy girl with adolescent pimples, who hurried to answer it. When she flung open the door, Dick Eherenson and his new wife Portia stood there, holding their baby. They had been married a week; the baby was almost a year old. Its name was Bach Partita.

In the bedroom, where a monstrous bed took up the entire floor space — room enough for three couples on it — God Geller was sitting cross-legged upon the dirty sheets, informing a rapt audience of four girls from Hunter College what the drug *peyote* was like:

"It's non-habit-forming and it's purely safe. The one drawback is that it tastes like hell. I mean, it's so bad the thought of it can make you puke."

"What's it made from?" one of the girls, a freshman with deep-black eyes, asked.

God Geller ran a shaky hand through his short, curly hair. "The *peyote* cactus," he answered conversationally. "We have it mailed to us from a nursery in Texas. It's illegal in California, you know. I used to blast off on it when I was in Hollywood. You know I was in one of the Bowery Boys movies, don't you — "

God Geller had once hitchhiked as far West as the Napa Valley where he had worked for two months hauling feed bags on a dude ranch. He had come back to astound his friends in New York with tales of his sexual prowess among the starlets, and his modicum of success in the cinema. He was paranoid.

" — the Indians have a religion based on the *peyote*. First you strip off the spines and the bark around the roots, and you cut them up, and boil them down into a tea. The stuff is too bitter otherwise."

"Is it really that bad?" one of the girls asked, her young face lit with awe.

God Geller made a steeple with his fingers, and pointed the edifice at her. "I can *tell* you how bad it is. When you drink it, you have to cut it with Hawaiian punch or tomato juice, and toss it off real quick, otherwise you'll barf right then. Your stomach can't hold it down for very long, maybe a half hour.

"*I've* been able to keep it down over an hour before I vomited it back up!" he chimed proudly. "But that's enough time for the stuff to saturate the lining of your stomach, and *then* boo-dow, it's like you were a God or something!"

A chemistry major, a girl with freckles and a large nose supporting horn-rimmed glasses, interrupted his panegyric. "What does the *peyote* cactus look like?"

God Geller looked at her with annoyance. This was the only one he considered a dog. He had been trying to impress the others. He answered her sharply, "The biggest is about the size of a fist, the smallest like a walnut. The thing *looks* like a mushroom head without a stalk; it's a root like a sweet potato."

He turned back to the good-lookers who hung on his every word, dropping his hand to the knee of one sophomore with large breasts.

"It like heightens your senses," he confided. "You see everything clearer, hear everything better, you just naturally *dig* more. The neons in the street look like little jewels, everything is better, it's just a great kick, if you can stomach the ghast of the taste."

"That bad, huh?" asked the sophomore. He moved his hand under her skirt slightly.

"Yeah, it'll make you puke every time. After a while you kind of build up a tolerance. It's worth it when you've been up on it for a few days, though. Great!"

He stood up and moved out of the room with her, into the darkened hallway. He had never sampled *peyote*; he had read

Huxley on the subject. But the sophomore had large breasts. It was an opener.

The Chem major was jotting notes in a pocket notebook.

The party was swinging, everybody was digging. Everybody but Spoof.

Spoof was feeling down. The party was a flake.

There was another bang on the door, and Spoof rolled over on his stomach. He was lying on a Mexican shawl stretched out near the dead fireplace. *Not more of these deadbeat creeps,* he thought. *What we have to put up with just to pay off the goddam rent.*

Floormat opened the door, and Roger "Teddy Bear" Sims stood there with a girl on his arm. One of the button-down boobs let out a low, long, two-note whistle, and Spoof rolled over quickly. She was fantastic.

It wasn't anything simple about her; it was more the overall effect. The moment she walked in ahead of Teddy Bear, her feet in their high heels carefully placed on the tilting floorboards, she was Irish to him. Whatever her name might be, she was simply Irish.

Spoof leaped up, his image passing rapidly across the now-peeling mirror standing at the side of the fireplace. It was a clever image, full of Machiavellian undertones; his eyes set deep and brown under his thick eyebrows, the planes of his gaunt face catching light and releasing it in a panoply of shadows. He wore a black walnut-colored crewneck sweater over a white shirt, and a pair of oatmeal-colored corduroy slacks that just lapped at the tops of his soft doeskin boots. He looked clean, and yet there was a Northern desire in his face. The look of the Visigoth and the Hun was there.

He was a writer with great talent and no drive. He lazed in the backwaters of New York, mouthing his philosophies and scrawling his sentiments in loose-leaf binders that might not ever get compiled into The Novel of Outrage.

But right now, as he stood up abruptly, he was a man, and what had come through the door was Irish; for him, perhaps for others, but especially for him, a sex symbol. This was Woman, and he had the scent.

Teddy Bear had been mobbed by all the unattached men in the place, all clamoring for an introduction.

Spoof stood near the fireplace, watching her face bobbing between their heads, waiting for the glance he knew would come, and when it did, she had been staring at him a long moment before he even realized it. "Irish" he said, loud enough for her to hear, because she was expecting it; but not loud enough for the others to make out.

She smiled that gamine smile, and they were mating, right then. Right then, they were doing it with their eyes.

Finally, he elbowed through them, said a vague excuse us to Teddy Bear, who worked for Pillsbury as a clerk and took his meager hedonism on weekends, and rescued the girl from the horde. They went out through the living room, into the hall, where he yanked open the door, and they passed through. Floormat, whose love was a rotting rose clutched between her teeth, watched them go with sorrow and a sour stomach.

Down the hall there was yet another flight of steps. He led her up, like a leaf borne unresisting, fatalistically, on a south wind. The trapdoor to the roof was easily thrown back, and it was only late summer.

Time of darkness.

Time of passion.

When they came down, she was his, and the party had subsided into mixed apathy and drunkenness. God Geller was under the dirty sheets with the sophomore, while the Chem major continued taking notes. The button-down boobs, each having made his try with the Salamander as a last resort, had noisily exited, damning Bohemians, and making plans for the White House.

Her name had been Lois Bishop when she had gone up that dismal flight of stairs; now, with tar stains on the back of her pencil skirt, her name was Irish, for all time.

The second time, under a bridge in Central Park, far uptown, she told him she *had* been a virgin the first time. He looked at her quizzically, and there was disbelief on his darkly handsome face. She recognized it for what she thought was pity, and soothed him with the information that a water bucket, at the age of twelve, had preceded him. But she had been a virgin.

The third time, at Valhalla, in the monstrous bed with its stiff, circular-stained sheets, she confided she was a Catholic. It annoyed him; he was a renegade Jew with no religion whatsoever. She toyed with the idea of converting; he ignored her.

The fourth time was a hurried thing, a demand made on her lunch hour that she paid simply because it was him, and she did hate the office and its eternally clacking typewriters — while this escape route seemed wide open.

The fifth time she told him about her parents in the Bronx. They lay side by side in the $3 hotel room in the hotel without a name, and she told him about her parents, and her kid brother, and the distance she had to walk each day to grab a bus to the subway station. She told him of seasons in Kansas City and the hard times and how her father had said New York was a jungle, but there were always bananas if nothing else in a jungle.

The sixth time she told him she was pregnant.

He laughed and went to sleep.

She had the baby on Riverside Drive, in the park, late at night, and left it head-down in a paper bag behind the stone wall bordering the sidewalk. For several months, since she had gotten large, she had lived in a cheap room in a residential hotel catering mostly to poor Puerto Ricans fresh in the city, and impecunious students at Columbia. She had used the name Mrs. Morris Walnack.

She had known a Morris Walnack in Kansas City when she had been a child.

Spoof had not called in three months, but she sent him a short note telling him what had happened.

He invited her to a party.

It was a bring-a-bottle party.

In the kitchen The Salamander was squeezing blackheads against the little mirror over the sink. PattyPeek was necking in a dim corner with The Green Hornet, who had recently grown a diabolical-looking red beard. Gig-Man had found Confucius, and PattyPeek was a passionate girl. On the Mexican shawl God Geller was sitting cross-legged (though his two-year active duty in the army had made them muscle bound and they cramped easily) picking out "Old Joe Clark" on the three-string banjo.

A Barnard girl was watching him rapturously.

Occasionally he winked at her.

The cats were clustered around a saucer of beer Shorty Jibbets had set out for them, and Boo-*dow!* was twitching just prior to what might be a cataclysmic feline epileptic fit. Shorty sat on top of the old TV in his undershorts, a towel from the Luxor Baths wrapped turban-style around his oddly shaped head, swearing he would fly the set to the Moon.

William Arthur Henderson-Kalish was pontificating at a trio of black musicians who had fallen in at a stranger's sidewalk-mention that someone had a few sticks up here. He was saying in loud tones: "Miro was a self-plagiarist. Just the same images, turned sidewise and stood on their heads. Nothing new. No *élan vital* in the later stuff. Now, if Heinrich Kley had ever left his little world of fantasy, he might have burst forth . . . "

No. 1, having found Maureen wanted sex and not culture, had gone back to the uneasy relationship with Stanley Reskoff, and now they lay together on the great bed, arguing softly about who should put the make on that sweet young boy from Connecticut Teddy Bear had brought from the Pillsbury office this evening.

Maureen lay drunkenly across Big Walt's lap, her mambo dress with its flaring hem about her ample thighs. Abruptly she pulled herself to a sitting position with one arm around Big Walt's neck. She screeched into the semidarkness of the living room:

"How many of you girls want to go to a party?

"A *real* party!"

She hung there absently for an instant, and in that instant Gig-Man rose from the shadowy corner, and with vitriol dripping in his voice shouted, "What the hell do you know about real parties?"

There was such hatred in his voice, that for an instant there was a dead, uncomfortable silence.

Then he followed it up with: "What the hell do you know about *anything*?"

Maureen started to say something, but Big Walt belched grotesquely at that moment, and put a meaty palm in her face, forcing her back across his lap. She lay there breathing stentoriously, and feeling pale.

Gig-Man found another can of beer and settled back into his corner.

Floormat sat in a straight-backed chair by the big living-room window, the rubber plants shadowing her, a pen in her left hand, a pad of drawing paper propped on her lap, and she drew things eating each other. Her face was dirty, and ink stains smudged her sausage fingers.

For a long time there was the sound of music in the loft, as Clifford Brown issued his ultimatum to the night. Then, when the world had rolled over him like a tank, his sounds were gone, and like life on Second Street, embalmed in its own inactivity, suffocated by its own inadequacies, pockmarked by its many intemperances and outright sins, all that was left was the memory of a muted trumpet.

*

There were many people at the party, and in one corner of the great living room, sitting on the lap of a boy she did not know, was a girl with dark eyes. Her hair had been hand-cut awkwardly, and though it did not dull the attractiveness of her features, it made her look strange, Bohemian, unclean and unkempt.

The boy had his hand on her thigh, and she was whispering to him of Kafka and dull moonlight, of what roaches think and how to escape the dullness of a regimented life.

The boy was not listening, but it did not matter. He knew what he wanted from this girl, and there was no doubt in either of their minds that he would get it, if he told her he loved her.

The girl had had a name once.

Now she was Irish, for all time.

Some diseases are more easily communicable than others, and the recruiting gets done come hell or high water.

It was a good party. There were lots of new faces.

Turnpike

Formless, some kind of heart-bearing creature all sense and instinct, I've swum my life through a sea as black as the motivations that have driven me. Limpid reason, dulled at birth, has played so infinitesimal a part in my doings, that I cannot truly say it has ever sent me with the proper tides. Bumped and jostled and once or twice I have cleaved to another entity in that lightless ocean, sucked it dry of whatever it had, and floated away. If I knew, if I had the faintest idea why I do what I do, why a man such as myself — and God knows I'm anything but stupid — cannot find direction and ethic it might save me from tomorrow. Better still, from tonight.

But tonight began three days ago, and tomorrow is as inevitable as the way it started.

Riding high in the cab of a tandem-axle semi; underneath me twelve big overweight doughnuts out of Goodyear; behind me seventy billion uncounted ground-up Brazilian coffee beans mixed with some mocha java and a little Guatemalan, packed in double-foil bags with turndown closures guaranteed to keep the grind "brewpot-fresh" all the way from the loading dock in mid-Manhattan across the turnpike route to San Francisco, California, where "brewpot-fresh" coffee is treasured, worshiped, bought at the very highest mark-ups in specialty gourmet shops. As pushed — like a pea with the nose down all the highways of tomorrow — in a 12-wheel, tandem-axle etcetera by this heart-bearing creature, this Neil Danzig, this truck driver with the soul of Rimbaud.

Riding high above the Pennsylvania Turnpike, somewhere just past King of Prussia (leave it to the stiff-necked, propermiened Dutch to preserve absolutely nothing), I pulled alongside the Mustang convertible with the blond girl driving. We matched speeds, just sixty, lane-by-lane. She drove with her face straight-forward and didn't look at the behemoth pounding along beside her. The top was down, her hair was loose in the flat, long teenage style, and it fitted: she was eighteen. Not a dime older.

I was fascinated; it was the best thing I'd seen on that imbecile stretch of turnpike with the unbroken concrete grey and mindless in front of me. I was able to drive and stare at her, both at the same time. The road went flat-out and the concentration was useless. Tunnel vision and road hypnosis were my excuses. Stare at the broad, and don't let the highway kill you. We fled along beside each other for half a dozen miles, and finally she looked up at me, right across the old man asleep on the other side of the front seat.

She had eyes as blue as a diesel exhaust, and a wet mouth. The hair was like a banner flying out behind her in the wind. She gave me a smile that was the end product of a million female mouths. I smiled back.

We kept abreast of one another for twenty miles, flirting with each other. I would make half-assed funny faces at her and she would toss back her head and laugh, the sound lost in the whipping backwind. We couldn't talk to each other, but it was somehow more satisfying than the usual fencing conversation a guy has to use when first he meets a girl. We got all that out of the way in the first twenty miles.

Finally, I caught her eye on one of our interchanges, and made a pantomime of a cup of coffee with my left hand. I pointed to her, then back to me. She shrugged, gave me a helpless little moue of resignation, and jerked a thumb almost into the left ear of the sleeping old man on the passenger side. Then she shrugged again. Sorry, Neil, but old dad is in the way.

We continued up the pike, and I kept urging her, all in dumb show. Finally, she nodded. Reluctantly. I pointed ahead to the next turnpike sign that was coming up on us. It said rest stop ten miles. She nodded and smiled, and we both decked the accelerators at almost the same moment. When we were within a mile of the rest stop, she fell behind, and I speeded up, and pulled into the service area a minute ahead of her.

Old juices were coming to life in me as I sat in the Howard Johnson's, waiting for her. She was a kid, but even sitting down, some of her concealed, she was some kid. The poor-boy sweater she was wearing showed me a tasty abundance of high, round meat. Her face was something you see in a television commercial, all lean and sleek and well-fed and clean. Eighteen, but as Pushkin put it: "Old enough to bleed, is old enough to butcher."

She came through the entrance and looked around.

Then she walked to me, without guile, and sat down. The waitress came with the two coffees, then.

"Is this a pick up?"

"That's what it's called."

"I think I'd like a piece of pie."

The way she looked at me, I knew it was there, if I could figure a way to get it. Cross-country, on turnpikes? Her in her little blue Mustang, me in that semi? It was impossible. She had a piece of pumpkin pie, with a scoop of maple-walnut ice cream.

"Who's the fellow you're with?"

"My father. He's very strict. We came from Pittsburgh. We're going to Sacramento, California. Some property he has to take care of."

I told her my name was Ken Schuster. She told me her name was Stephanie Lane. We grinned at each other in a mako-shark sort of way. I told her my name was Jack Norton. She told me her name was Jane Doe. We both laughed. We didn't bother telling each other the truth. It wasn't that kind of conversation.

"Too bad we can't find some place to stop along the way, to get to know each other better . . . " I suggested.

She shrugged. "It's very hard."

My little mind went ker-whump and I felt gears clashing, as the nativity the crucifixion and the resurrection all merged into one. "If we drove all day, and kept each other in sight, we could stop over in the same motel tonight."

"What about . . . ?"

"Your father? How about you let him do all the driving. He doesn't look like he can cut three, four hundred miles of hard driving and still stay alert. Then when you suggest overnight, he'll go for it. Do you take separate rooms when you stay overnight?"

She shook her head, and addressed herself to the sweet things. Then she licked the corner of her mouth with her tongue tip. It was a singular movement.

"Usually a room with twin beds. But, yes, I guess that would work, about his driving. He has a bad heart, and he can't keep at it too long, he gets tired fast. And his reflexes aren't too good, that's why I've been driving. How'll I know which room is yours?"

That simple. We had it all planned that simple. "I'll leave my light on. At that hour, there shouldn't be any others on. And I'll keep an eye out so you don't wander into anyone else's room."

"Why, Mr. Schuster, Mr. Norton, Mr. Mickey Mouse, I think you must believe I'm some kind of loose woman or something."

She smiled a smile that was not intended for an eighteen-year-old face, got up, and walked away. The sound of her nylons rubbing at the thighs set me up erect, and I watched the way her body smoothed and rolled as she stopped by the candy counter to buy some chewing gum, giving me time to pay the check and get to the truck just after she'd slid behind the wheel of the Mustang. The old man raised up, looked around with total disorientation, murmured something to her and she said something back. Then he nodded, thumbed his sleep-sticky eyes with a pair of weathered claws, and she got out, went around to the passenger side as he slid under the wheel. She got in and they peeled off. Badly; he swerved around the gas pumps. *You have an exhausting five, six hours ahead of you, old pop*, I thought, smugly.

That day I kept in sight of them straight across the beefy middle of Pennsylvania, the dead face of the turnpike staring up at me vacuously. One road sign after another, no rest breaks, and the old man must have been pleading. But she kept him going, on and on, and there I was, hanging back so I could get my big hands around those breasts of hers, bend her double and work off the road strain I'd been building for I didn't know how long. And then, as we passed over the line into Ohio, with night bombarding us, I got the most eerie feeling. What was pulling me on like this? Why was I so hot to get this little teenie-bopper? I'd seen the swingers before; they peppered the bars off Times Square every Saturday night, in from Jersey where the age limit was higher. But why this one? What song had she been silently singing that got my groin all tingly? What emptiness was there in me, what wrong bell bonging, what snail crawling through my inward side, what height I hadn't reached, what door slammed when I was a child, what act I'd begun and never completed, what vision I'd had that had been shattered for me . . . what meal had turned rancid in my belly, what bill had never been paid, what game had I chanced everything and been taken like a patsy . . . what wind had chilled me, what sun had scorched me . . . all uselessly, all senselessly . . . that had brought me through four years of college to the day of graduation when I'd run shrieking into the fields of reality and never gone back for the passport into the big time? What was it, that made me follow through the night that blue Mustang with the waving banner of yellow hair? What was it, and would it kill me?

We pulled off the turnpike just east of Cleveland. I passed them doing seventy and in the rearview I could see the eyes of her dear old father, like a pair of mushrooms grown in somebody's basement.

The Red Coach Motel was a U-shaped complex, twelve little ticky-tacky boxes, with a VACANCY sign burning vermilion in the night. I plowed in across the gravel and got my room as quickly as possible. I watched from the window as they emerged from the office and hesitated till they spotted the room number. Five down from me on the long arm of the U. They went in. I took a shower.

There I lay on the tacky bed, the phony farm-furniture furnishings all around me. The hurricane lamp, the borax bureau in imitation Quaker, the hooked rugs, the antique hat rack from Sears. I lay with the towel wrapped around my middle, and the light on. My arm thrown over my eyes. I didn't count time.

Finally, the footsteps, and the door opened.

She didn't wait for bugles or sightings, for banners unfurled or stately pavannes danced. She came across the room throwing the door closed behind her, and off came the trench coat. She was naked underneath, and she fell down on the bed, right on top of me, one leg dumped over mine, the moist heat of her coming straight through the towel.

And then she moved.

And then she mewled.

And then she attacked.

Once, down in Biminy, I went to a cockfight. It was one of those threepenny operations where the foam and the blood spattered high; and the higher and foamier, the more the swine around the taffrail leered. The winner got the loser down and stripped him, and they watched. Flesh came off bit by bit, all matted with blood-soaked feathers; and the eyes, like little bits of soft jelly, running down off the killer-beak.

She attacked.

Hard inner thighs, locked around my waist. Arms that pressured me tight to her hard little belly. The breasts hanging over me and then suddenly rolling, and the breasts squared flat against my chest. The mouth an open wetness, all good wine and musky. Teeth clenched, breath sucked in heavily, and pinwheels of color that went cascading over me like sparklers from a kid's dynamite stick on a holiday outing. And *that* word; yeah, that word, the one with the eff opening, over and over again, and begging. Then a pow!

Another pow!

A string of oil wells gushering, wetness all over everything. "It's a shame we have to wait for tomorrow night," I said, drying myself. "Ten doesn't seem like nearly enough." She looked at me in the bathroom mirror. "He gets nappy about two in the afternoon. Where on the map does that put us?"

I laid her in Galesburg, Illinois.

I laid her in Omaha, Nebraska.

I laid her twice in Arizona, Flagstaff and a little town without much of a name near the Grand Canyon.

That old man, that father of hers, half-conscious from driving and sleeping, dogging it behind the wheel while she was getting her backside and her brains banged out in every two-bed twitchery along the Great Divide.

She popped it to me, the big cross-country hustle, in Salt Lake City. The Mormon fathers would have crapped.

I said no, forget it, that wasn't my bag. So she showed me a new trick. It was very close in there, very strained. I couldn't remember my answer after a couple of hours.

So here I am now, on this rainy night with the rain coming down like rain never came down before, sending cars off bridges and pedestrians over like nine-pins. Here I am on this high-fatality night in the parking lot of a California motel, loosening the lug nuts on the left front wheel of that blue baby Mustang, so she can ask that old man — who never was, and never had been her father — to drive into the next town across that fatal damned slippery careening sure-death turnpike and get her a certain medicine from a druggist that will stop the sudden cramps she planned to have, way back in Salt Lake City.

Here I am loosening the lugs so her old-man husband — who had heard the same song, so much earlier than I did — can go off and get himself killed and the investigation started that will sure as hell show someone loosened the lugs and I'll be grabbed, and all that coffee won't get to the gourmet shops.

Here I am, doing it, all for that hard little ass back there on the motel bed. And what I want to know is, why? Why, dammit, when I know I'm going to get skewered for it, without a prayer in the world? If I knew the answer, I could put down this lug-wrench and get in my truck and cut out of here. But I don't know why.

And never have.

And never will.

Is it ladies-first in California gas chambers?

Hey . . . what's her name?

Sally in Our Alley

They found this child, this Sally, lying on her stomach, behind the garbage cans. Somebody had tried to separate her from her head, and they'd come pretty close; looked like a dull bread knife.

Actually, I'd have found her myself in a couple of hours, when I came to sweep out the rear doorway at 3126 McMurdo Alley. I'm the janitor there. I mean, it's not the best job in the world, but they give me the basement apartment at 3128 rent-free, plus twenty-five a week, so I janitor it up for the old Polack who owns the buildings. It gives me time to finish my epic.

I'm writing this epic poem about the destruction of the Great Wall of China, and you can yuck, but it's a subject that's needed talking about for a helluva long time. Besides, I *like* being a poet; it's easier than working.

McMurdo Alley is glutted right now with the beat element. A bunch of lazy ne'er-do-wells all talking about Hegel and Kant and Nietzsche and writing The Great American Whatchamacallit. They'll never do it, of course, they're not like me, they're all phonies. Besides, they like to party it too much. Well, so do I, of course, but my work . . . you know, that's big with me, too.

I just janitor to keep eating. It helps.

But that has nothing to do with this Sally kid. The two who found her were Whipper Georgulis (his first name is Philoctoden, but who the hell can pronounce *that*?). And Betty January. That isn't *her* name, either, but who needs a last name like Manzenetti to be a stripper. You see what I mean? Phonies, all of them.

Anyhow, they were out in the alley, having left a party upstairs in the Tower Suite, which is what Bernie Katz calls his pad. Be kind enough not to ask what they were doing down in the alley, behind the garbage cans, as it was a rainy night, and whatever they were doing, they would be doing it messily.

So Whipper and Miss January (as she's billed) found her, oozing into a puddle, and they called the cops. As well as the rest of the damned neighborhood. This January kid has a great set of screamers on her; she even woke old Mrs. Perlmutter, who hasn't heard a sound since Alf Landon got his ears pinned back.

Then the fuzz descended on us, stringing up ropes to keep everyone back, and all the bearded ones yelled bloody murder because the Alley was the only way into most of their pads. The fuzz had a rough time, let me tell you.

It went that way for a couple of days, with them dragging everyone down to Homicide East, and asking questions you'd at least think they'd offer haggis or baggis for answering. But they drew a blank.

Because the funny damned thing, for a whore, nobody knew who this Sally's customers were. None of the artists knew her; they had enough amateur talent around ever to go pay for it. In the Alley, payment in cash is a rarity. Everybody had seen the trade slouching up to her door, but no one knew who.

Finally, my turn came, and they took me down in a prowl car, sitting between two yo-yo cops whose faces would have looked great on the lions' heads in front of the Public Library.

They ushered me into a dark little room, sat me in a chair as hard as the Polack's heart, and went away. There was a glob of fat and slime behind the desk, and the nameplate read LT. B. C. KROLL.

Let me tell you, this Kroll character was so far out, he'd automatically have to have a ticket stub to get back in.

"You want to help us, Spivack?"

"The name is Snivack. My cat will get hungry if I'm not home in an hour."

"Screw your cat. You want to help us?"

"Since when do the badges need help from impecunious poets?" I demanded, crossing my legs.

"Since now," he answered, staring at my thong sandals and my dirty feet.

I uncrossed my legs.

"I didn't do it," I said automatically. Philo Vance always said that, and I figured I'd best get on record before the ranks got cluttered.

"Not very well you couldn't."

"How do you know? What's the matter, I'm not good enough?" I was offended.

"Not unless you have abnormally long arms. Your alibi was in here yesterday, and she had corroboration." He seemed damned smug about it. I was still piqued.

"Aggie never could keep her yap shut."

"Nice-looking girl."

"Mind your business, cop. My sex life is nobody's business."

This Kroll got up from behind the desk; "got up" isn't the best way of describing it, but I have a gorge that becomes buoyant easily. So Kroll "got up" and came around the desk. He must have weighed as much as a small Percheron.

"You know what we found in Sally James's apartment?" he asked. He wanted to tell me, so I saw no reason to be nasty and not wonder. Besides, he could have beaten the hell out of me. Have I mentioned that brutality frightens me? I'm basically a very gentle person. My art demands it.

"A set of bagpipes?"

"Who the hell's been writing your material? Goodman Ace?" He was getting peeved. I was sorry I had jested with him. The constabulary in our precinct was never known for its riotous sense of humor, and Homicide East could only be the kings of the bland stare.

"All right, I give up," I fell in with him with a thump, "I'll *play* your silly little game; *what* did you find in Sally James's apartment?"

Had he said a matched set of cockatoos or a full symphony orchestra, I couldn't have been more rocked. I pride myself in being rather blasé. Even a no-vacancy parking lot in that little apartment off McMurdo Alley wouldn't have thrown me as much as what Kroll said.

"That's crazy," I answered him, "what kind of a whore would

use a set-up like that? Or was she having an abortion pulled on herself?"

Kroll shrugged and offered me a cigarette. It was so dim in his office, I didn't see it coming: it was abruptly like getting a fence post thrust into my eyes. I took it out of reflex, and when I couldn't figure out what to do with it, it dawned on me that I didn't smoke.

"She had the bedroom set up as an operating room. What we think now is that somebody was performing an illegal on her, and something went wrong, she made a fuss, and the doctor used something sharp on her.

"The trail of blood shows she managed to get from the bedroom to the alley before she collapsed. Almost impossible, but she made it . . . and then dropped."

I thought it was about time I ferreted out my place in this little saga of gore and sex. "What's that got to do with me?"

"You get around in the Bohemian section, Snivack. They trust you; they think you're nuts, but they know you. We're going to need help on this thing. We want you to get some leads for us. No detective work, just a little judicious spadework."

"What're ya, crazy or something?" I started. "I'm no cop. What good could a janitor do? You better get somebody else."

Kroll leaned over my chair. "Do you know how old Aggie is?"

"When do I start?" I mumbled. Aggie never *could* keep her mouth shut.

The next week was a series of low blows for me. I felt like a minor-league Herbert Philbrick, spying on all my friends in the Alley. First, I got so annoyed at Aggie — she came sneaking down to my pad at six one morning when her mother went off to empty waste baskets at the Crane building — I tossed her out on her underage can, and she stood in the Alley yelling she was going to dispense her favors in the future to Bernie Katz. That got back to her old lady, and she being of the shotgun set, it was nip and tuck for a few hours later that day.

Then Priscilla and Teddy, the lesbos on the second floor at 3126, had their monthly falling-out, and this time — since Teddy was playing the male — Priscilla came tumbling out onto the fire escape howling murder, rape, incest, carnage, and I had to go up and separate them.

I came away from *that* gallant effort with a handsome shiner. Right eye.

As though I hadn't found my share of aggravation, the union came around and demanded to see my card. I hedged; I didn't have one. So they sent around a pair of bully-boys who proceeded to convince me of the merits of joining the janitor's union. Left eye.

Three young toughs from Gulliver Street caught one of the three ballerinas who lived at 3128 on the front stoop, and gave her a real hard time. When I tried to scare them away they yanked shake-knives on me and I decided cowardice was the better part of living, which cut me off from the three ballerinas.

So it went, through the week, helter-skelter, sort of devil-may-care digging my own grave.

Then came Saturday night, which was always big for parties in the Alley, and Scat Bell, the ex-Mr. Newark who had discovered he had a psyche and had moved into McMurdo Alley to nourish it, decided to import talent. He had heard about a whole colony of Zen-oriented poets from way Uptown, and had convinced them to come over, to read their stuff with a jazz background.

Half a dozen boys from the neighborhood got their instruments together, and we had a pretty fair combo. It promised to be a fine bash, with everybody letting their beards grow, and the chicks dying their hair stringy black to go with the turtlenecks.

Interest was running high, particularly when Scat told us one of the boys coming from way Uptown was The Hooded One.

This made no sense whatever until he informed us this guy was really far out; he wore a hood like an excommunicated Ku Klux Klanner. They said he was the beatest, like he had the word and the word was TRUTH! So we were all looking forward to his showing up and reading the stuff. Hood and all.

Seeing as how it had been a rotten week anyhow, it was no surprise that as I was emptying the trash cans behind 3126, Kroll should emerge from a doorway.

"Hey," he commanded with a syllable. I set down the can full of beer bottles and muscatel flagons, and walked over to him.

"Fancy meeting you here," I said. "Am I overdue?"

"Did you find out anything for us yet?"

I spread my hands. "I told you I was no Nero Wolfe." I regretted having referred to the 1/4-ton detective because Kroll *did* look like Nero Wolfe. He was pretty stout in the rex.

"Any of these characters," he saluted both buildings in the Alley with a sweeping gesture, "ever go to college to study medicine? None of them have any police record, except Yarbrough."

He was referring to Pastey Yarbrough, who had a thing about stealing from the five and ten. He'd been picked up so many times, Woolworth's was thinking of making him a tax exemption.

"I don't know. I can find out, I suppose," I said.

"Do it, Snivack," he said, sliding oozily into the doorway from whence he'd come. "Time's getting short. The police commissioner is howling for action."

"This is *my* concern, your job?" I demanded with outrage.

"You aware of the rap for statutory rape in this state?"

Funny how you can suddenly develop an interest in the affairs of your fellow man. Humanitarianism, that's what it is, goddam humanitarianism.

I decided the night of the party, Saturday, was the time to find out if anyone had practiced medicine, or if they'd been to college for it. I had a very subtle plan all laid out. Scintillant, it was.

The party was in The Tower Suite, and somehow or other Bernie Katz had persuaded Aggie's mother to let her attend. I more or less sulked in a corner while the usual crowd had their good time, seeing Aggie was playing the barefoot contessa bit again, on the table with her underwear showing.

The usual crowd consisted of Weep For Me, who was maybe the ugliest girl in the world, who had a lech for Scat Bell, and who made it a point of demonstrating her affection for him at least once every party, by throwing herself under his feet as he walked past. This sometimes proved unfortunate, for if Scat was hammered, as was his usual performance at social gatherings, he would pointedly ignore Weep For Me and stomp across her prostrate body.

Eventually, someone would help her up and either take her to the couch to rub her with Ben Gay, or haul her down to the Lying-In Hospital where she'd be admitted under some pretext or other.

The usual crowd: Enrico Massetti, who was the grocery boy in the neighborhood, and who thought he was the new Caruso. He had had his name legally changed from Bruno to Enrico to aid his career. He was pitiful. Whipper and Betty January, either of whom seldom came up for air, and who seemingly *waited* for parties so they could fall down in a corner and copulate. Someone once suggested they use the bedroom, and Miss January, after breaking the impertinent's nose, advised him to take his dirty mind elsewhere.

There were about thirty others, of course, all neighborhood regulars who found in the Alley those things so dear to the existence of a liberal-minded, intellectual beat type: stimulating conversation, artistic atmosphere, cultural contacts, cheap booze and chicks.

The party was in full flower when Scat was called to the apartment's door; he came back with a grin that wasn't entirely drunkenness plastered across his ruggedly good-looking face. "Hey, like everybody," he announced, "you know who that was at the slammer? It was our Zen Men and they're here to wail a while."

Scat always was impressed by pseudo-hip jargon. We indulge him; he has a *wealthy family.*

"So . . . come on in, Zen Men," he chirped, as though he was the moderator on *What's My Line?* And in violent contrast, through the doorway came these three weirdies. Everybody made small applause, and the poets clustered together by the wall. One of them was real short, with a lot of hair. He didn't have much forehead. The second one was a Negro with a gigantic wart on his cheek, and a patch over his left eye. He had a violent tic in the wartcheek, and he clutched a sheaf of papers to his bosom with ferocity.

The third poet was The Hooded One, and he was about six feet tall, with muscular hands, and a black sack-hood, gathered by a drawstring, around his head. He wore a very sharp low-crown snap-brim with an Alpine feather-pin in the band. Perhaps he wore it to hide the fact that he was masked, on the street.

I could see where it might cause talk.

Scat got up on something (it turned out to be Weep For Me) and, standing there, announced that these three major poets of rebellion were here to impart truth, man, like to *us!*

He announced the first one as Flo Goldknecht, and the hairy midget came forward with a malevolent smirk on his ratty little countenance.

"My first poem," he said, in a voice that brought back memories of the grave, from my first incarnation, "is called 'Respects to a Shallow Parade'. It's kinda short, to sort of get you in the mood."

He pulled a crumpled sheet of paper from his jacket pocket, and smoothed it between his hands. Then his hair — for lack of a forehead — pulled down, and he began to read. This is what he read:

> *Roaring through midtown streets,*
> *Brawling balloons of sound. Smite*
> *the caustic unawareness of the teletypes.*
> *Throw from your gray-flanneled*
> *balconies the arthritic conscience of*
> *Nervous souls in jeopardy.*
> *Oh! Sensuality of intent!*
> *Cascading down, homage for a spent icon.*
> *Waltzing to earth with false bravado,*
> *Can you smell my hunger of defeat?"*

He was perspiring, because he had read it in a great voice, with much compassion and clenching of hand. His voice had gotten deeper as he read, and if it was a mood he was trying to evoke, he evoked it. I was scared out of my wits. I didn't stay to hear his second poem, "Puke."

I went into the kitchen where Art Penny and his current wench Vania were on-lap enjoying each other's affections. "Beg pardon," I mumbled and helped myself to a beer from the sink. It wasn't quite cold, having been left on top of the cracked ice mound. But it was better than "Puke."

When I went back in, having heard applause, Scat was introducing Jathrath Hamutt, the Negro with the wartcheek. His first poem was "Essence of Peaceful Non-Existence" and it began:

> *When I am young, and the flesh-eating oldsters*
> *Cry for my humanity . . . then do I suck dry the*
> *Marrow of aggression with a carbine in my*
> *Anointed fist and the blind upstaring eyes*
> *Of my designated victims bright as stars in*
> *A field of slime . . .*

I had another beer.

When I came back in, I noticed that everyone was in a state of great anxiety, and I supposed it was because The Hooded One was now about to regale us with *his* efforts. I imagined they'd be called "Upchuck" or "Garbage" or something equally as charming, but when he came forward and began to speak in a quiet, dark voice, there was meter and rhythm and sensitivity in his work.

"The Opening" was his first poem, and it was a solemn, honest tribute to virginity, and the morality of innocence. It made some of the more loose types in the room look uncomfortable.

His second was "Respite" and it effectively damned the uselessness of war without being vitriolic. As a poet myself, I had immense respect for this hooded man, whoever he was.

We listened to them, and for a few moments after he had finished them, I leaned against the bookshelf with growing awareness that this was a major talent. How ugly he must be, under that hood, to be able to write such gutty, such effective stuff. He was the essence of what has been misnamed "beat," for there was a strength in defeat in him.

I had completely forgotten my scintillant ruse to find out if anyone was a doctor in disguise. I had planned to cut my finger and see who knew the most about first aid. Now it didn't seem like such a good idea. I was enjoying myself immensely.

Then Aggie got up from where she was sitting cross-legged on the floor, and she threw herself at The Hooded One.

"You're cool!" she squeaked, and her arms went around his neck. Aggie is a nice kid, a real sweet girl, well brought-up and that sort of thing, but she has one small character flaw: she's a nympho.

And the slightest little thing can set her off.

The next thing we knew, she was smothering his hood with kisses, and he was trying to break away from her. His poems fluttered all around his feet as he flailed at her, and Bernie Katz was starting to get up, muttering, "Aw, c'mon, Aggie, knock it off . . ."

When a peculiar thing happened.

Aggie tried to get his hood off, and he straight-armed her as best he could. It only served to help her cause, and as she fell on her back, half of us were watching her thighs, and the other half were looking at The Hooded One.

A seismic gasp went the length of the room. And then The Hooded One had a knife in his hand, a switchblade, and he pressed the stud, with a *phwip!* the blade came up, and he screamed:

"You! You're all alike! All of you! All you rotten women! You can't let a man have his art! You've got to ruin him! I wanted my art, but she gave me *this . . . this!*" And he plucked at his face. Then he jumped for the white-faced, terrified Aggie.

I don't know what happened, how I managed it, but I grabbed a book from the bookshelf at my shoulder, and brought it across in a wide sweep, catching him full on the nose. He went down like the *Andrea Doria*.

Later, I saw it was a copy of *Under Milk Wood* by Dylan Thomas. For a poet as beat as The Hooded One, it somehow seemed apropos.

Kroll showed up at the party, the following week, of all people. He mentioned something about a public citation, but I poo-poohed it; I had my reward; Aggie was back in the fold. Of my arm.

"The funny thing about it," I said to him as we sipped beer in the kitchen, "is that Sally wasn't a prostitute at all."

"Mmm," he agreed, slurping, "but who'd ever think a female plastic surgeon would be living in McMurdo Alley? And a renegade at that."

"We always thought the guys who came to visit her were clients. I guess they were, but of a different kind."

Kroll finished the beer and squashed the can with one hand. "This Hooded creep was really buggy," he admitted, watching Scat and Weep For Me. Scat was trying to stuff a dirty sink sponge in Weep For Me's mouth to stop her protestations of love. "He went for plastic surgery, and she misunderstood. Did it just the opposite of what he wanted."

"Yeah," I mused, "pretty weird. You'd think the guy would be happy to look like that. But he wanted to be ugly, so he could commune with God, or whatever it is these beatniks want to do. Couldn't stand being a good-looker. Said it destroyed his work, his oneness with his art. Pretty bad."

Kroll nodded. "Well, I got to go. Just wanted to stop over and thank you for your help."

"Any time, Lieutenant," I waved as he went out the door.

Fattest man I ever saw.

I sat there a few minutes, hearing the sound of the party in the other room. What a weird world it was. A female plastic surgeon, carrying on illegal operations in McMurdo Alley, everyone thinking she was a whore, and when a screwball slices her up, they find her operating equipment, and think someone came to perform an abort on her. How weird.

The weirdest part of all, though, was the cuckaboo with the hood. He wore it because he detested what he looked like. She probably hadn't done too much to him, only shaved and altered select parts of his kisser, but what kind of a nut is it that gets sore when he turns out to look like Rock Hudson.

I mean, how beat can you get?

The Silence of Infidelity

William: thirty-one years old, five feet ten inches tall, weighing one hundred and seventy-seven pounds. A slight bulge just under his belt due to an affinity for pizza with pepperoni. A man who once considered elevator shoes, though he didn't really need them. A man with heartburn and a bank account of $612.08, jointly entered in his wife's name. A thin scar that runs from his wrist to his inside elbow, which he got in his early twenties, in a threshing machine on an Iowa farm. William was happily married to

Madelaine: twenty-nine years old, five feet six inches tall, weighing just over one hundred and twelve. A woman with rich chestnut-colored hair, and friendly brown eyes. A comfortable woman, who kept a clean home, and worked part-time in a shipping concern, as ledger recorder. A woman with definite tastes in reading matter and the type of breakfast cereal kept in the apartment. She had two children, both girls, named Roxanne and Beth, whom she treated fairly, impartially, and lovingly. She had seen her husband rise from stock clerk to manager to district advisor for a group of cooperative grocery stores. She felt deep within herself that she had aided his climb by being a good wife and an understanding companion. They had been happily married for ten years.

There was a third person.

The Woman.

"We're out of ketchup, Bill," Madelaine's voice reached him in his chair before the television set. The smell of lamb chops filled the five-room apartment, and the kitchen seemed a magical country composed of nothing but delicious odor.

"Want to send Roxy down?" he asked, turning his attention from the news.

Madelaine's voice was ever so lightly tinged with worry. "No. Bill, would you mind running to the corner to get some? The neighborhood's getting pretty wild, and you just never know. We'll be eating in a few minutes . . . would you?"

He swung up out of the chair with a short bemused half-chuckle. "Sure, honey. Be back in five."

He didn't bother to slip on a topcoat, it was the end of October, and though the nippiness was in the air, still it was warm enough for a stroll to the Puerto Rican *bodega* on the corner for a bottle of ketchup.

He rang for the elevator, and lit a cigarette as he waited. If the blankness of a mind constantly thinking can be called blankness, then blank his mind was. No thoughts surged to the top, yet a vague feeling of security, of relaxation, ran through him.

On the street, he walked briskly, stepping in and out of the shadows without conscious awareness of them. Yet his thoughts agreed with what Madelaine had said. The once-wealthy neighborhood had deteriorated. Stately apartment buildings had been cut up into single rooms and rented out to Puerto Ricans, fresh from the boats. And though he had no malice in his mind, though he did not dislike a people for its race, still they were new to American New York, and their habits were not the most sanitary.

Madelaine had been wise in not allowing Roxanne to walk these streets, even at seven o'clock.

In the *bodega* he said a friendly hello to the Puerto Rican owner, a drooping-moustached fellow named (inevitably) Juan. They exchanged cursory pleasantries over the counter as Juan slipped the ketchup into a bag, and accepted the coins.

William stepped out of the *bodega* and crossed the street against the light. Far down, at 80th Street, a stream of cars double-eyed brightly toward him, and he stepped to the curb rapidly.

He walked up from the corner, toward his apartment building, passing the bus stop. The Woman was there, at the bus stop, waiting. He saw her as he approached, and even then his interest rose.

It was that simple, without fanfare and without preamble. She was tall, slightly taller than he, wearing black patent-leather high heels that seemed a trifle higher than any he had seen before. Her legs were slim and well formed, what he could see of them below the tweed of her skirt. The wedge of skirt that showed beneath the thigh-length leather car coat was tasteful, and matched perfectly, somehow, with the steel-gray leather. She had the collar up, and it collided with the shoulder-length blond hair that fell in soft waves.

Her face was half-turned away from him, and he only caught a sheer glance of uptilted nose, blue eye, and full mouth. It was, more than anything, the way she had her feet set, that made him stop.

As he passed, he looked back over his shoulder, and saw she had one foot turned outward, the way the fashion models do it when they are being studiedly fashionable. He stopped and there was something about the street light that cast a sheen across those few inches of nyloned legs. His eyes rose to her face; she stared at him fully.

He gripped the ketchup bottle tighter, for she didn't turn away, as a woman should who is being stared at by a stranger on the streets. She watched him intently, and there was an arch to her well-formed eyebrows. Her eyes said something to him. William was by no means a deeply perceptive man. His blood speeded up, and he felt a quivering in his legs. Thoughts flashed in and out of his mind like bright fish in a clear stream.

Then the Woman smiled.

Her full, rich red mouth curved upward, and her hands, which had hung at her sides till now, rose to smooth her hips. At that moment the thought crossed William's mind that she was a prostitute.

But as her hands moved, he retracted the thought. No, not a prostitute. A Woman, yes, but not a whore.

Almost without realizing he was moving, he stepped back toward her. Very close they stood for an instant, and he saw the

swell of the car jacket over her breasts. Her figure was hidden
by the bulk of the steel-gray coat, yet he was certain it must be
magnificently proportioned.

He could smell the faint muskiness of her, and it filled his
head with an aphrodisia that made him stagger mentally.

As he stood next to her, staring into her symmetrical, unlined,
sensuous face, she wet her lips. It was a slick, quick, razored
movement that abruptly brought to mind pictures of women
lifting their skirts, showing their bodies. It was a completely
sexual movement, and the pale tonguetip slipped out and in
again in an instant.

He knew then that she wanted him to come with her.

Not a word had been spoken, yet he knew what her eyes said,
knew what the positioning of her feet meant, knew what that
wicked little tongue had ordered in its journey.

She turned away and walked back down toward the corner,
looking over her shoulder once, to let him know she was leading
him. He started after her, and the thought of Madelaine and the
kids and the dinner scurried out of his way. He watched the fine
taut line of movement as her legs scissored inside her skirt, and
the pain hit him in the deepest, most remote area of his belly.
The Woman was reaching him.

She turned up the steps of the one brownstone apartment
house, and he followed quickly. She opened the door with a key,
and led him up three flights of stairs, to another door.

She opened this one with the same key, and reached around
the inside of the jamb, flicking on the lights.

He stepped inside, and she shut the door, locking it quickly.

The apartment was tastefully furnished, without being either
ultra-modern or period. It was a conglomeration of furniture, the
kind of assortment a person collects having moved many times
in many cities.

She took his hand then, and removed the bottle of ketchup
in its brown paper bag, setting it on a table near the door. She
led him to a sofa, where he sat down, unbuttoning his jacket and
jerking up the creases of his pants leg as he sat.

She walked quickly to the portable radio plugged into the
wall, and turned it on. A newscaster's voice broke in. She turned

the dial rapidly, bringing in a program of quiet dinner music, but the sound of the newscaster's voice had started him back along the track of the past ten minutes. It had been no longer than that since he had left his apartment, left Madelaine with the lamb chops, and Roxanne spoon-feeding Beth.

Yet he didn't seem to care. He was making as big a decision as he had ever made. He was changing the course of his life, and he knew it. He was raising a barrier between himself and the life he had led with Madelaine, as surely as he sat here, yet he didn't care.

He knew this was the way it was, *because* it was.

He did not consider the idea of sin, and he did not consider the idea of adultery. This was real, it was true, it was the way he must live.

Then the Woman turned away from the radio, and unwound the belt that knotted her car coat closed. She stripped off the jacket and hung it carefully in the closet.

At that instant he wondered where she had been going, to be waiting at the bus stop, and if it could have been so unimportant an engagement that she could break it to bring him here like this, a stranger.

But he also knew, in that instant, that she had wanted *him* . . . not just any man, not anybody, but *him*.

Him, pure and simple and direct and true. The way it should have been. The way it was meant to be. The way the world saw it and the way it was going to be. The way it was.

She faced him, and he was assured of her beauty. It was not a cheap or a superficial beauty. She was a handsome Woman, right through and down as deep as anyone could wish. She was not ashamed, for there was nothing to be ashamed of, and she knew what was about to happen, even as he knew.

William watched as she unbuttoned her sweater, folded it precisely on the chair beside the table. He watched with growing expectation, but without a feeling of lechery as she reached behind her and unfastened the brassiere of pink material. He stared calmly at the shape of her breasts, so warm and inviting, and as she stepped close to him, signifying he should unzip her skirt, he knew this would not be the last time he would see the

Woman. He knew, as his fingers touched the warm metal, that he would see her again, and whether on the subway, or on the street, or in the pharmacy, it would always end like this. That they would never say a word, and that they would never know each other's name, but that it would be just like this over and over again.

And it was right. It was the way it should be.

She slid the skirt down off her hips, the silky sound of her slip rustling making the only sound over the quiet dinner music so typical of his apartment down the street.

She folded the skirt properly and laid it beside him on the sofa. She put her thumbs between the silk of her slip and the dark blue of her pants, and pulled down the half slip. It went atop the skirt, and somehow *that* seemed so right, also.

She took him by the hand and they went into the bedroom. As he watched in the filtered light from the living room, light that cast an aura around her, touching the faintly blond hairs that covered her body like down, she turned back the covers of the bed.

Then she sat down on the bed, and unfastened her stockings, removed her shoes and took off the nylon hose, the garter belt and, finally, raised herself so she could slip out of the dark blue underpants. Then she lay back on the bed, perfectly flat, like a painting of exquisite gentleness.

Afterward, she went into the bathroom and locked the door. He knew what she meant. That it was through for this time, and that she wanted no money, that she had done it because she had done it, and there were no recriminations, no apologies, nothing to be said. It was done, and she had wanted him as William, with a false plate, and with heartburn and with a bank balance of $612.08. Jointly in his wife's name.

He dressed quickly and left the apartment, not even taking notice of the number on the door. He would know it when he came again, for he would not come alone. He would be led by her, and he would never come there unless she *did* lead him; that was the silent bargain they had made.

He knew every line of her body, as well as he had grown to know Madelaine's in the ten years of their marriage. He knew the feel of her hair and the scent of her body. He knew where every bit of furniture stood.

He walked out onto the street, and the air had turned chillier. But he walked slowly, feeling the sting of the air as he drew it into his lungs.

There had been nothing said, but the message was there for always.

He opened his apartment door with his key and walked in. Madelaine hurried out of the kitchen at the sound of the closing door and stared at him oddly, hands on hips, eyes sparkling.

"Bill, where were you? I've already eaten, and Roxanne too. We went ahead. The chops are cold. I'll have to heat them for you now. We ate them without ketchup. Where were you?"

William handed her the bottle of ketchup in its brown paper bag, and kissed her lightly on the cheek.

His mind was quiet, and there was a feeling of fulfillment that mounted to his chest as he said, "I met an old, old friend. We had a few things to say to one another."

And he did not lie.

Have Coolth

Once upon a when, Derry Maylor had been cool. But that was past, and now there were long, thin dark spaces when he walked. Even the night was quiet for him; no sounds of the boo-*dow* in his head. He had taken to squareness, and wore his collar turned up.

How does a man blow his coolth?

It takes a combo of many littles. Like the chick with the eyes so green and so razor-slim the little kids ask her like, "Are you Chinese?" It takes the loss of all your bread and the loss of all your steam and most of all, the loss of your virility.

Get creamed once by a badass chick, and you've had it. Derry Maylor had had the course. Now came the times when the drums were quiet, and the horns didn't blow, and the faint cha-tah of the sticks could not be heard. Rose had been her name, and Rose was her name, but Rose wasn't right.

Try Bitch.

Which is the worst of all, man, when you blow piano that's more than piano, and the chick takes your blood and your liver and wraps them up for 89¢ a pound — (any buyers?) — then you got to stay away from the lofts where the men are blowing and the smoke is warm and thick; then you got to stay away from the Sweet Lucy and the good Guatemalan shit and the honk and spike and the speed and the Good Book because when you come down off them, you got the blues so bad more worse you want to puke. Then you got to stay away from it all, like the piano, because the piano has been Mama and Poppa and home and life and all of it so nice. But what you got now?

You got *tsuris*.

Derry Maylor was about medium height . . . this is the make on him, so dig. He had eyes set up under his brows, so unless the light was with them, you knew he had no eyes. But when the light was right, then dig, they were as blue as something Tatum tinkled. His nose wasn't merely a blow-station, it was a monument. Cyrano and Derry Maylor were blood brothers in the Society of Snot-Sockers. But it didn't look bad, that was what made it swing so; it was a nose like larger than life. It was straight and squared at the tip, and it came down at you like a hungry buzzard, but it swung, and that counted. His mouth was very strong, but very thin; and all that, with the high Cherokee cheekbones, made him look rough and cold and with it.

But was he?

Not now, he wasn't. Once, but Rose, and *whamm!*

No, he was a loser now.

That's why he was mugging lushes in the Village.

For piss money. For pennies.

That was how I met the Tiger. I always called him the Tiger because he had a scrapbook he showed me once, with some pix from when he was at Middlebury, with all that sophomoric jazz in the room he shared with a guy he called the Bear. All fancy liquor bottles and like that. But that had been in the days when he had been another Derry Maylor, and the world was smelling like Air Wick.

I met him in the Village, most strange.

I mean, he tried to mug me.

He came out of this dark little side street off Bleecker, and came sneakity up behind me, like I played it cool. This cat didn't. He just didn't. I mean, he came on like gangbusters. Down came the duck and burped and said the secret word, "I'm gonna lick you one up longside the head and take your bread man," so I just naturally turned on him when he got close enough and had this leather glove full of nickels raised to whomp me, and I said, "Shit, man!" And tagged him one right on that monumental bazooz of his.

He did a back flip and swam the length of the pavement, just for chuckles.

I mean, like I got a nasty temper, so I picked him off the sidewalk and shook him a little till his eyeballs registered UNCLE, then I set up that kook against the building wall and belted him again.

I got to learn to control my temper, for true.

After a while, after about half my Viceroy was gone, he picked himself off the deck, shook his head like a St. Bernard what wonders who swiped his cask, and tried to take me out with a strong left. I ducked and caught him around the shoulders in a loving clinch.

"Baby, you want a mouthful of bloody Chiclets, you keep peppering my good nature. I'll kill you, baby."

So the Tiger just naturally settled back, because when you're being hugged close by a two-hundred-pounder you make all your decisions for Christ.

When I saw the light of sense flick in his eyes, I turned him loose. I dug this guy, and the first make I got was one of chagrin. Like this cat was really ashamed; I asked him, "You got bills to pay or is this a hobby?"

He shook that bony head of his, and in the faraway streetlight I caught a glimpse, for the first, of those blue eyes. They were but tired.

"You got a name?"

He wouldn't say. I felt more sorry than anything else for the guy, but what could *I* do? Not only was I not my brother's keeper, I was almost not my own keeper sometimes, what with public relations being as slow a game as it is.

"Well, watch yourself, Cootie," I laid it down, and made to split. "The next mark might tear your head off. Try getting a job, hey?"

I started to walk away, and I heard this odd voice behind me, and the guy said:

"I haven't eaten in three days, mister."

It was so *goddam* pathetic, I stopped. I would have backed up without turning around, I didn't want to catch the expression I *knew* he had on his face, and put a buck in his hand, but there was something strange in his voice. Something sullen, and yet very hip. It was like a *way* of talking, that gave me the tip this guy had it.

"You want some coffee?" I asked him. He gave me a weary peck with that beak of his. So . . .

I took him to Jim Atkins and we fell down on a pair of straight-blacks, till I saw the way he was hollow-cheeked and miserable.

"Come on, man," I said, clapping him on the shoulder. We went over to Eighth Street, to a little delicatessen I know, and walked through to the back where Cummerbund holds dominion over a twelve-table kingdom. Hardly anybody but the hip go to the delicatessen to eat, and Cummerbund is part of the reason those who do go come back often.

Cummerbund isn't his name, but his real name is so easy to forget, and that silk cummerbund is so incongruous, it fits — so why fight it? It's a good place to talk.

I ordered a hot plate of matzoh ball soup for him, and when Cummerbund had brought it — nodding to me in recognition, which warmed me — I put in a request for two hot corned beef sandwiches — lean — two orders of blintzes, two slaws, and a couple more coffees. While he shoveled it all in, I sized him up and decided this was a good kid.

He looked as though he was with it.

Over a cigarette and a second coffee, I tried to feel him out: "You got a name?"

He didn't look up from the java, but he said, "Maylor. Derry Maylor."

We sat and gabbed, and after a while he started to open up, and gave me a little of himself, and it came up seven that I'd dug this kid before.

"You ever play any piano?" I asked.

"Some," he said, and it clicked.

"You used to be the fourth in Con Whitney's Quartet, right? Played the Vanguard and that one side for Bethlehem, right?" He gave me the nod again. It was like a salute by a buzzard.

Then I *knew* the kid was okay, because he had talent, not the kind of gaff the Village phonies put out, but the real thing. So I became my brother's keeper. So sue me.

Derry Maylor, the Tiger, came back fast. All it took was a

strong hand because when it came down to it, he was pretty weak in the clinches.

Working as a freelance public relations man for a grab bag of second-rate attractions — like Lulu Seeker, The Girl with the Educated Crotch, so help me that's how they bill her in Jersey City — I didn't make much bread, but man, did I have coolth.

Part of the coolth came from taking my fee out in trade at low joints like The Hedonist Union, a down-the-stairs bôite featuring prices too sour and jazz too sweet. But I got it mentioned in the columns from time to time, and once in a while *CUE* did a restaurant piece mentioning it; I was being paid what I was worth.

Usually, I took my pay out in meals. I bought my own bicarb. Giulio, the chef, was a worse cook than my mother, and she had been only the last in cooking. Burned water.

Giulio was worse. But it was free.

So I took the Tiger down to see Frankie Sullivan, who owned the joint, and in a burst of fantastic dynamiting, sold him on the kid. Sullivan started the Tiger at fifty a week, backing him with three pick-ups from around town who were pretty well known. It wasn't a smash at first, but that was how Miles and Bird and Cannonball had started, so I waited. I figured he had it, and when he had enough under his belt, he'd start to shine.

I was right. The kid began to make real sounds. By no sheer coincidence Derry Maylor was living with me, and I saw him every morning when I got up to start pounding my rounds, so I'd ask him, "How they swinging down there?" And at first he'd just nod sleepily from the Castro and turn over. But in a few weeks, he started to tell me things:

"We hit a couple good ones last night. Richie was really fine on Monk's 'Midnight,' and I think Tad'll be a great stick man one of these days . . . " then he'd realize he'd been exposing himself, and flip over in the sack. But he was coming back up the road, and that swung.

A couple evenings, when The Hedonist Union was closed, we'd make the scene at The Five Spot or Birdland or The Jazz Gallery and the kid would dig. If I knew someone there, I'd have them invite him up for a sit-in, and the kid just glowed. It was like great. Once he even sat in with Mingus at The Showplace. Far-out, but rewarding.

Let me tell you about the Tiger's music.

It was more than him. It was like his nose; bigger than life. When Derry Maylor slid onto the bench, and hunched down, there was a bomb about to go. He'd crack his knuckles, and let his hands rest on the white keys for an instant, waiting for the nod from whoever was heading up the set. Then he'd dip his head to pick his way through the intro, and start letting it out from under his fingernails.

The sounds were full sounds. No histrionics, no Liberace or Ahmad Jamal stuff, none of that. It was more like a progressive Waller, if you can put a make on that. There was gut in it. He flatted himself constantly, and the riffs were all minors. It was big tone, what he played, and there was the whole fist in it, not just a pinky at a time. It made you hear that piano over everything else, but at the same time the combo was top ride, the Tiger didn't try to upstage them. Yet he was the horse and they were the riders. Without him, they'd of been walking, it was that simple.

When they turned him loose for a solo, he cut in on the upbeat and struck away like trampling down the vineyards where the grapes of wrath and like that. He was so good it caught you in the stomach and you got all hot and prickly in the palms of your hands because they were beating on the tablecloth.

That was Derry Maylor's music.

It was all him, and more than him. It took from everyone in the joint at the same time, and sucked it out like some ego-eater, and fed it back richly and many-colored clean. It was a talent you could identify, and there wasn't any question is that Monk or is that Evans or do you dig Powell in the left hand. It was all Tiger, none but Tiger, this Tiger and period.

He was coming back. But strong.

One night, I'd cut my rounds early that day and had caught some sack time, I fell in on The Hedonist Union to pick up on some Maylor. He was good that night, really mellow like Jell-O, and when the second set was done, I sent word round to him by a juicehead named Juicehead, and the kid made it to my table.

"Nutty, man," I greeted him, holding it out. He took my hand, and gave me that self-effacing little beak-nod. "Really great, specially on 'Hotshoe.' Whose number is that?"

"A thing Shorty Rogers recorded from a Brando movie a couple years back. Like the changes we got on it?"

I gave him a thumb-and-forefinger okay and he smiled. We sat and had a few on the rocks until he had to make the next set. I dug all evening, and when he was finished, when the night was like a big coal chute, we staggered home to my pad, going oo-shoobie-doo all the way like a pair of wet brains.

But when we fell upstairs, the Tiger couldn't sleep. For the first time since I'd met him, he seemed willing to talk about himself. So I grabbed off a couple vitamin B-complex caps that helped dispel the foggy-foggy-doo settling in on me, and I picked up what the kid was laying down:

I never had much (he said) but the piano. You know how it is, you come from a family with dough, and they're good to you and everything, send you to a good school, but you just don't swing. You know, it's like you're a round peg not nearly square enough. And they don't dig, they keep saying make something of yourself, and stop screwing up. So you try, but it's no go. Then one day you get enough guts to cut out and you hit the big town with five bucks and a couple of hands of piano. That was the way it was with me.

(He got up, then, and went over to my hi-fi and shook out an Australian Jazz Quintet side and laid it on the turntable. Then he took it off before it could play, and got out an Eric Dolphy thing, "Outward Bound," and laid it on. We sat there for about two minutes, digging the slow, new stuff of Dolphy's horn and he started in again.)

It was a rough row at first (he wet his thin lips) but after I hit with Con at the Vanguard it all looked cool. I cut one for Bethlehem and Hentoff said it was swinging. They had Feather do the liner notes, and it looked like I was on my way. Then Con found Rose somewhere and she started to sing with the combo.

(I could tell it hurt him to talk about her.)

Man, I want to clue you, this Rose item was it. She had green eyes, and they looked Oriental, you dig? Her skin was like some kind of china or something, so clear and smooth. And her hair was auburn almost bloody when the spots dug her. I wanted her so bad, you'll never.

For a while I thought she dug me, too. We made it together pretty often, you know. Like she wasn't a tease, and she had this great body, man. Then one day, she came up to my pad while I was practicing, and she put the eye on me, and finally got to the pitch which was Derry would you mind letting this friend of mine who's a pianist try a few sets tonight with Con, so I gave her the nod, and she brought in this kid from Hollywood who had a name out there, and next thing I knew he was sitting on the bench, and I was hoisting 'em from the floor.

Derry Maylor finished his story, and I stared at him, because I knew who he meant. The kid was now voted high in the *Down Beat* and *Playboy* polls for ivories, and the chick — Rose, I couldn't even remember her name, she hadn't been much good vocally, really — had cut her own throat; she'd built this new kid and he'd tossed her like she'd tossed Derry.

I felt sorry for the Tiger, but it was a dying hurt now. It was going away like the sounds of the blues when it's fade-out time. I gave him some bonded sauce, and when he conked, padded him for the dark.

I knew he'd be okay. He'd spilled his gut and now it was clear. I liked the kid . . . don't ask why, except maybe it was my kid brother Pete who'd gotten it from a semi when he was thirteen. Maybe, but I don't know.

Trouble wore a sheath, and had a pair of cans like the headlights on a fire engine. She was waiting for me at Brioni's, a little espresso house I beat the drum for occasionally. She was sitting with Eddie Brioni at one of the chess tables, a cappuccino in front of her, and I glommed her immediatest because she had green eyes.

Like slitty green eyes.

Like this had to be a Rose.

Oh no, I dug inside, *oh no!*

"Hey, flack-artist!" Eddie Brioni stood up as I approached. "Got a little lady here says she wants to meet you." I walked up to the table, her eyes locked with mine, and stared down at her. God, was she gorgeous. It made my belly muscles tight just to see her. The Tiger had put the make to her proper, she had this great body, and her face was all shadows and green, slim eyes.

Brioni was still bubbling. "And this is Miss Pardo. Miss Rose Pardo." He introduced us again, as if it hadn't taken the first time, and said he'd move out because we probably had but lots to talk about. Brioni's a nice guy, even when he isn't overcharging, but sometimes I'd like to flatten him.

I sat down, making sure the creases were right in my Continentals. She was sizing me. I was big and I knew it. Now there were two of us who knew it.

"What can I do for you, Miss Pardo," I asked.

"I've heard a lot about you," she said slowly. Her voice was butter on a stack of hotcakes. It rated five stars in *Down Beat*. It was the seventh wonder of the Western world. I dug. It was easy to see a guy like the Tiger blasting his beret over a twist like this. What but sweet type of music we could have made together, but I dug a memory of what she'd done to the Tiger, and I knew this kid was a green bottle with a death's-head on it.

"Oh?" I played it cool.

"Yes." I had never heard it like that before. Made my feet feel funny . . . and other parts of me, too. "I hear you handle Derry Maylor."

She didn't waste any time.

"Where'd you hear that?"

"The Stem," she answered, waving a slim hand out toward the darkening street. "Some of your clients told me I might find you here. I've been waiting."

I knew what Lindbergh felt like with all of Paris waiting. It must have been the same. She breathed, and the bodice of her sheath did tricks. I yelled to Eddie for a cup of espresso. I had to do *some*thing.

"So. You've been waiting. Something I can do for you?"

She nodded, and the dim lights played over her auburn hair. Bloody wasn't the proper word. Try ruby. Not that either. Something, but not that.

"I want to see Derry again."

I gave her a look that would have made a cigar-store Indian join a union for protection, and fed her a flinty "No!"

She leaned across the little chess table, and what her breasts did as they scrunched against the black and red squares made me feel checkmated. "I've got to see him, don't you understand?"

"No!"

"I love him."

"No!"

"I want to set things right with him."

"No!" Eddie brought my coffee.

So I took her to see the Tiger, naturally.

So I'm a weak character. It was those goddam green eyes.

I hadn't realized it, but The Hedonist Union had become a very hip spot. It was mostly Derry Maylor, of course, and not my public relations work, but Frank Sullivan wasn't sure which it was, so he had kept us both on, and Derry was pulling down three Cs a week now. The Union was drawing big crowds every night, and Sullivan was thinking of adding another dining room, if he could purchase the wrought iron goods shop on the other side.

I hadn't realized how big it had gotten, but apparently *Rose Pardo* had. She moved in against Derry like a blotter to a puddle of ink. And she soaked him up in the same way; I got to call it a spade, the chick had coolth. Almost more coolth than anyone I'd ever seen. She wound that guy around her painted fingers like he was saltwater taffy. But he liked it, and that was what counted.

I didn't say anything, even when he set her up in a pad in my building. She spent most of her time around our joint, cooking for us, and not doing much of anything; when they wanted to ball I either checked out or they went up to her apartment. It seemed like a sweet little set-up, and as long as she didn't try to hurt the kid, it was okay with me.

So I sounded like a big brother, so what? So sue me.

The night it all came down, Chicken Little, was like any night. Derry was at the Union, and I was alone trying to figure a new angle for The Girl with the Educated Crotch now that she was out of the cooler on that holding rap. I'd told Lulu a hundred times to stay off the junk or I wouldn't handle her any more, but she was hooked, and once a hophead always a hophead, no matter how good they peel.

The doorbell rang and I got up to answer it.

Rose stood in the doorway, wearing a pair of jeans and one of Derry's white button-down shirts, tied in a bow at her bare midriff. I stepped back and she came through. It made me feel like I had a case of dandruff all over. She was something, even in jeans; especially in jeans. I could see every muscle on her.

"I want to talk to you," she said. She had stopped right in the middle of the room, with the lights behind her, giving her a halo of sorts.

"So talk."

"I want a job singing at the Union."

She didn't beat around it any. I had an idea in the back of my weak brain that it had been something like that all along, but this was the first she'd said about it.

"So go apply. Frank Sullivan does the hiring."

"He's married." The way she said it made it sound dirty.

"Last I heard, that ain't no crime."

"I can't get to him. And I'm not that good to make it on talent alone."

I was rocked; I'd heard about chicks who laid it on the line, but this broad was just *too* much. She didn't even seem to mind facing the truth that she didn't have the wherewith to make it on her own.

"So you came to me. I'm supposed to get you in."

"Sullivan'll listen to you. He always does. He's a grateful slob."

This kid was sweet but deadly. Like a box of poisoned chocolates. My eyes must have been wide.

"So why should I do it for you? Far as I'm concerned you can rot."

"Because if you don't, flak-man, I break your Tiger. I break him inside like a cheap dish, like I did the last time. Only the last time I suckered myself; I know better now. I'll do it right this time."

"You know something, girl," I asked her.

"What?"

"You stink!"

She chuckled then, deep in her throat, like a cat that knows it's got a special deal and has ten lives, not just nine. "I can be nice, too, flak-man." She started to undo the knot at her belly.

"Hold it, sister," I said. "Nothing you've got can make me change my mind."

She got it undone, saying, "I always like to pay a man for his labors."

"I'm not going to do it."

"You want to see Derry a stumblebum again, mugging lushes in the Village for doughnut dough?"

"You bitch you. Lousy stinking . . . "

"Listen, mister," and her tone dripped blood, "I know what crap is. I was born lying in it and it's been in my smelling ever since. I've got very little to trade on besides my shape and my voice. My voice isn't so hot, but my backside is! You have to lie down with a lot of old dogs in this life to get what you want. I've been lying down for a long time now, mister, and I'm weary. I'm just weary enough to ruin your little piano player for good. I tagged onto him once as a meal ticket and got straight-armed by a bastard when I thought I was on the way up.

"But it isn't gonna happen this time."

Now what happened next is my fault, I know it.

There was such red-hot hatred in her voice, she became the most appealing witch I'd ever dug. And she'd been unbuttoning that white shirt all along, it was open and you *know* she wasn't wearing a bra.

I don't even remember grabbing her, but the next thing I had her mouth and she was plastered against me and we went over onto the sofa. The slammer went bam against the wall and there was the Tiger standing in the doorway.

"Rose, why'd you call me to come — "

He stopped, and the growl that came out of him was half-human. I tried to get free of Rose, but she had her damned legs twined around me, and I was stuck! The Tiger came at us, and grabbed my collar and ripped me off the sofa. I was twice as big as him, but I'd never met anyone who wanted to kill more than him.

He caught me one straight in the right cheek and I sailed back against the wall. I slid down the wall and just sat there for a minute, too stupid to do anything.

He went after her, then, and picked her right up by the neck. I saw what she'd wanted to do; to break us up. If she could split us, she could move in on me and get an in at the Union. But it hadn't worked that way. The Tiger had picked up his guts somewhere, and now he was kill-mad.

He had her by the throat, and he was banging her auburn head against the wall, while her tongue came out of the side of her mouth . . . she was dying.

"Tiger!" I yelled, and got up from my Little Jack Horner corner.

I grabbed him and pried his thumbs off her jugular. Then I spun him around and took him out with one solid bolo to the mouth. He collapsed against me and I let him slide down my body.

Rose was able to move around by now, and she was dragging herself to the kitchenette. I was too stunned by the arm Derry had laid on me, too knocked out by the events of the past few minutes to know what she was doing.

But when she stood over him with that butcher knife in her goddam hand, I knew what she was thinking, what she wanted to do. The girl was off her nut; she wanted to make it so bad, she didn't care who got drug in the process.

"Kill him!" she said, and pushed the knife into my hand. I stood looking at him for a moment, at the kid who reminded me of my dead brother Pete, and the talent he had all boiling in those hands, and the way this woman would stop nowhere to get what she wanted, and she said, "Go ahead, you big bastard! Go ahead, for us!" and she jammed her hot body against me, so I used the knife.

*

It's all in having coolth, the way I see it. There are some people who got to get somewhere, even if they don't know where that somewhere is. And there's others who aren't meant to get at all.

Those are the kind that brodie when the gaff gets too thick. You dig?

I mean, some people are just meant to take a blade in their gut, and others are meant to take the blame. So that something worthwhile can go on.

The Tiger's playing at Basin Street this week, you said? See what I mean . . . he's got it. He's got the talent, and that's more important than one flak-man named Brenan.

That's Brenan with one "n" in the middle.

The warden gave me a record player and a couple of the Tiger's sides with Trane as a last request, you know. I thought that was kind of sweet of the old guy. He and I had quite a few gab sessions about Bix and the old days.

He's a good joe.

I don't think I dig this haircut, though. I never liked a baldie — even if it's just in one circle on the back of my head. And look what that razor did to my Continentals. These slits'll never catch on, man.

That's Brenan with one "n" in the middle.

I guess I'm just a flak-man at heart. Any publicity is good publicity, like they say.

So stay cool, man, I gotta split.

I got a date. A hot date.

RFD #2

8 May 1975

Talmadge Services, Inc.
545 Fifth Avenue
New York, NY 10017

Dear Sirs:

A friend of mine, whom I prefer not to name, has told me that your organization might be helpful. I am given to understand that your company has certain **added** services to offer, in addition to the useful private investigation.

There is a person I am very much interested in having located. He is a rather troublesome person, and if you have any service that might (I hope you'll pardon my frankness) put him off me, I would be very glad to have all particulars.

I do not know if you have such an **added** service, but if you do, I would be most happy to send you any information you might need about this person.

It is quite a problem to me, and I worry about it continuously. I hope you will be able to do something for me.

I will wait impatiently to hear from you.

Yours very truly,
(Miss) Loretta Parish

May 10th, 1975

Miss Loretta Parish
RFD #2
Stimson, Ohio

Dear Miss Parish:

In reply to your letter of May 8th, we are not quite certain what you mean by an *added* service, but since Talmadge Services is equipped to handle all business of this type, from location of missing persons to detective work, I'm certain we can offer some help in this matter.

We are always ready to aid a client. If you wish to send us the particulars in this matter, please send them airmail, first class, in a sealed envelope. You will hear from us soon, at which time we can more readily discuss remuneration.

Hoping we may be able to assist you, we remain, most respectfully yours,

Harrison Talmadge,
for Talmadge Services, Inc.

HT:lt

12 May 1975

Talmadge Services, Inc.
545 Fifth Avenue
New York 17, New York

Dear Mr. Talmadge:

I have your letter of May 10th, and am herewith enclosing particulars concerning the man I wish you to find. Frankly, I'm not so concerned about locating him as I am in making certain that he does not trouble me again. The man's name is Philip Grademan, and his last residence was Taunton, Massachusetts, where he was employed in the service of a Mrs. Margaret Constable.

Mrs. Constable, now deceased, was the widow of Leonard

Constable, the restaurant man. She was a wealthy woman, and very fond of books; Mr. Grademan was a rare book expert who was employed to maintain and catalog Mrs. Constable's library. I was also employed at that time by Mrs. Constable as a confidential secretary.

Philip Grademan and I worked for Mrs. Constable for two years and our relationship was always cordial. However, when Mrs. Constable died of acute enteritis, he accused me of falsifying her will. If you wish to learn the true facts of this affair, I am sure you will be able to unearth them in the inquest proceedings of her death, February 14, 1975, Taunton. It was a case of pure envy, since Mrs. Constable favored me in her will with a bequest of $60,000, and gave Philip Grademan only a very fine set of books.

Nevertheless, Philip was very incensed about what happened, and made several wild threats to me after the inquest. When a series of suspicious accidents began to occur to me, I was certain that Philip intended me harm. I did not take my suspicions to the police, and do not wish to do so now, as I have a horror of becoming involved in a public scandal. **I'm sure you understand**. Instead, I left Taunton and changed my name (if you check the court proceedings, you will find it listed as Elizabeth Fernig).

I am very happy here in my new surroundings, and have purchased a fine home, and would be completely content with my lot if it weren't for Philip Grademan. I have no real **evidence** that Philip is actually looking for me, but I am convinced that he is, and that he means to do me harm. I can never be really happy until I know that Philip Grademan will let me live my life in peace. I am not a well woman. My heart is weak, and I suffer from high blood pressure. It is impossible for me to flee this man, and this sense of uncertainty makes life difficult.

I cannot supply you with a photograph of Philip Grademan, but your sources of supply must be better than mine. All I can tell you is that he is tall, dark-haired, and slightly balding at the temples. He has a small, pear-shaped birthmark on his left hand, above the knuckles. He has nice, even features, but I always thought his mouth was rather cruel. His one interest that I know about is his love of books; this might provide a clue for you, as to his whereabouts. I know that he is no longer in Taunton, because some friends of mine there informed me that he left town the week after I came to Stimson.

Please tell me if there is any other information you require and, most importantly, whether you can do more than just **find** this man.

Yours very truly,
(Miss) Loretta Parish

May 13th, 1975

Miss Loretta Parish
RFD #2
Stimson, Ohio

Dear Miss Parish:

Just this note to let you know we are looking into your problem, with an eye to definitely clearing this matter up to your satisfaction. Enclosed is a standard table of payment for our services.

However, while my sources are checking back — we have accepted your kind suggestion to check the coroner's inquest transcript in Taunton — I should like to make certain precisely what services you will require of us.

My associates and myself, having reviewed your letters, are puzzled by your references to whether " . . . we can do more than just find this man."

We wish to establish that we are a reputable firm of some years standing. However, for special clients — such as we now feel inclined to consider you, in the light of your special difficulties — we have a number of special services.

If you would care to be more specific in this one particular, I am certain we can arrive at a mutual understanding.

A further statement of our progress will be sent you as soon as our sources have reported.

Checks may be made payable to the undersigned.

Most respectfully,
Harrison Talmadge,
for Talmadge Services, Inc.

HT:lt
enc: Rate Table

16 May 1975
Talmadge Services, Inc.
545 Fifth Avenue
New York 17, New York

Dear Mr. Talmadge:

I'm sorry not to have replied to your letter immediately, but I have not been well.

I appreciate your desire to have me make a specific request concerning Philip Grademan, but this is a delicate matter, as I'm certain you understand.

I can only repeat that unless this man is **permanently** prevented from bothering me, and accusing me of crimes, and actually threatening my life, that I can never look forward to a peaceful existence.

I'm afraid that this is the most I can say, and if it is not sufficiently clear, perhaps we had better conclude the entire transaction.

Yours very truly,
(Miss) Loretta Parish

May 18th, 1975

Miss Loretta Parish
RFD #2
Stimson, Ohio

Dear Miss Parish:

Please do not misconstrue, or take offense at my request for clarification. You must be aware, I am certain, of the delicacy of the nature of our business.

I feel impelled to reassure you that anything written or conveyed to us, in any form, will remain exclusively confidential, and at the termination of our business, all your correspondence will be returned. You can be assured our own reports remain in secret file, where no one will ever gain access to them.

The attitude of Talmadge Services, Inc. has always been: "The client's confidence is sacred. We must assume the role of doctor or counselor. The confidence must never be violated." We at the Agency hope you, too, will feel this way about us.

I believe we understand each other perfectly now, Miss Parish.

To be sure, we will handle this problem to its logical end, and publicity of any sort would be as damaging to us as to you. Discretion is all-important, to both of us.

In any event . . . the extra days during your indisposition have allowed us to procure the transcript of the inquest, and the preliminary reports of our field man. We are now preparing the latter for your consideration.

I wish to remind you that no check has been forthcoming, and while we wish to satisfy our clients, our field work is quite expensive. I'm sure this reminder will suffice.

Hoping you feel better-disposed, I remain most respectfully yours,

Harrison Talmadge,
for Talmadge Services, Inc.

HT:lt

May 22nd, 1975

Miss Loretta Parish
RFD #2
Stimson, Ohio

Dear Miss Parish:

I wish to thank you for your check, which more than covers our preliminary work. I am certain you will find our work as thorough as you might have wished.

Our primary report is enclosed. However, a brief summary reveals the following: there *was* some question, at the inquest and subsequently (which you could not have realized, having moved from Taunton so soon after Mrs. Constable's unfortunate death) as to the circumstances surrounding her death. Now we certainly do not wish to pry, and have no desire to tread where it is not our province, but to more clearly establish for our own purposes just what action Mr. Philip Grademan might take, we must know all particulars.

It is not our belief that you are withholding any details of this matter, but perhaps you might recall a few things both about the situation in Taunton, and about Grademan in particular, that might abet us.

We are happy to have you with us as a client, and wish to once again reassure you that at the conclusion of our transactions, your problem will be *permanently* solved.

While we await any further data from you, we will proceed with the tracing of Mr. Philip Grademan.

Once again, yours most respectfully,

Harrison Talmadge,
for Talmadge Services, Inc.

HT:lt
enc: Primary Field Report-6pp.

24 May 1975

Talmadge Services, Inc.
545 Fifth Avenue
New York 17, New York

Dear Mr. Talmadge:

I really must protest the insinuation in your letter that the facts I reported concerning the Taunton situation were not complete.

First of all, it was **only** logical for Mrs. Constable to make me her heir, since I was employed a full year prior to Philip Grademan. I was more than just a secretary to her, I was a friend, while Grademan only tended to her books. She knew he was more interested in the library than herself, and so naturally her sentiments lay with me. Also, Mrs. Constable recognized that I, being a woman, and in ill health, did not have the means, available to Philip Grademan, for self-support.

I suppose that what you've run across is the nasty gossip circulating in Taunton concerning the fact that I prepared Mrs. Constable's diet for her — she was on a low-salt, low-residue diet, and supervision was necessary — which has led several local busybodies to imply that her death was perhaps not merely a matter of ill health.

Also, you may have heard that the relationship between Philip Grademan and myself was more than mere friendship. I can assure you that I loathe and despise Philip Grademan, and I would not be made unhappy by the realization that I might **never see him again.**

I suspect that this man is mentally unbalanced, because of his conviction that Mrs. Constable's money should have been willed to him. A man like that is capable of the most drastic crime, and I urge you to take appropriate action at the earliest possible opportunity. If further remuneration is required, I am willing to meet any reasonable request.

Yours very truly,
(Miss) Loretta Parish

May 30th, 1975

Miss Loretta Parish
RFD #2
Stimson, Ohio

Dear Miss Parish:

Good news! We believe we have picked up Philip Grademan's trail. Our man in the field has had reasonably little difficulty tracing Grademan. He has made a habit of stopping in every antique bookshop within the area he happens to be, and this pattern of behavior will simplify our task immeasurably. His actions lead us to believe he is not too concerned about anyone knowing his whereabouts. This is a result of a lucky coincidence that occurred two days ago.

There is a certain amount of cross-reference between all tracing agencies, which facilitates location, and we had a note from the Superior Detective Agency of this city, mentioning that a Mr. Paul Gestler was trying to locate Miss Elizabeth Fernig, late of Taunton, Massachusetts.

The similarity of initials cannot be mere coincidence, leading us to believe that Grademan is, indeed, trying to locate you as you suspected.

Needless to say, we did not reply to this note, and we are hastening our efforts. This has met with some difficulty, for Grademan (if Gestler is Grademan, and we believe he is) mails his checks to the Superior people from a professional mailing service, to which the Superior Agency sends its reports, and this firm will not, under any circumstances we have been able to devise, inform us where his letters originate. However, we believe his movements are at random, following any leads the Superior Agency might unearth, and hoping to stumble on you both through their activities and his own.

At any rate, our man in the field will continue to track Grademan, and any further developments will be related immediately to you. He left Pittsburgh, Pennsylvania, a mere week before our man reached there.

Be assured that we are sparing no effort in this matter, and your more than generous remittance will afford us a great deal of leeway in hiring the best possible men for the job. And when we have located Grademan, your situation will clear up very nicely.

In passing, I thought I might clarify a point made in my letter of May 22nd. The rumors circulated in Taunton about you were not precisely as you imagined. The rumors said that you had induced Philip Grademan into a plot to kill Mrs. Constable, giving him the impression that Mrs. Constable's will favored you both equally. This is supposed to account for Grademan's anger, when he discovered that you were the sole heir, and he merely your beneficiary.

While these rumors have reached us, both as hearsay and as the by-products of our field man's reports, we wish to assure you that none of this is our concern, and it remains a confidential section of this investigation.

We are certain, of course, that all such rumors are just that: rumors. We are with you, here at the agency, in spirit as well as action.

Hoping you are feeling well these days, I remain most respectfully,

> Harrison Talmadge,
> for Talmadge Services, Inc.

HT:lt
enc: Secondary Field Report-12pp.

1 June 1975

Talmadge —

For God's sake, if Philip Grademan has detectives looking for me, then I'm in terrible danger. You must do something right away!

> *Loretta Parish*

June 3rd, 1975

Miss Loretta Parish
RFD #2
Stimson, Ohio

Dear Miss Parish:

Please calm yourself. Our men are working on this matter full-time since your checks have allowed us to more than double our activities.

Grademan was seen in a bookstore in Canton, Ohio, not more than five days ago, and we have every reason to expect that he has received some definite information from the Superior Agency. We are trying to get some inside information there ourselves, as to just what progress they have made in finding you. We will, of course, do everything in our power to forestall their activities.

A further report is enclosed, and I can only re-state my assurances that you have nothing to worry about. With our men on his track, he can't go far without our finding him. We are trying every bookstore in every city within a hundred miles of where he was seen, on the chance that his bibliomania will make him turn up there. And when he is located, the total discrimination of this Agency will be employed in quietly eliminating his danger to you.

Please be calm, and be assured we are with you all the way.

Yours most respectfully,
Harrison Talmadge,
for Talmadge Services, Inc.

HT:lt
enc: 3rd Field Report-8pp.

4 June 1975

Talmadge,

    I repeat . . . I'm in terrible danger! You must find Grademan at once. Before he finds me. Spare no expense but hurry — Please advise at once!

Loretta Parish

June 6th, 1975

Miss Loretta Parish
RFD #2
Stimson, Ohio

Dear Miss Parish:

    I feel you are becoming unduly emotional about a situation that will soon be cleared up nicely. In that respect I have good news for you again.

    Grademan was traced as far as Columbus, Ohio, which seems to be narrowing his track of approach. We are confident he will be turned up shortly. Then our *special* service will return the value you have paid out. We have hired a man for this single service alone. However, the cost of this expert was slightly higher than anticipated. You will find a bill enclosed to cover this factor. I trust that it will be satisfactory to you.

    We hasten to remind you that all transactions are strictly private.

    Certain you'll understand, I remain most respectfully.

Harrison Talmadge,
for Talmadge Services, Inc.

HT: lt
enc: 4th Field Report-16pp.
Bill for Services

June 9th, 1975

Dear Miss Parish:

On the 7th he was in Dayton. On the 8th (yesterday) he was in Springfield. His searching is bringing him closer to you and, accordingly, our men closer to him. Our operations are swinging into high gear.

Hurriedly,
H. Talmadge

NJ133 PD-NY NY 10 530PME
MISS LORETTA PARISH-
RFD #2 STIMSON OHIO

1975 JUNE 10 AM 7 09
HAVE LOST TRAIL, BE ADVISED OUR FRIEND HEADING YOUR VICINITY. LETTER FOLLOWS.

TALMADGE

June 10th, 1975; 6:00 PM

Miss Loretta Parish
RFD #2
Stimson, Ohio

Dear Miss Parish:
Having received my telegram I hope you took immediate steps to protect yourself. Our man lost Grademan's track when he disappeared in Springfield, Ohio. We feel certain now that Grademan has received definite information as to your present whereabouts.

We believe the most prudent thing to do now is to advise us immediately, and we will provide another of our services, which is protection, in the form of an agent.

In point of fact, our Mr. Schneider, who has been closest to Grademan through this entire affair, is now in your vicinity, and if you will advise by return mail or telegram,

we will have him proceed immediately to you, to act as your guard. I might also note the bill for the hiring of our "special" agent has not yet been paid.

Respectfully yours,
Harrison Talmadge,
for Talmadge Services, Inc.

HT: lt
enc: Protection Rate Table
     Bill for Services

COLONIAL BOOK SHOP
16 Cherry Street
Stimson, Ohio

August 2, 1975

Talmadge Services, Inc.
545 Fifth Avenue
New York 17, N.Y.

Gentlemen:

I am sure you will be saddened to learn of the passing of Loretta Parish, *neé* Elizabeth Fernig, who succumbed to an ailing heart last June.

As the beneficiary of Miss Parish's will, I have recently discovered, among her effects, several statements for services rendered by your organization.

Please find check enclosed. I'm sure you will be as happy as I to mark "finis" to these outstanding charges.

Yours most respectfully,
Philip Grademan, Prop.

"BOOKS ARE FRIENDS"

No Fourth Commandment

"I'm going to kill my father," said the boy.

"If I ever find him, I won't bother to tell him who I am, or say hello, or anything. I'll just walk up and kill him." He was a tall, thin kid, with a hungry look in his green eyes.

"But *why?*" I asked. "Why do you want to kill your father?"

"You should see my mother. She looks like she's fifty."

I still didn't understand. "So?"

"She's only thirty-six."

He didn't say anything more, and I didn't think I should bug him, so I went back to picking the strawberries. I've been out on the road enough years to know when to leave a body alone when he don't want to talk. But this kid was different. I was kind of drawn to him — I don't know why — maybe 'cause I never had no wife and kids his age.

It was one of those real warm, pleasantish days when you know there ain't no place better to be than on a farm.

Even so, I felt a chill. The sun was beating down on me, naked to the waist in the middle of a strawberry crop, I was sweating like a pig, and I was chilly.

The chill started in my chest — way inside — and worked out. It was that kind of chill. It was that kid, that's what it was.

The way he'd said it. That he was going to kill his old man. It made me wiggle. I've heard lotta men say they was gonna kill someone else, but it was the first time I'd heard anything like that!

I'd never thought too much about the Fourth Commandment. *Honor thy father and mother* just hadn't applied to me — my folks got killed when I was a kid. But I knew what it meant, and it was one of those things that seemed natural, and there wasn't no reason to dispute it. But when I heard that kid say it, I felt all funny. He shouldn't of said something like that, it wasn't right.

I looked over at him.

He was down on his hands and knees, working the next row, with his berry bag over his shoulder and his hair tumbled into his eyes. He looked to be about fifteen, sixteen, with a long, loose body that was decently muscled, but pretty thin. He looked like he was always set to run. Like a racehorse chomping at the bit. He never did run, he just looked like he wanted to.

Nobody knew where he'd come from, and mostly, nobody asked. Almost all the boys in the fields were roadwalkers and runaways and, of course, a lot of field-followers trailing the crops, so it was smartest just to keep to yourself and not inquire.

But he was different. You could tell. There was something about him — something hungry. One of the men, fellow named Jan who'd been to college, was talking about the kid over supper; said the boy looked like a wild animal huddled up in an unaccustomed cage. I couldn't of put it better myself. This Jan was smart, and he said the kid was starved for affection.

Well, Hell, ain't we all?

The kid stuck his hand through the bushes and plucked a handful of ripe berries off. He hadn't been so good at it the first few hours in the fields. Anyone could see he wasn't a regular crop-man, but after a bit he'd watched us with those sharp green eyes, and pretty soon he could six-pluck a fistful as well as the rest of us.

"Where you from, kid?" I asked.

He looked over at me, and puckered his lower lip. I don't think he knew he was doing it. He gave a strong blow and his dirty brown hair went out of his eyes for a second. It fell back in a long branch, and hung there.

He settled back on his haunches, pushing the hair away with force, and said, real slowly, "Up near Cedar Rapids way."

"That's in Iowa, ain't it?" I asked.

He nodded, breaking a dirt clod in his hand.

"Thanks — thanks for . . . the . . . other day," he stumbled, his face turned down in shadow.

I knew what he meant. The fight. He'd gone nuts, for no reason, when he'd heard the boss's wife, Miz Fenkel, talkin' to her little boy in German, and I'd hadda pull him high off before he'd smashed the poor woman.

There hadn't been no reason for it. He'd just started for her. I'd slapped him once, good and hard, and the craziness had died out of his eyes and he'd settled back without a word.

But it hadn't made sense.

"I — I — thought," he mumbled, and then stopped. He tried again, " — it seemed for a minute she was . . . but it wasn't . . . " His voice died off again and he sat there idly fumbling with the dirt.

I did something I don't do, usually. I started to pry into another man's business. "What's your name, boy?"

He looked up, then. He looked at me long, and I could tell he wasn't just thinking about now. I'd done him a favor, sure, but he didn't know me from Adam. I was just another field bum, pickin' strawberries. He was thinking, what if I tell this man my name, and in the future, and what'll happen, and is there a reason not to tell, and then he said, "Holloway. Most call me by my first; that's Fair."

"Fair Holloway?"

He nodded. "What's that short for?" I asked.

"Fairweather." He seemed embarrassed.

"Nice name," I said, and went back to my berries. That was enough prying for then. I didn't want to scare him off. I kinda liked the boy. He seemed grateful I stopped, too. I saw him give me a short look, then he bent over his rows again.

Natchitoches, Louisiana's a piece down from Cedar Rapids. A strawberry farm is a good ways from the home this boy must have come from, too.

While I picked, I wondered about him. I wondered more than I think I've ever wondered about anyone. Any kid would say he was going to put his old man down, like that, in that real matter-of-fact talk, was something pretty odd. Besides, I liked him. He seemed like a nice kid, aside from what he'd said, and except for his goin' after Miz Fenkel that way.

I finished that row, not even minding the sun, or the

mosquitoes, just thinking, and started on another line. The kid stayed right next. He didn't go off to work another string. I liked that. He seemed to get along with me, too.

We worked till the sun was good and high, and starting down a bit, then they called us for supper. I got up, slow, because I ain't as young as I used to be, which sounds like what everybody else says, but it's true. I'm getting on. It won't be too many years I can keep running the crops this way.

I been running 'em a long time, and maybe the reason I'd taken an interest in the kid was that I'd been on the road alone all those years, and I saw myself in the kid a little bit. I don't know, maybe that was it. Maybe not. But I liked him, and I figured he needed a friend.

The boy was ahead of me, swinging his berry bag from his hand, kicking at the dirt, pushing his hair out of his eyes. "Hey!" I yelled. He turned and stopped when he saw it was me. His eyes were wary, and every line of his blue-jeaned body suggested running again.

"I'll walk over with you," I said, coming up. We started walking again, and he didn't say a word, so I didn't figure it was my place to do otherwise.

Our feet sank into the summer ground slightly, giving a sort of springiness to our walk, that even our heavy boots couldn't take away. It was good to be alive.

I stole a look at Fair Holloway out of the corner of my eye. He was a hungry-looking thing, like I said. His face was long and tanned from the sun, and it came to a point at the chin. His cheekbones were high and his nose was straight and thin as a finger.

His hands hung loose and open by his sides, but they had a way of knotting up — sudden-like — for no particular reason at all. He seemed and looked like an ordinary enough kid.

And he wanted to kill his father.

We came up to the house, and Fenkel, the man'd hired us, was out back with his wife, ladling out soup to the first batch of field workers.

We dumped our bags into a trough the hired girls would use when filling the berry boxes, and sat down at the big table.

There was soup, and biscuits, and chittlins, baked potatoes and fresh peas. Corn on the cob, cranberry sauce, two kinds of preserves, and hot, black coffee. Then Miz Fenkel brought out half a dozen good old-fashioned Dutch Apple pies and we cleaned 'em up in short time.

Once, she was saying something to her husband in German, as she served us, and I saw Fair tighten up again. He made like to rise a little, and I put my hand on his shoulder, hard, and he seemed to snap out of a dream. He sat back down again real slow, and shook his head a couple times. He ran his hand through his hair, down across his face, and gave me a sort of sick white smile.

Right about then I figured I'd stick with the kid some. He needed a friend real bad. He needed someone to keep an eye out for him.

There was usually a horseshoe game going after supper, for a half hour or so, and most of the men were over watching. I didn't bother joining them. I wandered over to where the kid was leaning up against the steel frame of a plow. I was drawn to him, somehow.

"They put up a good spread here, don't they?" I said, coming up behind him.

He spun around, half-dropping, his hands tightening, and glared at me. Those sharp green eyes were slitted up like a catamount's, and his tongue kept flicking in and out, in and out.

For a minute there I was petrified. I'd never seen a kid that looked so old. He could have been a thousand years old in that minute. With the hate of a thousand years all ready to brim over. Then he saw it was me, and all that stoking died down. I could see the scare and fury simmer out from behind his eyes and he wiped his hand across them, as though they were burning. "Yeah. Yeah, they put up a real fine spread." He sounded bone-weary.

I sat down right by his feet, with my back against the plow. He gave me a funny look. The kind of look a man who is alone always gives someone breaking into his loneliness. But I tried again. "Why do you want to kill your old man?"

He looked me that slow, careful look, and then pursed his lips. He was weighing it again, I could see.

"I'm just curious, that's all," I said. "If you've got reasons, why then don't tell me. I was just curious, that's all."

He slid down, then, and went plonk in the dirt right next to me.

I thought he was going to silence, but he started in talking and pretty soon I'd of had to stop him with a gag in the mouth to shut him up.

"My father went overseas near the end of the Second World War," he said, "and he met a *fraulein*." Way he said that kraut word I thought it was all the nasty stuff in the world, all in one word. He sounded real strange when he talked about it, like someone older than fifteen, sixteen.

"Yeah," I urged.

"He married up with her, over there, and then brought her back here. Then he married her again, over here, just to make sure it was legal. Only trouble was," and his face drew tight, "he was a bigamist. He was still married to Maw." His face was white and stretched, as though someone had it out on dryers in the sun. It was real harsh and tight, with the lines under his eyes and around his mouth like ink.

I wondered how a young kid could look so old.

I wondered what he'd been through to know words like bigamist. He told the story quick, and it seemed he knew what he was going to say even before he said it. I wondered how often he'd told this story.

"My mother slashed her wrists once, and stuck her head in the oven a second time." He winced when he said it, like it hurt in his stomach. "But she couldn't die, cause she loved that man too much. He came home one night and made a big scene that broke her heart for real, then he ran off somewhere, and was gone with that *fraulein* of his."

Then I understood why he'd tried to jump Miz Fenkel. The kid just hated German women. He was in a bad way. He could get real sick if he was to let a thing like that rule his whole life. I wanted to help him, but I didn't know how.

He'd stopped talking, and had begun playing with the dirt

between his outstretched legs. It was difficult to keep thinking of him as a young kid. He didn't say any more, and I knew that was the story.

"How long you been looking?" I asked.

"Four years," he said; real quiet.

"Ever found track of him?"

"Little bit. Words here and there. I always follow up what anyone says. If they tell me an American's living with a German wife, I always go there. That's why I came down here, but Old Man Fenkel ain't American, he's German." He seemed disappointed, somehow. "I'll find him," he finished.

He stopped cold. I knew that was all. I wasn't going to get any more, and it was a polite way of sayin', don't ask for no more.

I didn't want no more.

All the next week we stayed pretty close together. The kid took a like to me, cause I didn't bug him, and he knew I understood his troubles. And I was glad to be around him — it gave me something to do, watching out for him.

But the berry crop played out in a week, and Fenkel paid us all off, and thanked us mightily. He'd made connections and had a pretty penny setting up waiting for him for the batch.

Day he paid us off, I didn't see Fair much. He got his stuff — just a few things — together in a beat-up old carpetbag and moved out of the bunkhouse. After Fenkel gave me my wages, I started to move out, slow, looking for the kid. I was just toting my blanket roll and some spare clothes. I moved out of the farm and down the road, looking both ways for the boy.

Then I saw him. He was up the road a few yards, walking slow, kicking the clods of dirt like he always did. I yelled to him.

"Where ya headin', Fair?"

He looked over his shoulder, and I was glad he didn't give me that catamount stare. He'd gotten real used to me during the last week, and we'd bunked down next to each other every night, so I kind of figured maybe I'd tag along with him, show him where the next crop was gonna be.

He answered, "Don't know, Harry. I was thinking of going

down to Lake Charles. Some of the boys said there was a peanut crop coming out around there somewhere." Then he wetted his lips like he did once in a while, and said, slow, like he had trouble getting it out, "I was talking to one of the hands. He — he said he thought there might be someone down there I'd want to see." He didn't look at me when he said it, kept staring at his dusty army boots.

There was a light in his eyes.

"Your old man?"

He nodded.

"How do you know it is?"

"I don't."

"Then why — " I began.

He cut me off. "I've got to find out. It might be. It just might." His voice fell to a whisper. "I've got to see."

"Mind if I tag along?"

He stared for a minute; he must have been wondering why a full-grown one like me wanted to chum up with a kid like him. But he ducked his head a little bit, so his hair tumbled again, and told me I could come if I was of a mind.

I had a mind, so we walked into Natchitoches together.

We caught a few hours' sleep in the bus station, and later that night we hopped a freight, which is real tough to do these days, and started for Lake Charles.

We lay in the boxcar, staring out through the slats of the construction, watching the fuzz of trees whipping past.

I didn't know for sure yet why I was going with this kid, but he was something I was interested in, and it'd been a long time since I'd been interested in anything.

It's lonely out on the road — and that's the way most guys like it. That way nobody makes demands on you. But this kid was company, and interesting, and he had worries, and he didn't ask for nothing. You could be with him and not worry about him making any demands.

And he needed a friend real bad. It's good for a man to be a friend, once in a while.

I looked over at him, lying on his carpetbag, staring with his eyes shut.

"The whole idea about Lake Charles is pretty slim," I said. It puzzled me. Someone back at the berry farm had told the kid he knew of a man that fit the description Fair gave of his father, with a kraut wife and all, and the kid had taken off like a big bird.

It didn't matter to me. One way was as good as another, but the way that kid shifted direction with the rumors was a strange thing.

He mumbled something in answer, but I didn't catch it.

"It probably isn't your old man," I continued. I could tell he wasn't listening.

All the time in that freight he'd just laid there with his head on that carpetbag, part of the time staring up at the stars through the slats, part of the time like he was asleep. I couldn't tell if he was or not.

Funny thing. I didn't try to talk him out of killing his old man. That was his business, and it seemed right that he do it, if he wanted to. The kid had built his life around it, that was easy to see, and if you took that away from him, well, hell, he'd of had nothing.

It was a kind of distant thing, really, that's why I didn't worry about it too much. It was like someone that says I'm going to China some day, but you know they'll never quite make it. It was like that with his killing his father. I didn't think he was going to find his old man. The United States is a big place. I was sure we'd never run into the father. I was pretty much sold on sticking with the kid, by this time. We got along, and it was a good deal.

All but the father business.

He was okay aside from that.

And then, I was sure we wouldn't find the old man.

I was wrong.

First night in town, that kid made like a bloodhound, and the trouble started brewing.

We got into Lake Charles and the kid said we'd better split up for a while. He said he had to check at some store or other for something, and we'd meet back in the center of town in an hour.

I didn't see no reason for splitting like that and I told him I'd come along.

"Look, Harry, you go where you want, and I'll meet you. I want to go someplace by myself." He was starting to catamount me, so I agreed. I went off looking for a greasy spoon to get some grub. That train ride had hungered me good.

In an hour, I was back sitting on a bench in the square where we'd parted. After a cop had told me to move on three times and I'd shifted benches three times, Fair came back.

His lips was drawn so tight against his face they looked like two lines of topsoil down a field. I knew he had something.

"He's here," was all he said, and started past me. He probably hadn't even come back through the square to meet me, that was most likely just the way to get where he was goin'.

I grabbed his arm. He was only a bit smaller than me, and he shook me off quick. "Don't be doing anything crazy now, Fair," I said, waving my hands around without any purpose.

He just looked at me like I'd told him to stop breathing. "Harry, don't you *understand*? That man's in this town. I have to kill him. Don't you understand?" It was so queer, to hear them words coming out of that young boy's mouth, in that kid's voice — *but them words!*

He started off, then, and I knew I couldn't say nothing. I still didn't believe it was his father, and I was hoping he'd stop when he saw that. I decided to just go along with him. You don't try and stop a person when they want to live their life that way. This was his problem — I was just along to see he didn't do anything crazy.

We walked out of town, and down a dirt road. We kept walking and every once in a while the kid would stop someone on the road or yell at a man in a field and ask him where Ernest Luber's farm was.

How did the kid know this Luber was old man Holloway with a new name? I couldn't understand it.

"How do you know it's your old man?" I asked him, trotting alongside.

"I know."

"But *how* do you know? You can't just take a poor description! You got to *know*!" I pleaded with him.

"I know!"

"Fair, watch yourself. You can't do something to this man, even if he is your father. That's for the law to handle." I was getting desperate. What if it *was* his father?

"The law didn't help my maw. Go look at her. Then come back an' tell me the law. Go ahead!" He snapped it out, and I knew I couldn't talk to him. He was set to go after this Luber.

It was all real queer. I liked that boy, and I had to stay with him, but I felt futile, and helpless, like I couldn't do nothing.

Every now and then I'd tell him to forget it.

He didn't even listen.

By the time we'd been walkin' a half-hour, the bandanna round his throat had been soaked to sogginess with sweat. He was on a kill day. His eyes showed it.

Finally we got to this Luber's farm. The mailbox out front said so in red, and the kid walked down the driveway, past a battered station wagon, and into the yard. There was a stubby blond woman peeling potatoes on the back steps, and a man chopping wood by a pile near the well.

The woman started to get up off the steps. "Hello. Can I help — " she started to say, but the kid was looking at the man, and his eyes had suddenly got real narrow catamounty. "Paw!" he screamed, real loud, and the man turned around sudden.

"Paw!" the kid yelled again, and the man looked at the woman in confusion.

"Who are you? What do you want?" said the man, and he must of seen something in that boy's eyes, because he backed up a step. He was a fairly short fellow, with thatchy hair, and dirty overalls on. His face was wide, and fat, and plumpy.

He didn't look nothing like what Fair had said his old man resembled.

The kid screamed something frightful, and the woman dropped her bowl of spuds. The man got a real angry look on his face and started toward the kid. The ax was buried in a cord of wood: he didn't have nothing in his hands, and that's what choked me up when I saw the kid pick up the scythe.

It had been laying near some tall grass. Someone'd left it there, and the kid stumbled forward with it, half-rusted and curvy in his hand.

"Stop, Fair!" I screamed. "That ain't your — " but I knew he couldn't hear me. He couldn't hear anything. I yelled to the pudgy man. "Take the ax! Take the — " but he didn't hear me either.

The man was pudgy, but taller than the kid, and he must of thought he could stop him, cause he came at the kid with a growl.

"Get off this farm, you — " the man started, and then that kid was on him.

God, I've seen 'em bad, but this was too much!

That kid was down on him for a good five minutes and I couldn't do a thing but watch. The woman screamed and screamed and screamed, but she couldn't do nothing, either.

We just watched, and the rust and blood made a funny look all mixed together.

The kid got up off the leftovers, and dropped the scythe. He stumbled toward me, all coated with it, like I wanted to vomit, and he stopped right in front of me.

"Paw. I killed Paw! I killed him, my paw," he said, staring at me real cool. He didn't seem to think anything about it.

"Paw," he said again, this time real low.

I hit him flush in the mouth with my fist, hard as I could.

They came and got him about half an hour later. They put him in the town jail and had Ernest Luber, his wife, and me come along to find out why this kid had killed a stupid hired hand by the name of Goeblick. Then somebody said hey didn't the kid fit the description of something or other and yeah, didn't he, so they sent out a wire, and got one back, and word to hold him, and me.

I didn't get much sleep in the jail that night. They wouldn't let me near the kid, and I couldn't hear him, and all I kept thinking about was *my God, that poor Goeblick!*

Next day came down to the jail some guy from near Chicago, said he was a doctor.

He wanted to talk to me, so I sat and listened.

I listened to him, then he listened to me. I told him where I'd met the kid and what he'd said and what had happened at this Luber's farm.

"You know that wasn't the boy's father," the doctor said.

"I know."

"Just a total stranger. A hired helper named Goeblick. Luber happens to be married to a German woman, but he was out in the fields when it happened. Goeblick didn't even resemble the Holloway boy's father."

"Oh, my God in heaven," I said, because I'd been saying it all night and it seemed the thing to say.

"His father has been dead for four years." That really got me.

"Does the boy know?"

"He should. He killed him."

I wanted to swallow my tongue. It felt so big and swollen and shapeless in my mouth that I wanted to swallow it. Somehow, I got the words right:

"T-tell me."

So he did.

Fair Holloway had caught his father as he was trying to leave his mother. The kid had walked in on the end of a real stinking farewell address by the old man, about a month after the stove episode. The kid had walked in and caved in the old man's skull with a heavy frying pan.

Then he'd kissed his mother, told her he'd find his father and kill him when he did. Then he left home.

They'd caught him twice, but not before he'd killed two more men, neither of them anything like the dead Holloway, and neither of them bastards like his old man. They just happened to be married to German women, and they happened to be in his way.

They'd caught the kid and put him away twice, and twice he'd escaped. This last time he'd been out for two months, and they'd lost all track of him. His trail was fairly clear, though. He'd gotten two more men.

"Don't he know?" I asked, and I'm afraid I was white around the face.

"No. Something went wrong. Here." He tapped his head like he thought I was too stupid to know what he meant. "The boy thinks his father is still alive. He's forgotten all the others he's killed. Immediately after the murders, he seems to go into partial amnesia, blanking out that area of experience completely. He knows enough to get away, but he thinks he's just hunting, hasn't found the man yet."

I was sick all through me. "He always seemed so quiet, and polite, and friendly — except for that thing about wanting to kill his father. Leastways he always was to me."

The doctor frowned. "Do you want to know something?" he said slowly. "There's a reason why he was always so respectful to you."

I didn't understand. "What?"

"You're a dead ringer for that boy's father. The dead Holloway."

"Oh, my God in heaven," I said again, so low he had to ask me what I'd said.

I went to say goodbye to Fair. I didn't want to, but I knew I'd do it, anyhow.

He was sitting in his cell, just sitting, not doing anything, just sitting. He looked like he'd of liked some dirt to crumble in his hands. There wasn't any, and I was sorry I hadn't thought to bring some. But that didn't really make sense.

"So long, Fair," I said, through the bars.

"So long, Harry," he said, from the bunk.

He'd lied about his name. It wasn't Fairweather. I should have known that, but I didn't.

"Well . . . " I began.

"Oh, I'll see you, Harry. I've still got to take care of something."

I looked in at him. He was sitting there calm and cool on the edge of the metal trough that was his bed, without any mattress, and I wanted to cry. That boy was only sixteen. He didn't know anything. He'd never seen anyone or known anyone but that father of his. He'd never seen me. I wanted to be a friend, but all he'd seen was his father.

I'd been out on the road a long time; no wife, no kids, no real home, and I'd liked that kid. I'd liked him. It wasn't right, it just wasn't right.

It's best to be alone on the road. Lonely is best.

I didn't want him to say what he was gonna say.

"I've still got to kill my father," he said, narrowing his sharp green eyes.

I turned away and walked away.

What was that? *It is a wise father who knows his child.*

What about a wise child that knows his father? Or a dumb child?

I should of had a chance — he should of had a chance. The lonely don't know. They never know. They just go on down the road, they just keep walking. I'm getting on, but I knew that kid'd never had a chance.

I headed out of town, looking for the peanut crop.

The Night of Delicate Terrors

In the sovereign state of Kentucky, Kin Hooker mused, hunching over the wheel, *it is possible to freeze to death and starve to death with a pocketful of money.*

In the back seat, Raymond cried out in his sleep, and Alma reached back to straighten the heavy car robe over him. "How's Patty?" McKinley Hooker said to his wife.

Alma straightened around and let air escape between her lips. She stared straight ahead through the windshield at the barrage descent of thick, enveloping snow that wrapped the car in a hush. He had to repeat the question; she did not look at him as she replied, "Still sleeping. How much gas we got?"

He winced at her grammar. That was the only thing about Alma that distressed Kin Hooker. But it was easily attributed to the degree of schooling she had received in Alabama.

"Should have enough to get us over the state line. Is gas more expensive in Indiana?"

Alma shrugged and went back to her absorbed sighting into the slanting white. In the back seat, Raymond turned on his side, moving closer to little Patty's warm body. They huddled together against the January bite that reached them despite the laboring car heater.

"Damned road!" Hooker murmured under his breath. They were traveling at a pitifully slow pace despite the firmness of the concrete dual-lane. A cold front had blitzkrieged down from the North earlier that evening, catching the hard, cold Kentucky countryside in a noose of below-zero snow and raging winds. All traffic had begun to crawl, with jack-knifed trailers and cars tossed this way and that in the ditches at the roadside. On every

turn cars spun out helplessly, leaving their inhabitants stranded .
. . for no one could himself chance helping anyone else, with the
risk of being stuck omnipresent.

Now the snow had piled along the inner lane, leaving only
the outer passable to the horde of traffic heading upstate. Across
the humped median, the traffic going South was in like shape.

McKinley Hooker's back hurt terribly, and his hands on the
wheel were cold. He felt a graininess in his eyes, and there was a
persistent throbbing in his right temple.

They had eaten all the food in the lunch basket earlier that
evening and now, as the dash clock read 2:25 A.M., they knew
they would have to find a motel for the night. Kin had been
driving since seven that morning with only infrequent gas stops,
and his back just under the shoulder blades, at the base of his
spine, in the area of the kidneys, was so sore he had slumped
into a half-crouch over the wheel, round-shouldered and
uncomfortable, from which he was not certain he could emerge.

And the blizzard was getting worse.

No gravel spreader or snowplough had come out yet, and
it was a safe bet none would till morning. In the meantime,
conditions were getting unbearable. With only one lane open at
all — and that covered with a veneer of ice — and snow drifting
in from the sides constantly, there was no telling how long even
their fifteen-mile-an-hour pace could be maintained.

They would have to find a motel. Someplace to eat, where the
children could get warm, where they could bed down to restore
their strength, for the balance of the journey to Chicago.

They would have to find a motel . . .

He tossed the thought like a wild mare shedding its rider.
Then he looked into the rearview mirror, and saw the futility of
the thought.

His chocolate face with its keen eyes and wide, white mouthful
of teeth stared back at him. And Alma was even darker.

He screwed his hands down tighter on the wheel.

There had only been three colored motels between Macon
and this lost point somewhere in the Kentucky darkness. Three
motels, and all of them disgusting. Kin Hooker sometimes
wondered if there was any point to fighting. This conclave in

Chicago, now. He had been selected by all of them as the Macon, Georgia, representative. He was to receive his instructions, and then one day . . .

He decided not to think about it. It was all in the future; a special kind of future that he never really thought would come to pass, but which he dwelled on in hungry-souled moments.

Right now, the problem was to keep alive.

"Kin, we gonna make Chicago tonight?"

"I don't see how, honey. It's a good four hundred miles, and frankly, my back is sore as hell right now."

"What we gonna do? You figure we can sleep in the car?"

He shook his head, keeping his eyes riveted to the faint twin beams of brilliance cast so feebly through the swirling curtain of snow. "You know we'd have to keep the engine running, and even so the heater wouldn't do us much good tonight; looks to be dropping fast out there."

"They gonna be a stop along here somewhere?"

He tossed her a fast glance. She knew it had come to this, too. It always did. They didn't talk about it, because you can't talk about the facts of life constantly without growing bored and despairing. "I don't think so. Maybe. We'll see."

He turned back just in time to apply the brake before he hit the rear of a farm truck. It was an old truck without taillights, and as he slapped the brake, then pumped quickly, the car lost its feeble grip on the road, and began to spin. He turned into it, and they managed to straighten without losing acceleration.

But for a shuddering time without measure, now that the danger was past, he sat rigid behind the wheel, his eyes locked to the road in shock, trembling uncontrollably.

It was decided, for him, then. They would have to stop at the very next motel or restaurant. He knew what would happen, of course. He was not a stupid man; in the secret crypts of his thoughts he often damned himself for not being a "handkerchief head," illiterate and content to let the white boss run his life. But he had grown up in Michigan, and it had been a good growing-up, with only a scattered few of those unbearable incidents he now wished to forget. Oh, there had been the constant watching of caste and conversation, of course, but that grew to be an instinctive thing. In all, it had been satisfactory, till he had been inveigled into going to work in Georgia.

Then he had learned the ropes quickly, as he was wont to phrase it. He had learned what the ofay meant when he said, "The lines of communication between the nigger and the white man." It was not plural; there was only one line. The line that read: *I'm the Massa' and you're the One-Step-Up-From-A-Monkey, and don't forget it.*

McKinley Hooker was not a stupid man, and now, because he had been chosen, he was an emissary to a conclave in Chicago. A very special conclave, so he had to make it.

There had been many years of taking orders, and now he had a new set of orders, the final wrinkles of which would be ironed out at Chicago. So he had to get to the Chicago conclave, and find out what the final instructions were to be; then he could carry the word back to his people in Macon.

Perhaps . . . perhaps it would be the beginning. The real beginning, where those who searched for the word would find the word, and the word would be *truth*. Perhaps. If all the gears meshed properly, then perhaps.

If he managed to stay alive through this January hell. He cursed himself for bringing Alma and the children along; but it had been clear all the way up from Georgia, and they had never seen Chicago. If they could only get to a motel. If . . .

Far ahead — or what *seemed* far ahead — lost in the crisscrossing lines of snow, he thought he saw a flamingo-flash of neon. He strained forward, and wiped at a spot on the windshield where the defrosters had not cleared away all moisture. The flash came again. He felt both a release and a tension in his stomach muscles.

As they drew closer the red flasher could be seen whirling atop the restaurant's roof, casting off its spaced bdip bdip bdip bdip of crimson. The redness swathed the ground in a broken band and was gone, to reappear an instant later.

The sign was forbidding, it said: EAT.

Alma turned her head slowly as Kin decelerated. "Here? You think they'll serve us?"

He rubbed his jaw, then quickly dropped the hand back to

the wheel. He had a day's growth of beard, and none of them looked too well-starched after being on the road. "I don't know; I guess they'll just have to feed us; you can't turn people away on a night like this."

She chuckled softly. He was still a big-town colored, in many ways.

They turned onto the snow-hidden gravel, and Kin pulled carefully around two gigantic semitrailers near the entrance. Then as they drew around the bulk of the vehicles, the sign that had been blocked-off winked at them. MOTEL FREE TV SHOWERS and underneath, in a dainty green worm of neon: VACANCY.

The semitrailers bulked huge, like sleeping leviathans, under their wraps of snow. It was getting worse. The wind keened around the little building like a night train to nowhere.

He stopped, and they sat there for a moment, letting the windows fog up around them.

Alma was worried, her brow drawn down, her hands in their knitted gloves interlocked on her lap. "Should we stay here while you go in?"

He shook his head. "It might have some effect if all of us went in together. Stir their hearts."

They woke Raymond and Patty. The little girl sat up and yawned, then picked her nose with the lack of self-consciousness known only to a child upon awakening. She mumbled something, and Alma soothed her with a few words that they were going to stop and eat.

Patty said, very distinctly, "I have to go pee-pee, Mommy."

It loosened their tenseness for a jagged second, then the implications dawned. This was another problem. *Well, let's tough it out*, Kin thought wryly, a prayer rising silently from somewhere below.

When they opened the doors, the sharp edge of the wind slashed at them, instantly dispelling the body warmth they had maintained in the sealed car. The children began to shiver, and an involuntary little gasp came from Alma, barely discernible over the raging of the wind and the constant downdropping of the snow.

"Let's go!" Kin shrieked, lifting Patty and charging at the Motel-Restaurant's front door.

He hit the door at a skidding run, turned the knob, and flung the door wide. Alma crowded in behind him, and slammed the door as Raymond moved in on her heels.

They stood frozen for a split second, till the shock of the bitter cold left them, and then, abruptly, their senses returned.

They stood there, the four of them, in the middle of the restaurant, and slowly, everyone had turned to stare at them.

Kin felt a worm of terror leave its home and seek warmth elsewhere. It crawled toward his brain as he saw the eyes of the men in the restaurant fasten on them. He knew what they saw: a nigger, a nigger's woman, and two little pickaninnies.

He shuddered. It was not entirely from the cold.

Alma, behind him, drew in a deep breath.

Then, the thick-armed counterman, leaning across the Formica counter-top, furrowed his brow and said, very carefully, so there was no chance for misinterpretation, "Sorry, fella, we can't serve you."

Then all the suppressed hopes that this time, just this one time of such importance, it would be different, that someone would let it slide, disappeared. It was going to be another battleground, in a war that had never really been fought.

"It's pretty bad out there," Kin said, "we thought we might get something hot to warm us up. We've been driving all day, all the way from — "

The counterman cut him off with a harsh Midwest accent, not a trace of drawl in it. "I said: I'm sorry but we don't serve Negroes here." The way he said it was a cross between Negro and nigger. His voice was harder.

Kin stared at the man: what sort of man was it?

A thick neck supporting a crew-cut head. It looked like some off-color, fleshy burr on the end of a toadstool stem. Huge shoulders, bulging against the lumberjack shirt, and a pair of arms that said quietly musclebound and muscled. Kin was sure he could take the counterman.

But there were others. Four men, obviously truckers, with their caps slanted back on their heads, their eyes coolly inquisitive, their union buttons on the caps catching the glow of the overheads.

And a man and woman at the end of the counter. The woman's pudgy face was screwed up in distate. She was a southerner, no question. They were able to look at you in a way like no other way. They were smelling hog maws and chitterlings and pomade. Even if it wasn't there.

Even as they talked, a waitress came out from the kitchen, carrying a plate with steak and home fried potatoes on it. She stopped in an awkward midstride and stared at the newcomers. Her head jerked oddly and she turned to the counterman. "We don't serve 'em, Eddie," she said, as though he had never known this fact.

"That's what I been telling 'em, Una. See, fella, we — uh — we don't serve your people here. Gas, we got it, but that's it."

"It's winter out there," Kin said. "My wife and kids — "

The counterman reached down and took something from under the bar that he kept concealed. "You don't seem to hear too good, fella. What I said was: we ain't in business for you."

"We need a room for the night, too," Alma inserted, a quavering bravado in her voice. She knew they would get nothing, and it was her way of having them turned down for everything, not just a lousy meal. Kin winced at her petty game-playing.

"Say, now, get outta here!" the waitress yelled. Her face was a grimace of outrage. Who *were* these darkies, anyhow?

"Take it easy, Una, just take it easy. They're goin'. Ain'tcha, fella?" He came out from behind the bar, holding the sawed-off baseball bat loosely in his left hand.

Kin backed away.

It was going to be fight this big ofay, and maybe get his brains knocked out, and even then not getting food and sleep, unless it was at the county jail . . . or going back to the car, and the cold.

There could be little decision in the matter.

"Let's go, Alma," he said. He reached behind him and opened the door. The cold struck him suddenly, sharply, like a cobra; he felt his teeth clench in frustration and pain.

Eddie, the counterman, advanced on them with the ball bat

and his arms like curlicued sausages of great size. "G'wan now, and don't be makin' me use this on yer."

"Is there a colored place near here?" Kin asked, as Alma grabbed Raymond and slipped past into the darkness.

"No . . . and there ain't gonna be, if we c'n help it. We got a business to run here, not for you people. G'wan to Illinois, where they treat a nigger better'n a white man."

He came on again, and Kin backed out, closing the door tightly, staring at the 7-Up decal on the door. Then the wind raced down the neck of his coat, and he hurried to the car.

The three of them were huddled together in the front seat.

"Daddy, I gotta go pee-pee," Patty said.

"Soon, honey. Soon," he murmured at her, sliding in. He turned the key in the ignition and for a moment he did not think the overheated, then chilled motor would start. But it kicked over and they pulled ahead, past the forms of the trucks, like great white whales sleeping in shoals of snow.

The road was worse now.

Cars were strewn on either side of the dual lane like flotsam left after the tide. Kin Hooker bent across the wheel, slipping automatically into the rib-straining position he had known all day.

His thoughts were clear, now.

For almost two years now, since they had started the idea, he had been undecided. Certainly it would be decisive, and a new world, and worth fighting for. But so many would be killed, so many, many, many who were innocent, and who had nothing to do with this war that had never been fought.

But it was all right, now. He had received his instructions, and he *was* going to make that conclave in Chicago. Somehow, he would drive that distance.

And even if he didn't. Even if he and Alma, Raymond and Patty should overturn out here, if they should freeze to death, or be cracked up, there would be others. Many others, all heading to Chicago this day, and all waiting for the final word.

It was coming.

Nothing could stop it.

They had done it their way for so long, so terribly long, and now the time had come for a change of owners. It had come to this and there was no stopping it. He had been uncertain before, because he was not a man of violence . . . but suddenly, it was right. It was the way it would be, because they had forced it this way.

Kin Hooker smiled as he studied the disappearing highway.

Like a million other dark smiles that night, across a white countryside.

A wide, white smile in a dark face.

Harlan Ellison®

Harlan Ellison® was recently characterized by *The New York Times Book Review* as having "the spellbinding quality of a great nonstop talker, with a cultural warehouse for a mind." *The Los Angeles Times* suggested, "It's long past time for Harlan Ellison to be awarded the title: 20th century Lewis Carroll." And the *Washington Post Book World* said simply, "One of the great living American short story writers."

He has written or edited 76 books; more than 1,700 short stories, essay, articles, and newspaper columns; two dozen teleplays, for which he received the Writers Guild of America most outstanding teleplay award for solo work an unprecedented *four* times; and a dozen movies. Currently a member of the Writers Guild of America, he has twice served on the board of the WGAW. He won the Mystery Writers of America Edgar Allan Poe award twice, the Horror Writers Association Bram Stoker award six times (including the Lifetime Achievement Award in 1996), the Nebula award of the Science Fiction Writers of America three times, the Hugo (World Science Fiction Convention achievement award) 8-1/2 times, and received the Silver Pen for Journalism from P.E.N. Not to mention the World Fantasy Award; the British Fantasy Award; the American Mystery Award; plus two Audie Awards and a Grammy nomination for Spoken Word recordings.

He created great fantasies for the 1985 CBS revival of *The Twilight Zone* (including Danny Kaye's final performance) and *The Outer Limits*; travelled with The Rolling Stones; marched with Martin Luther King from Selma to Montgomery; created roles for Buster Keaton, Wally Cox, Gloria Swanson and nearly 100 other stars on *Burke's Law*; ran with a kid gang in Brooklyn's Red

Hook to get background for his first novel; covered race riots in Chicago's "back of the yards" with the late James Baldwin; sang with, and dined with, Maurice Chevalier; once stood off the son of a Detroit Mafia kingpin with a Remington XP-100 pistol-rifle while wearing nothing but a bath towel; sued Paramount and ABC-TV for plagiarism and won $337,000. His most recent legal victory, in protection of copyright against global Internet piracy of writers' work, in May of 2004—a 4-year-long litigation against AOL et al.—has resulted in revolutionizing protection of creative properties on the Web. (As promised, he has repaid hundreds of contributions [totaling $50,000] from the KICK Internet Piracy support fund.) But the bottom line, as voiced by *Booklist* in 2008, is this: "One thing for sure: the man can write."

And, as Tom Snyder said on the CBS *Late, Late Show*: "An amazing talent; meeting him is an incredible experience." He was a regular on ABC-TV's *Politically Incorrect* with Bill Maher.

In 1990, Ellison was honored by P.E.N. for his continuing commitment to artistic freedom and the battle against censorship, "In defense of the First Amendment."

Harlan Ellison's 1992 novelette "The Man Who Rowed Christopher Columbus Ashore" was selected from more than 6,000 short stories published in the U.S. for inclusion in the 1993 edition of *The Best American Short Stories*.

Mr. Ellison worked as a creative consultant and host for *2000^x*, a series of 26 one-hour dramatized radio adaptations of famous SF stories for The Hollywood Theater of the Ear; and for his work was presented with the prestigious Ray Bradbury Award for Drama Series. The series was broadcast on National Public Radio in 2000 and 2001. Ellison's classic story "'Repent, Harlequin!' Said the Ticktockman" was included as part of this significant series, starring Robin Williams and the author in the title roles.

On June 22, 2002, at the 4th World Skeptics Convention, Harlan Ellison was presented with the *Distinguished Skeptic Award* by The Committee for the Scientific Investigation of the Paranormal (CSICOP) "in recognition of his outstanding contributions to the defense of science and critical thinking."

To celebrate the golden anniversary of Harlan Ellison's half century of storytelling, Morpheus International, publishers of *The Essential Ellison: A 35-Year Retrospective*, commissioned the book's primary editor, award-winning Australian writer and critic Terry Dowling, to expand Ellison's three-and-a-half decade collection into a 50-year retrospective. Mr. Dowling went through fifteen years of new stories and essays to pick what he thought were the most representative to be included in this 1000+ page collection. Along with *The Essential Ellison: A 50-Year Retrospective* (Morpheus International), Mr. Ellison's first Young Adult collection, *Troublemakers* is currently available in bookstores.

Among his most recognized works, translated into more than 40 languages and selling in the millions of copies, are *Deathbird Stories*, *Strange Wine*, *Approaching Oblivion*, *I Have No Mouth*, *& I Must Scream*, *Web of the City*, *Angry Candy*, *Love Ain't Nothing But Sex Misspelled*, *Ellison Wonderland*, *Memos From Purgatory*, *All The Lies That Are My Life*, *Shatterday*, *Mind Fields*, *An Edge In My Voice*, *Slippage* and *Stalking the Nightmare*. As creative intelligence and editor of the all-time bestselling *Dangerous Visions* anthologies and *Medea: Harlan's World*, he has been awarded two Special Hugos and the prestigious academic Milford Award for Lifetime Acheivement in Editing. In 2006, Harlan Ellison was named the Grand Master of the Science Fiction/Fantasy Writers of America.

In October 2002, Edgeworks Abbey and iBooks published the 35th Anniversary Edition of the highly acclaimed anthology *Dangerous Visions*.

In the November 2002 issue of *PC Gamer*, Ellison's hands-on creation of the CD-Rom game *I Have No Mouth, and I Must Scream*, based on the award-winning story of the same name, was voted "One of the 10 scariest PC games ever." ("I Have No Mouth, and I Must Scream" is one of the ten most reprinted stories in the English language.)

June 2003: A new Edition of *Vic & Blood*, published by iBooks in association with Edgeworks Abbey, collected for the first time both the complete graphic novel cycle *and* Ellison's stories including the 1969 novella favorite from which the legendary cult film *A Boy and His Dog* was made.

December 2003: Ellison edited a collection of Edwardian mystery-puzzle stories titled *Jacques Futrelle's "The Thinking Machine*, published by The Modern Library.

October 2004: A new edition of *Strange Wine*, published by iBooks in association with Edgeworks Abbey.

May 2006: Ellison and Oscar nominee Josh Olson (for his adaptation of *A History of Violence*) collaborated on a teleplay "The Discarded" (based on Ellison's short story of the same name) for the ABC television series *Masters of Science Fiction*.

November 2006: A new edition of *Spider Kiss*, published by M Press, in association with Edgeworks Abbey. The second book in the M Press /Edgeworks Abbey series, *Harlan Ellison's Watching*, was released in a new edition in 2008.

March 2007: Based on Ellison's work, *Harlan Ellison's Dream Corridor (Volume Two)* is released. Ellison introduces a dozen tales in this new collection, featuring adaptations of some of his greatest stories by some of the most respected names in comics, including Neal Adams, Gene Colan, Richard Corben, Paul Chadwick...and the very last work by the late, great *Superman* artist, Curt Swan.

April 2007: A special world premiere screening is held of *Dreams With Sharp Teeth*. For more than twenty-five years, documentarian Erik Nelson (*Grizzly Man*) has been interviewing Ellison and friends [including Josh Olson (*A History of Violence*), Neil Gaiman (*Anansi Boys*), Dan Simmons (*The Terror*), Peter David (*Fallen Angel*), Michael Cassutt (*Tango Midnight*), Ron Moore (*Battlestar Galactica*), and actor Robin Williams] to produce a feature-length look at the life and work of Harlan Ellison: *Dreams With Sharp Teeth*. In 2008, the documentary was featured at The South by Southwest Conference and Festival, The Edinburgh Film Festival, The Independent Festival in Boston and opened at both the prestigious Lincoln Center in New York and The NY Film Forum. In celebration of his 75th birthday, *Dreams With Sharp Teeth* premiered on the Sundance Film Channel and was released on DVD in May 2009.

Harlan Ellison lives with his wife, Susan, inside The Lost Aztec Temple of Mars, in Los Angeles.

Lightning Source UK Ltd.
Milton Keynes UK
UKOW042028020413

208560UK00001B/23/P